A Narrow Margin of Error

Faith Martin

ROBERT HALE · LONDON

© Faith Martin 2013
First published in Great Britain 2013

ISBN 978-0-7198-0797-8

Robert Hale Limited
Clerkenwell House
Clerkenwell Green
London EC1R 0HT

www.halebooks.com

The right of Faith Martin to be identified as author
of this work has been asserted by her in accordance with the
Copyright, Designs and Patents Act 1988

2 4 6 8 10 9 7 5 3 1

Typeset in 10.75pt/14.5pt Palatino
Printed in Great Britain by the MPG Books Group,
Bodmin and King's Lynn

CHAPTER ONE

Hillary Greene lay staring up at the bright, water-dapple patterns that were cavorting across her ceiling. The dawn light streaming in through her narrowboat's windows was definitely becoming stronger now that late April was threatening to give way to early May. She sighed as she turned over on her single bed, and squinted at the tiny travelling clock on the shelf just underneath the porthole.

It was barely 6.30. She could sleep in for another hour at least. Or even two, if she felt so inclined. Now that she didn't have to get in to work until dead on nine o'clock, such luxuries were becoming commonplace for her.

Since retiring from the police force over a year ago, she'd travelled England's canal system for a while, before going back to work as a civilian consultant to Thames Valley's Crime Review Team. CRT handled cold cases, something that had become popular with the public since the advent of several television crime series that showcased their work. Reality was rather different, of course, with the bulk of the CRT's work being done in the forensics field, which tended to generate a lot of paperwork and deskwork, neither of which were her favourite pastimes.

Although she missed her days as a DI with the privileges that it brought, she was gradually becoming used to some of the bonuses that came with being a civilian again – no unpaid overtime being one of them. And although she still sometimes felt herself to be neither fish nor fowl, since she had no powers of arrest, she enjoyed being back in the saddle to the extent that she was working murder cases again.

Albeit ones that were years old and as cold as yesterday's left-over rice pudding.

Her phone buzzed and she frowned at the inoffensive ceiling again. It couldn't be work-related – the corpses that now had first call on her time had all been dead for many years. And working in CRT meant that nothing could ever be that pressing – her current caseload simply didn't carry the same sort of urgency that breaking cases carried with them as a matter of course.

And the call couldn't be related to her private life either: she didn't have one. So it couldn't be a friend, calling to ask her to meet up for lunch, or an over-eager lover keen to meet up and do a bit of smooching. Besides, at this time in the morning, who the hell would have the energy? Since hitting the big five-oh just recently, Hillary Greene did not consider herself to be a spring chicken anymore.

Which meant it could only be *him*: her friendly neighbourhood stalker.

Just what she needed.

She sighed and reached for her mobile, flipping it open and checking the highlighted box. Yep – number withheld. It was him all right.

Since he only texted, she hit the appropriate button and watched the words light up her screen.

GOOD MORNING, BEAUTIFUL. CAN'T WAIT TO SEE YOU. WEAR SOMETHING BRIGHT AND COLOURFUL JUST FOR ME, THEN I KNOW YOU'LL BE THINKING OF ME. LOVE – YOUR ONE AND ONLY.

Hillary's arm flopped back down on the bed, the phone still held listlessly in her hand. She'd have to save this latest message and show it to Steven Crayle, the detective superintendent who ran a small team within the CRT, and was her immediate boss.

It was Crayle who got to make the arrests and bask in the glory. Not that she minded the basking part – he was welcome to handle the press and be patted on the back by the top brass. Being in the limelight had never felt like her natural habitat, although she'd been forced into it from time to time during her career, which had always been – technically at least – widely successful.

So when she'd made the decision to return to work, her old boss at the Thames Valley Police HQ, Commander Marcus Donleavy, had been only too pleased to welcome her back. Morever, she suspected that he had ordered Crayle to give her only the cold cases that covered murder and the more serious crimes.

She'd solved the very first murder case he'd given her just a few weeks ago, but, unfortunately, she'd somehow managed to pick up an 'admirer' in the process. Both she and Crayle were inclined to think that it was someone at the station. Whether a working officer, or a member of the civilian staff, they weren't yet sure.

It had started off with flowers mysteriously appearing on her desk, then Valentine cards, then written messages that were left, creepily, on her narrowboat, *The Mollern*.

The texting was relatively new, and had only started last week, but she was becoming bombarded with them.

He was upping his campaign.

With any chance of going back to sleep now thoroughly shot to hell, Hillary rose and took a rapid two-minute shower in the tiny cubicle that comprised practically all of her minute bathroom, then slipped into her underwear and stood before her wardrobe, thinking.

Should she wear something colourful or not?

On the one hand, the thought of pandering to the creep made her flesh crawl. But his messages were getting bolder and the one this morning had more or less openly admitted that he'd be seeing her some time today – presumably at 'the office'. And whilst the HQ at Kidlington was vast, with potentially hundreds of male suspects, there was just the chance that if she did wear something bright, she might just catch some male eye giving her more notice than was strictly necessary.

But did she really want to feed his fantasies? Already her stalker seemed to think they were engaged in some sort of secret, romantic affair. Which meant that he was a fantasist as well and, possibly, even seriously mentally ill. If she showed up dressed to the nines, did she really want to reinforce his sick fixation on her?

She donned a black skirt and black tights, and pulled out a matching black jacket. Her hand lingered over her choice of blouse. She could wear a brightly coloured one – which might or might not be construed as a message.

Or she could go monochrome with something in white, which would send a message of a far different sort. But on the other hand, did she really want to antagonize him? Or would going for the white option make him angry enough to react in some way, thus broadening their chances of catching him?

Decisions, decisions, she thought, her lips grimacing wryly. Come what may, she had the feeling that no matter what she did, her choice wouldn't please Steven Crayle.

As she stood there in the early morning light, the sunlight catching her long, bell-shaped cap of dark-red hair, Hillary Greene contemplated the thought of Steven Crayle with decid-edly mixed emotions.

Then, angry at herself for all this dithering, she reached inside the wardrobe for a faux-silk blouse in emerald green and slipped it on. Then she donned the jacket and went aft to her small galley kitchen in search of a meagre breakfast.

Since retiring and taking to the canals, she'd lost nearly a stone in weight, and didn't want to put it back on. Although she still retained a rather curvy, hour-glass figure that made most men look at her with more than a passing interest anyway, she had no desire to become even more curvaceous.

Again she found herself contemplating Steven Crayle. Did he like his women to be fashionably thin? Or not?

She scowled down at her brown-bread toast, spread with that tasteless stuff that was supposed to have the sort of fat in it that was actually good for your cholesterol levels, and found herself silently cursing all men. Be they stalkers, or handsome, younger, detective superintendents.

In his office, Steven Crayle glanced up from his chair behind his desk as there came a sharp tap at his door. A moment later it opened to reveal a young woman with long, lushly curling brown hair and a pair of big pansy-brown eyes to match.

'Vivienne,' Steven said briefly. He'd given up telling the girl she was supposed to wait to be summoned before barging into his office, and hoped against hope that when she applied to be accepted for formal training next month, she was turned down.

In this age of cut-backs and stringent budget restrictions, the CRT was manned by very few serving, fully paid-up members of the force, such as himself. Instead, his own small team-within-a-team down here in the bowels of the station consisted mostly of retired officers working to a strict timetable of hours, and young wannabes like Vivienne Tyrell, who worked part-time, got paid a pittance, and were supposed to be getting on-the-job-training for their pains. Which was, in turn, supposed to help them secure a job in the police service, when they could actually afford to get around to recruiting new, young officers.

Vivienne, who was now twenty, and still had no idea what she wanted to be when she grew up, handed over a folder and made sure she leant down over the superintendent's desk to do so. Obligingly, her low-cut V-neck sweater in fluffy apricot wool revealed a deep, creamy cleavage. Her brown eyes fixed firmly to his face as she watched him open and read the contents of the file, willing him to look up at her.

She knew he was forty-one years old, because her friend who worked in personnel had looked him up for her. And she knew from the usual hot-bed of station-house gossip that he was divorced, and currently available.

But not for much longer, if she could help it. The problem was breaking through that sexy cold reserve of his.

Vivienne liked her men older. And gorgeous. And Steven Crayle, at six feet tall, and with to-die-for thick, dark, floppy brown hair and dark-brown eyes, was so gorgeous he actually made her mouth water whenever she looked at him.

'Thank you, Vivienne, that looks like you've done a good job. Be sure Jimmy gets it before he sets out to interview the parents.'

Vivienne nodded. Jimmy Jessop was the old man of their team, and he'd been working on some old rape cases for the last few weeks. It seemed all she did was boring computer searches, background research and scut work. But if it kept her in Steven Crayle's orbit all day, she wasn't going to complain. Now, if only she could just get him to notice her!

It was so frustrating – he was so her type. He always dressed in these cool, expensive suits and silky ties, and was a class act through and through. His watch was as slim as an After Eight mint, and the expensive cologne he used smelt so good it should carry a government health warning. He was one of those men who was so effortlessly elegant that all her friends would die of envy if she could just hook him.

Her eyes dropped to his hands on the folder, now reaching out to hand it back to her. He had long, sensitive fingers – what her mum would call a musician's hands. And he could play a concerto on her any time he wanted.

'Was there anything else?' Steven asked, an expression of mixed amusement and annoyance on his face as he caught her mooning down at him.

'Hmm? Oh, no, sir.'

Steven nodded, then sighed as there came another tap at the door. 'Come in.'

Vivienne saw Steven Crayle's face become utterly expressionless, and she turned quickly to see Hillary Greene standing in the doorway. 'Do you have a moment, sir?'

'Of course,' Steven said, then turned back to the younger woman. 'Vivienne, don't forget to give the file to Jimmy.'

Vivienne flushed with resentment. Hadn't he just told her that? She wasn't likely to forget, was she? There was nothing wrong with *her* memory – she wasn't one of his wrinklies, after all, like Jimmy Jessop or Hillary Greene, who had to be forty if she was a day.

Shooting Hillary a smirk as she swept by, she gave an extra toss of her head for good measure, sending her luxuriant curls flying.

Hillary watched her go, biting back a grin. Everyone in the station knew that Vivienne was trying to seduce Crayle, without much success. Someone really should tell her that the superintendent was too ambitious to ever be caught out doing the sexual tango with such a younger woman, and a member of his staff at that.

Steven Crayle sighed. 'Shut the door, Hillary. Come on in and have a seat.'

'Sir.'

Hillary did as she was bid, then slid into the chair in front of his desk. Wordlessly, she brought out her phone, scrolled down the screen to the saved message, and handed it over.

Steven read it with a grim, tight expression on his face. Briefly, his eyes flicked to her jewel-bright green blouse, then back to the screen again.

As she'd come to expect from her new boss, he didn't miss a trick. But he didn't comment on her choice of dress either. Instead he said flatly, 'He's getting more confident.'

'Yes. But that could be a good thing,' Hillary agreed cautiously.

Steven nodded. 'He almost as much as admits to being a work colleague here,' he mused, tapping the mobile phone thoughtfully.

'Yes, I noticed that too.'

'You decided to play along, then? With the green blouse?'

Hillary shrugged. 'I didn't see that I had much to lose.'

Steven followed her reasoning effortlessly. 'I doubt he's going to be so obvious as to make some comment on it.'

'No, but I might catch someone ogling me.'

Steven's lips twitched. In his opinion, practically every man at the station probably ogled her – and some of the women too, for that matter.

'You want to try and actively flush him out?' he asked, after a few moments' thought.

Since she'd first brought the problem of her stalker to his attention, they'd tried several things to identify him, including setting up a hidden camera at her locker. In the past, he'd left her 'gifts' there, but he'd been too wily to be caught on film. Neither could their combined surveillance catch anyone out following her, and he was canny enough with modern technology to leave no visible trace of his activities.

They were both now of the opinion that he must be a seasoned stalker, since he had it all down too pat for Hillary to be his first victim.

'Nothing else seems to be working,' Hillary said, with understandable frustration. Knowing you were being watched was a war of attrition that played havoc with your nerves, no matter how calm you were under fire. 'You got any ideas?' she asked curiously.

Crayle shrugged. 'I might have.' He shifted a touch uncomfortably in his chair. He *did* have an idea, but he wasn't sure that he wanted to share it with her just yet – mostly because he was not sure of his own motive in coming up with it.

When Commander Donleavy had first told him that Hillary Greene was going to be joining his team, he'd had decidedly mixed feelings about it. Of course, a lot of officers retired early, then found themselves at a loose end and missing the job. Joining the CRT as civilian consultants was a good way to stave off boredom and earn some extra cash. Jimmy Jessop, for instance, was a prime example. At sixty-two, he'd retired on a sergeant's salary, only for his wife to die barely a year later, leaving him alone in a home that had fast begun to feel like a prison. He'd been only too glad to return to work, and there were many more just like him who had done so.

But Hillary Greene was hardly a typical CRT recruit. For a start, she'd been a full DI, and little less than a station legend, when she'd retired. Famously married to the bent copper Ronnie Greene, she'd been investigated by an internal committee when Ronnie's illegal animal-smuggling racket had been uncovered. Of course, she'd been in the process of divorcing him when he'd died in a car accident, and she'd been cleared of any suspicion of knowing what he'd been up to.

Secondly, her arrest and conviction record was second to none – literally. Eveyone knew that Donleavy rated her as one of the best investigative detectives in the region.

Then she'd been shot in the line of duty, and had won a medal for bravery.

And when her best friend and commanding officer, Philip ('Mel') Mallow had been shot and killed whilst standing right beside her, she'd stood firmly behind his widow, her former DS, when she'd shot and killed her husband's killer. Some even said that Hillary Greene had saved Sergeant Janine Mallow from going down for it, since Janine had, for reasons that had never really been fully explained at the time, called her old boss Hillary Greene to the scene whilst still holding the smoking gun, as it were.

And in the aftermath of that very public and messy affair, Hillary's immediate boss, who'd sworn to see both her and Janine Mallow fed to wolves, had for some reason, been mysteriously sidelined to the outer reaches of Hull. Meaning that Hillary must have had something on him.

All of which raised her standing sky-high with everyone at HQ. The rank and file really rated her for standing by her own, showing guts in the face of all kinds of crap, and knowing her craft. And the brass rated her for her successes.

Consequently, when she'd retired, the whole station house had seemed to go into shock.

So when Donleavy had told him that Hillary Greene was coming back, and was, moreover, to be landed in his lap, the situation had needed some serious mulling over. Donleavy had also all but ordered him to give Hillary only the cold murder cases. And nothing loath to oblige, he had promptly handed her the coldest, hardest murder case on the books.

Then he'd sat back and watched her successfully solve it. He still wasn't sure whether he admired her, or resented her. But had a sneaking suspicion it was both.

And it certainly didn't help his dilemma any, to find himself growing more and more physically attracted to her. Even though she was older than he was; they looked the same age, and she had a hard edge to her that was tempered by a sense of humour that unexpectedly appealed to him.

There was also an aloofness to her that drove him to distraction sometimes. He knew he was a good-looking guy, and was honest enough to admit to himself that he was used to women making a play for him. But Hillary Greene tended to observe him with a certain wry mockery in her level gaze that had him going hot and hard in some very annoying places.

So when she'd picked up a stalker, and he'd found himself thinking of a possible way for them to flush him out, he was not sure if it was his brain or another part of his anatomy that had come up with a solution.

Hence his reluctance to discuss it with her.

But when he looked up to find her regarding him steadily he took a deep breath and decided to go for it.

'You and I could always go public with a relationship.'

Hillary Greene blinked. She almost said 'What relationship?' before common sense took over. 'Oh. You mean pretend to be going out with each other and see if it presses his jealousy buttons?'

Steven Crayle nodded. 'That's got to be his default setting, isn't it? Don't most stalkers have a problem with their ego? And it's clear from his texts that you and he are already in a item – at least in his sick mind you are. So if he does work at the station, and he starts seeing us going out and about together, it might make him lose his cool enough to do something reckless.'

Hillary nodded slowly. 'It might just work – and the gossip mill in this place will certainly help feed the fire and keep the pressure on. The way the desk sergeants alone like to speculate about everyone's private life would put a bunch of old women to shame.'

Crayle laughed. 'Tell me about it.'

'Then again, if we were too convincing, it could just piss him off to such an extent that he just gives up on me and goes on to make some other poor woman's life a misery,' Hillary pointed out. 'Which isn't exactly the result we're after.'

'No. I want to catch the little pervert as much as you do. Well – think about it and let me know if you'd like to go ahead with it. In the meantime, I've got another murder case for you.'

And so saying, he reached into the top of his in-tray, and pulled out a thick beige folder. 'This is just the preliminary dossier.'

Hillary gave a wry smile. 'I know. Let me guess – there are boxes and boxes of more stuff waiting for me in the stationery cupboard.'

The stationery cupboard was what she called her office – since that was what it had been before becoming her office.

Steven Crayle's smile utterly lacked sympathy. 'They wouldn't all fit in there. Most of them are in the main office,' he admitted, without missing a beat.

It was the main difference between taking on a fresh new case, and taking over a cold one, Hillary mused an hour later, as she contemplated the piled-high documents concerning the killing of Rowan Thompson. When you're presented with a person whose dead body has only just been discovered, all the information to be gathered is stretched out ahead of you, and in the pursuance and gathering of it, if you were lucky, you would find the killer.

But when you are handed a cold case, all of it has already been done for you. The autopsy has been performed and the results are in; the reams and reams of forensic information are neatly catalogued, the witnesses have all been seen and interviewed, in some cases many times over, and the deceased family and friends have all been contacted and questioned.

And through the blizzard of paperwork, and many years later, you are supposed to go over someone else's case, and follow in the footsteps of some other Chief Investigative Officer who has already tried and failed to solve the crime.

Hillary sighed and poured herself another cup of coffee and re-read the initial reports, trying to get her own take on what she was being told, and gazing at the scene-of-crime photographs whilst trying to imagine herself actually there.

The facts were simple enough.

Rowan Thompson had been just twenty years old when he was killed on December 21 in 2001. The photographs of him – both alive and dead – showed him to have been five feet nine-to-ten inches tall, with spiky fair hair and big brown eyes. A good-looking kid, Hillary acknowledged, he was originally from Birmingham, having been raised in a typical middle-class home in Solihull. He'd been bright too, which is why he'd won a place at one of Oxford's many colleges, where he'd been reading PPE – Philosophy, Politics and Economics. According to his parents, he'd wanted to be either a banker or a stockbroker – and maybe go into politics later in life.

Hillary gave a wry snort and sipped her coffee. With the way the economy was nowadays, if he had lived to make it in the banking world, he'd have probably been widely loathed and vilified by one and all by now. But he'd been spared any of that.

Instead, someone had taken a large pair of sharp scissors and had buried them deep in his stomach.

He had been rooming, along with several other students, in a Victorian property not far from Keble College, where the old house, like many others of its ilk, had long since been converted into bedsits. He was due to go home to Solihull the next day, for the start of the Christmas celebrations with his family.

Instead, his parents had spent the seasonal holidays arranging his funeral.

Hillary picked up a picture of the murder victim taken when he was still alive. It was a group shot, taken in his bedroom at the murder site and the four other people in the frame comprised the other students who shared the house.

She began to make her own notes – part of the process of claiming the case as her own.

Marcie Franks had been twenty-four years old at the time of the killing, and was thus a post graduate student, who was studying for a D.Phil. in biochemistry. In the photograph she was standing to Rowan's right, and stood just fractionally taller than him. She had long brown hair and brown eyes, and regarded the camera with a steady, slightly bored look on her face. She and Rowan were not touching, she noticed, but her arm was casually slung around the waist of the man beside her.

Dwayne Cox was by far the best-looking of the bunch, and at six feet in height one of the tallest. With black hair and blue eyes he must have presented serious competition for Rowan, and she wondered idly if the murder victim had been jealous of him. From the quick run-down she'd given the notes so far, Rowan had had a voracious sexual appetite. And although he was good-looking himself in a more quirky, almost gamine kind of way, Cox was much more classically handsome. At twenty-one, he was a year older than Rowan, and was in his final year of reading experimental psychology.

Darla de Lancie matched her cute name, and was tiny – perhaps five feet – with red hair, freckles and big green eyes. She had a heart-shaped face and in the photograph had her arms flung around Rowan Thompson's neck, and was giving the camera a wide, infectious smile. She was also, according to the CIO's notes, the victim's main girlfriend. The CIO at the time had been Detective Inspector John Gorman, and he'd made it clear that Darla de Lancie knew full well that she did not have exclusive rights on the promiscuous Rowan, and had to be well up on the list of suspects. She was also a year older than Rowan, and was in the process of gaining a BA in English literature.

The odd man out in the photograph was easily Barry Hargreaves. A mature student, at the time of the killing he'd been forty-one years old. Six foot two and balding, he looked like the construction worker he'd been until having what DI Gorman clearly thought was a somewhat typical mid-life crisis. Hargreaves, married for twenty years with teenage twin daughters, had apparently woken up one morning and decided that he should put his brains to better use, and had taken A-levels in mathematics and physics at night school. He'd left regular school at sixteen in spite of a raft of excellent O-Levels in order to earn money, and had, until then, never seemed to regret it. He'd gained a place at one of the newer colleges through the auspices of some government scheme or other, and was in the first year of a three-year course in Mathematics.

Idly, Hillary wondered if he'd ever finished the course, and wondered what he was doing now. But then, no doubt, within the next few days she'd be finding out, for all four of them were suspects in Thompson's murder.

Along with the house's owner, sixty-four-year-old Wanda Landau, who lived in the basement flat, it seemed unlikely that anyone else had access to Rowan's room.

Wanda Landau had discovered him in his room at about ten o'clock in the morning. He'd been lying on the floor, roughly halfway between his bed and the sofa, with the scissors which had killed him lying beside him. From the crime scene photos, it was obvious that the room had been used as some sort of workshop, for swathes of coloured fabrics draped a lot of the unfashionable, brown wood furniture, and a sewing machine was set up on his table.

Gorman quickly established that Darla often made her own clothes, and tended to use Rowan's room to do so, because it was bigger than her own, and gave her more space.

She'd admitted that the scissors were hers, and were kept sharp in order to cleanly cut the silks and satins that she preferred.

Forensics had discovered that whoever had killed him had washed the scissors at the small washbasin beside the bed – and probably their hands too – before tossing the scissors down beside the body and leaving.

Gorman had ascertained that it was almost certain, due to the amount of blood at the scene, and the probability of arterial spraying, that the killer must have had a considerable amount of blood all over him – or her. But no witnesses came forward who could remember seeing anyone in the area at the time, walking down the street with blood on their clothing. Of course, it was the middle of winter so the killer could have taken off their coat, stabbed Rowan, and then donned probably a long coat to cover their bloodstained clothes.

Or, far more likely, it was someone in the house. Although Rowan's bedroom door had not been locked – and indeed, according to Gorman, the rest of the students were also in the habit of leaving their individual room doors unlocked – Mrs Landau always kept the main front and back doors locked, as well the door to her own flat.

So it seemed unlikely that a stranger would have been able to just wander in and gain entry that way, and Wanda Landau was adamant that she'd never let anyone in that morning. Rowan had been seen by all the others earlier on, and the ME had put the time of death at between 8.45 and 9.00 in the morning.

Of course, it was always possible that Rowan had answered the front door and let the killer in himself, but again the landlady's evidence seemed to rule this out. She'd heard no one enter the hall whilst she'd been in her flat, and no one had rung the main doorbell. But she'd admitted that Rowan could be 'a sneaky little so-and-so' especially when it came to smuggling in girlfriends.

Not that she barred her 'boys and girls' from having friends in: it was more likely that he wanted to make sure Darla De Lancie was kept in the dark about what he was up to.

So it was possible that Rowan had let a woman in and had taken her up to his room for some hanky-panky, and got far more than he'd bargained for. Gorman seemed to think that it was also possible that, given the victim's habit of bedding anything agreeable, an aggrieved boyfriend or a cuckolded husband might also be responsible. Although why Rowan would let in a male rival, of course, couldn't be ascertained from the facts available.

According to Gorman's notes, Thompson was something of a sexual athlete, not averse to experimentation and had a voracious appetite for sexual kicks with very little sense of discernment.

From time to time, Hillary caught a whiff of distinct disapproval in Gorman's rather dry, rather pedantic notes, but since the man was now dead, and thus couldn't be consulted, she couldn't be sure how much Gorman's own prudish nature had coloured his judgement of the victim.

But from the little she'd read so far, Gorman was nothing if not thorough.

Her coffee finished, Hillary turned to the first of the forensic reports.

The room, as was to be expected, was awash with fingerprints, nearly all of them belonging to the victim, his girlfriend, and the other housemates. Some were traced to an electrician who'd been called in to see to a fault the previous week, others that were much older were never tracked down. But given the history of the house as a student residence, there was nothing much unexpected in that.

Likewise, the victim's clothes had many fibre traces on them, some inevitably from the carpet, some from clothes that were a match to Darla de Lancie's, but again, given their close relationship, that was hardly earth-shattering. And since there was no way of knowing when the traces had been left on the victim, there was no way to put Darla actually at the scene at the time of the killing.

The only blood found on the victim belonged to the victim. Sometimes, with a stabbing, the killer cut himself, and thus left valuable DNA behind. But in this case, the murder weapon hadn't been an unwieldy knife, but a neat pair of scissors, complete with rounded plastic handles, making it almost impossible for the killer to wound himself in the stabbing process.

The medical report was the usual mixture of hard-to-understand medical pronouncements, but the summary at the end made it clear: there was only one blow – but it had been delivered deep and low, probably in an up-and-under underarm movement, and with a fair amount of force. A woman could certainly have done it, since the blades penetrated the lower part of the abdomen, where it was mainly soft tissue, where you wouldn't encounter bone or any other obstacle that would have required brute force to penetrate.

The victim had died of blood loss and shock, so again, no surprises there, but one thing did stand out.

Tox screens showed that Rowan Thompson had minute traces of some sort of drug in his system that the labs hadn't been able to identify. Gorman, of course, had been straight on to Thompson's GP, but the murder victim had not been prescribed drugs of any kind for a medical condition. In fact, Rowan seemed to be in the peak of health, and the only time he'd consulted his GP had been for regular screenings for various STDs. He'd been clear of those too, so he had obviously been a careful boy.

That left a whole raft of illegal drugs to consider.

Hillary sighed cynically. It was Oxford, he was a student, and a young man who probably thought of himself as immortal and, moreover, was the kind who liked to experiment. Where the hell to start? On the party scene nowadays there were always new drugs popping up overnight, some even technically legal. The law seemed to be constantly playing catch-up when it came to outlawing designer drugs.

No doubt Rowan had taken something either at a rave, or a private party, or just between friends – probably sometime within forty-eight hours of his death.

But since the ME made it clear that the unknown drug could in no way have contributed to the cause of death, Gorman hadn't wasted too much time pursuing it.

Hillary could understand why, but she didn't much like it. She trawled through the boxes of stuff to find Gorman's personal notes, and was glad to see that he'd copied the information and passed it over to the narcotics squad, but she could find no follow-up on it from them.

She made a mental note to get either Vivienne or Sam Pickles, the other young wannabe on her team, to see if they could find any report on it from the drugs squad. It would probably come to nothing but you never knew.

If Rowan Thompson was a regular drug user, he must have had a dealer. And drug dealers and murder went together like whales and pilot fish. Perhaps he'd refused to pay up, or had grassed on the dealer to someone, or, even worse, taken his business elsewhere.

People had been killed for far less.

Apart from that, science wasn't able to help much. Although the public was used to seeing crime shows where forensic science wrapped up even the most baffling of cases in one hour flat, with some very fancy microscope work and a scrap of esoteric knowledge, real life was seldom that cut and dried.

And although a lot of the CRT's work consisted of reopening cases when new advances in technology made re-examining retained evidence practical, there were the odd cases, like this one, where simple, good old-fashioned detective work was needed.

And it was this little niche that was Steven Crayle's own. And now hers.

'OK, Rowan,' Hillary said to the photograph of the cheeky-faced youngster who'd been in his grave for nearly a dozen years now. 'Let's see if we can't find out who killed you.'

CHAPTER TWO

At the end of the day, Hillary wearily pushed the stack of folders aside, and stood up to stretch. She had taken a mountain of notes from the Thompson case, and had a list of to-do's for her team tomorrow that would make Vivienne grumble for a week at least. She'd already informed them that they had been handed another murder inquiry, which had met with considerable enthusiasm from Sam Pickles, a vague excitement from Vivienne, and quiet satisfaction from Jimmy Jessop, the retired sergeant she'd begun to think of as her right-hand man.

Tomorrow the hard work began in earnest. She'd already set all of them on the task of tracking down the current whereabouts of the various witnesses and asked for any updated background information on them to start being collated. Since there would be little help from the new advancement in forensics, this case, she could see, was going to rely very heavily on the fact that new eyes were taking a look at it, coupled with any fresh information witnesses might be able to offer.

Which wasn't as forlorn a hope as some might think. Often, the passage of time could be a good thing, in that people who might have been more reticent at the time of the murder now felt more at ease and less threatened by the passage of over a decade. People who might have kept silent from sheer fright or unease might now be persuaded to talk. They might not even be aware that they knew anything of significance, which was where Hillary's overall view and experience came in. All she needed was to spot one little thread to unravel, one loose end that had never been tied in, and the case could suddenly come alive.

One thing was for certain: if she could not get any new insights, or didn't have luck on her side, the case was going to stay closed. And she was realistic enough to know that you couldn't win them all. She'd struck gold with her very first case for CRT, but that didn't mean her second case was bound to follow suit. If her close rate was only 20% on these hard-nut cases that Steven Crayle was determined to give her, then the brass would be happy with that.

Not that she wouldn't take it personally if she failed to find Rowan Thompson's killer. She knew herself well enough to be aware of just how much it would rankle to have to accept defeat. But it was way too early yet to even conceive of such an outcome. She let her mind wander over the case as she'd found it so far.

Gorman had dithered between Barry Hargreaves and Darla de Lancie as his chief suspects since their motives seemed the strongest, but in the absence of any forensics, witnesses or a confession, the case had stalled. But the fact that Gorman hadn't been able to find anyone else who might have wanted the student dead, didn't mean there hadn't been one. If she couldn't find his killer at the house where he lived, then she'd just have to widen her net. But that was listed firmly in her mental 'last resort' file.

She glanced at her watch, saw that it was just gone five, and sighed. Ever since Steven had come up with his rather cocka-mamie plan to lure out her stalker, she'd been considering its merits.

She'd been the target of her stalker for nearly two months now, and it was clear that his campaign was only escalating. At first, she'd been prepared to wait a while, to see if it would fizzle out of its own accord. But that was clearly not going to happen. All their other efforts to discover his identity had crashed and burned, and she was growing more and more impatient to knock this thing on the head before it got really out of hand.

But was Crayle's idea to pretend to be an item actually likely to work? Or was she just fighting shy of it for reasons of her own?

She was well aware of her growing attraction to Steven Crayle. And unless she missed her guess – and she rarely did – it was not exactly a purely one-sided state of affairs. So if they 'pretended' to get together, she could well see it veering off into the realms of reality. And wasn't that at the back of his mind too?

And technically at least, there was nothing to stop them getting together. They were both single and old enough and mean enough to tackle an affair. Now that she was no longer a DI, Steven was not even her superior officer, so there'd be no reason for the top brass to suck the air in through their teeth with disapproval.

She'd just never particularly liked the thought of mixing business with pleasure in this way, that was all. She'd rather they just dated, or just set out to get her stalker. Combining or blurring the line between the two just seemed to be asking for trouble to her. On the other hand, some sort of definitive action needed to be taken. She had the feeling that this was going to get very nasty, very fast, and that her *admirer* was going to start making her life very miserable before he was through. And her instincts had always been pretty reliable.

'Oh, to hell with it,' she muttered and, grabbing her bag and coat, she walked through the maze of subterranean corridors to Crayle's office and knocked on the door.

There was no answer. She reached into her bag for her mobile and, as she headed upstairs, speed-dialled his number. It was answered on the second ring.

'Crayle.' His voice was low, almost whispered.

'Guv, it's me. Wonder if I could have a word.'

'I'm in a meeting. I'll get back to you in half an hour,' he said tersely.

Hillary said thanks and hung up, her lips twisting wryly. So much for the beginnings of a sweet romance.

She drove back to Thrupp, parking in her favourite spot in the local pub's car park, and walked down the towpath. She could see the dark splash of crimson blooms lying on the top of *The*

Mollern from several yards away. She carried on stalwartly walking, snatched the gift of fifty red roses from the boat roof and carried on up the towpath.

When she reached *Ivanhoe* she tapped on the roof and waited. A moment later, her next-door neighbour of five weeks standing poked his head from the door in the stern. Alfie Bix, a pensioner with a penchant for producing fine crochet work, grinned back at her. He used his boat as a mobile shop, and regularly sold his wares to the tourist hotspots at Henley-on-Thames and Stratford-upon-Avon. 'Hello, lovely lady.'

'Hello, Alf. Didn't I hear you say that you and Betty had a wedding anniversary coming up?' she asked, waving the roses under his nose. 'These any use to you?'

Alf happily accepted the gift and asked her down for a drink of his home-made cowslip wine. Hillary, who'd already sampled it – and the headache that followed – quickly refused.

Back on her own boat, she made herself a cup of coffee and list-lessly contemplated dinner. Beans on toast? Or go for something really flashy, like Sainsbury's own frozen lasagne? She was still thinking about that one ten minutes later when her phone rang.

'Sorry about that,' Steven Crayle said. 'What's up?'

'I was thinking about your offer – to see if we can lure out my admirer. I want to take you up on it.'

There was a moment of surprised silence on the other end of the line, then his voice came back, as smooth and unruffled as ever. 'OK. What about starting tonight? You had dinner yet?'

The Plough and Anchor on the outskirts of Islip, a small village not far from Kidlington, had a good reputation for food, was cheap and on a mid-week night at least, didn't require a reserva-tion. It was also a fairly well-known spot for coppers to frequent, which was why Steven and Hillary had chosen it.

He'd picked her up from her narrowboat, which he'd been curious about, and found himself admiring it in a neutral sort of way. He could see that it suited her perfectly, and he could see the attraction of taking long weekends in it, or the odd week's holiday, but probably not living in it on a daily basis. He was too tall and liked space and light – the boat would probably begin to feel too claustrophobic after a while. His own house in Kidlington, that funnily enough also enjoyed a view of the canal, suited him just fine. It was big, modern and, since his wife had moved in with her new man, had been redecorated from top to bottom in the style that he preferred,

He drove a very nice mid-range black saloon car, which he negotiated around Islip's quirky road system with ease. Finally parked in the small and nearly full pub car park, he glanced around casually.

'Let's hope there's someone here to spot us and gossip about it,' he said mildly. And then, aware that that might have sounded, at the very least, less than gallant, added quickly, 'Not that I would mind taking you out any number of times.' He stopped, realized that hadn't exactly helped matters any, and added awkwardly, 'I mean, I'd be happy to see you regardless of the circumstances.'

Hillary, enjoying the unusual sight of the suave Steven Crayle floundering, suddenly grinned. 'You ever heard of that well-known advice? When you find yourself in a hole—'

Crayle laughed and nodded. 'Stop digging. Right.' They climbed out of the car and walked towards the pub. He was dressed in a dark-blue suit with a cream shirt and mint green, black and cream tie. He looked good enough to eat, Hillary thought, with a certain wistful pang.

She too had been careful in her choice of clothes, and had worn a long, very dark green velvet skirt, with a pale lemon silk top. With her hair pulled back to reveal dangling ear-rings, and with slightly more lavish make-up than she usually wore, she knew she looked good. Too good for this just to be a casual meal with a mate, anyway, which was the impression they were out to give. Anyone they knew seeing them together couldn't help but realize they were on a date.

As they entered the pub and walked to the bar, she was slightly surprised by how full it was. She asked for a white wine spritzer, and then waited whilst Steven was served at the bar.

'We've got a table in the conservatory area,' he said a few minutes later, handing her a glass. 'We might as well go through. And, by the way, I'm sure the fat bloke with the combover sat by the bar with the big-boned blonde is in Traffic.'

Hillary glanced that way, and vaguely recognized the man who was pretending not to notice them. 'Yes, I think I've seen him around,' she admitted.

'So, mission already accomplished, what say we have a nice time, and enjoy the meal?' he said, checking out the table numbers, and glad to note that theirs was a quiet table for two, lit by flickering candles, tucked away in a far corner.

He pulled out her chair for her, and Hillary sat down with a smile.

Good enough to eat and a gentleman to boot.

Tonight was going to be interesting.

The next morning, Hillary arrived in the office at a few minutes to nine. Vivienne, unsurprisingly, had not yet turned up for work, but both Sam, a tall, lanky, sandy-haired lad doing a sociology and economics degree at Brookes University, and Jimmy were in.

'Guv,' Jimmy nodded. 'We're making progress on the stuff you gave us yesterday. We've got a list of witness locations for you, and the background we've got so far.'

'Good.' Hillary took the list from the grey-haired man and ran a quick eye over it. 'Wanda Landau still lives in the same house?' she asked, with just a hint of surprise in her voice. In her experience, a lot of people moved house when someone was murdered on the premises. But perhaps it had not been financially possible for the landlady to move. Either that, or she was a tough old bird, the kind who'd be too stubborn on principle to be driven out of her own home. Or maybe she just hadn't cared enough about Rowan for it to bother her. Whichever it was, she needed to find out.

'Seems so, guv. She's still renting out all four rooms to students as well, though she must be in her seventies by now. Still, it's a good income for her, innit?'

Hillary nodded. 'Yes. Well, we might as well start with her. It'll give us a chance to check out the house for ourselves as well.' She glanced up, her gaze going between Sam and Jimmy.

Jimmy, as the experienced officer, would be more use to her, but she was well aware that she was supposed to be giving Sam as much experience and on-the-job training as she could.

'Sam, you want to drive?'

The youngster didn't have to be asked twice, and Jimmy grinned at Hillary as he shot up and scrambled eagerly for his notebook.

'Jimmy, hold the fort. And you might as well take the time to get acquainted with the files while I'm gone, and start up the murder book.'

The murder book was a new folder, set up by herself, and all members of the team were expected to keep it updated with any new information they came across in the course of the investigation. This meant that everyone was kept up to date, and could see the progress of the case at a single glance, lessening the chance of a possibly important fact slipping through the net, because someone had failed to mention it or see its significance at the time. Overseeing it was an important job, and since this was going to be a difficult case, Hillary could sense, she wanted Jimmy on it.

'Guv,' he agreed.

Outside, the sun was shining, and as they walked through the foyer, the desk sergeant began to whistle cheerfully. The tune, though somewhat garbled and less than tone-perfect, was instantly recognizable as the old Hot Chocolate classic *You Sexy Thing*.

Hillary shot him a look and saw the old reprobate wink back at her. Bloody hell, she thought, that was impressive, even by station-house standards. And then she thought back to last night, and Steven Crayle's expert, lingering kiss in the car park, under the boggling gaze of the man from Traffic, and knew she was actually blushing.

Which, naturally enough, didn't go unnoticed by the desk sergeant.

'Bloody hell!' she hissed. She couldn't remember the last time that she'd actually felt her face go warm over something like that.

'Guv?' Sam said.

'Nothing, forget it,' Hillary said sharply and threw him her car keys.

Sam's face fell. 'We not taking my car, guv?' he wheedled hopefully.

'No, we'll take mine,' Hillary said firmly, and led the way to Puff the Tragic Wagon, her ancient Volkswagen Golf.

Sam sighed and quietly joined her, praying the old heap would actually start. Somewhat to his chagrin it did – as good as gold.

Number 8, Kebler Road, was not far from Oxford's South Park, and was situated in a quiet street, lined with Victorian terraces and lime trees. On a warm spring morning, the traffic was surprisingly light, and Sam, much to his surprise, was able to find off-street parking quite close by. Hillary paused at the pavement to let a stream of bicyclists go by, then trotted across the road and looked up at the house where Rowan Thompson had lived and died.

It was a skinny structure of mixed red and cream brick, with a bay window on the ground floor and what was obviously a converted attic in the eaves. Steps led down to a small basement patio, and up to the main door.

Hillary went down the steps, admiring the black wrought-iron stair rails, and the terracotta tubs full of scarlet geraniums and blue lobelia that lined the flagstone patio floors. The whole area was shaded by a sweet, fresh-smelling lime tree, and in the summer would be the ideal place to set up a small table and chair with a glass of wine and a good book.

She rang the bell and waited. In her mind, she'd pictured Wanda Landau as the archetypal landlady, rounded, curly-haired and inquisitive. But the woman who answered the door failed to meet the criteria on all three counts. She was easily as tall as Hillary, with an elegantly lean figure encased in a simple wrap-around navy-blue dress, and her hair was a straight-cut platinum blonde in colour. Her make-up was discreet but flawless and she wore simple but expensive gold jewellery at her ears, throat and on her fingers.

'Yes?' she asked coolly, with no visible interest on her high-cheekboned, still-beautiful face.

She knew from reading the files that Mrs Landau had been sixty-four at the time of the murder, which meant she must now be well into her seventies. But she looked at least two decades younger, and Hillary wondered what plastic surgeon she went to for help to achieve the miracle.

Who knows, now that she'd passed the big five-oh herself, she might need his name some time soon.

'Mrs Landau?' Hillary held out her ID card that identified her, not as a detective inspector any more, but a civilian consultant with the Thames Valley Police. 'I'm Hillary Greene, this is Mr Sam Pickles. We're part of team currently taking a fresh look at the murder of Rowan Thompson.'

'Good grief! Well, in that case, please come in.' The voice was pure Oxford, that curious mixture of slightly country accent, mixed with upper-class accent, that somehow came out as being totally classless. She moved to one side, smiling at Sam indulgently as he carefully sidled past her in the narrow doorway.

'Go on straight through. I think Ferris is still in the lounge doing his homework – perhaps we'd be better off just there, to the right, in the kitchen? I can make us all some tea.'

Hillary obediently veered to the right and found herself in a small, but well-appointed and cheerful kitchen in shades of lemon and cream, with mint-green units and marble worktops. The white-tiled floor made the most of the somewhat restricted light in the basement flat, and gave the impression of spacious elegance.

Although Wanda Landau might have been reduced to giving over the bulk of her house to paying guests, she obviously knew how to maintain her standards of living.

'Darjeeling all right?' she asked, going to the kettle and filling it from the tap.

'Fine, thank you. Milk and one sugar for both of us, please,' Hillary acknowledged, then nodded at Sam to take a seat in the corner. She was pleased to see the lad open his notebook and take out his pen, under the cover of the table. Good, he was learning fast. Witnesses very often clammed up when they realized their words were being noted down by the authorities.

'Poor Rowan. I've never forgotten him, you know,' Wanda said, crossing over to a tall fridge and removing some skimmed milk. 'It doesn't seem like more than ten years ago since it all happened.'

'No, I'm sure it doesn't,' Hillary agreed. 'Time has a way of getting away from all of us. What can you tell me about him? I know you must have gone all over this before at the time, with Inspector Gorman, but don't worry about that. Just tell me what immediately comes to mind when you think of him,' Hillary said, keeping it determinedly vague. If you asked a specific question, you very often got a specific answer, and at the moment she was just fishing, and casting about for anything interesting.

'Oh, probably his cheeky grin,' Wanda said, returning to the table with two china cups and saucers. She moved to a cupboard and retrieved a sugar bowl, and two spoons from the drawer underneath. 'He had a certain kind of charm about him – you probably wouldn't remember an actor called Tommy Steele but he had that sort of way about him. Little-boy, mischief-maker, but with a heart-of-gold feeling about him.' Wanda smiled briefly, and then, hearing the kettle boil, set about pouring boiling water into a teapot. Eventually she brought everything together to the table and all the activity stopped.

As she took her seat with a small sigh, she suddenly looked her age. 'Mind you, it was probably all only skin deep. A bit of an act, perhaps. He was young, you see, and the young have a way of being ruthless, don't they? Not that they mean to be, they just only think of themselves.'

'I understand,' Hillary said, taking a sip of her tea, and wishing it was full-blooded coffee. 'He had a girlfriend at the time, but I suppose he led her a right merry dance.'

'Oh he did, yes. Little Darla – a lovely girl. She was head over heels in love with him, poor thing, but even I could see he had a string of others dancing to his tune. And I was never one to…. Oh, hello. Something the matter?'

She turned as the door to the kitchen opened, and a teenager poked his head in. He could have been any age from a gangly fourteen to as much as eighteen. He had close-cut hair, in the current fashion, and a silver ring through his left eyebrow. He was wearing skinny jeans and a much-washed, fashionably faded black T-shirt.

'This is Ferris, my grandson,' Wanda introduced them.

'I've got to get off to school for my mocks,' the lad said, his eyes running without interest over Sam before coming to rest on Hillary.

'He's doing his A-levels this summer, aren't you, sweetheart?' Wanda said, with grandmotherly pride. 'Four of them. He's already been offered a place at Hertford if his grades are high enough.'

'Congratulations,' Hillary said. A place at Hertford College, one of the many that comprised Oxford University, was something to be proud of indeed. 'What do you want to read?'

'Engineering. Got any crisps, Gran?'

Wanda got up and went to a cupboard, coming back with a large silver-foil packet and an indulgent smile. 'Don't eat them all and ruin your appetite for dinner. I've got fresh salmon and I'm making that dill sauce you like.'

'OK,' the lad said, and withdrew without another word.

'Ferris! Manners,' Wanda called, and they all heard a vaguely mumbled 'goodbye' waft back from the depths of the flat.

'Boys,' Wanda said, then forced a brief laugh. 'Not that I can lay the blame for his lack of charm on anybody else. I was the one who raised him, but what can you do? Youngsters nowadays – still, rebellion against the status quo is part of the rite of passage of growing up, isn't it?'

Hillary nodded, not interested in Ferris, and determined to get things back on track. 'Yes. You were saying something about Darla and Rowan?'

'Oh – oh yes. Only, as I was about to say, I don't really interest myself in the students who live here. I'm not their mother, after all, and what with having had Ferris to look after, I simply don't have the time to concern myself with their comings and goings. So long as they pay the rent on time, don't cause any damage, and are reasonably quiet, that's really all I ask for. I rather think Inspector Gorman was disappointed that I couldn't give him chapter and verse about the private life of all the students who were here at the time Rowan was... well... I mean, as I said to him, I'm just not the nosy kind.'

Hillary nodded and took another sip of tea. No doubt someone like Wanda would consider it far too grubby and embarrassing to live vicariously through the young people who shared her home.

'You're a widow?' Hillary asked gently.

'Oh yes – more than thirty years now. Geoffrey worked in insurance. He left me this house, and, rather oddly considering, very little in insurance money.' Wanda Landau laughed. 'Daddy always said he was the least reliable stuffed shirt he'd ever met. Daddy was a farmer – we had a few acres out near Witney way.'

Hillary nodded, seeing it all. A well-to-do daughter of minor landed gentry, Wanda had married beneath her, and had been reduced to renting out her nice house in Oxford to students. She could well understand why she'd have as little to do with the never-ending flow of youngsters as possible. She and they must have virtually nothing in common.

'But Rowan seemed to have made an impression? You seemed to know him quite well,' Hillary probed delicately and, to her surprise, the sophisticated elderly lady blushed slightly.

'Well, yes. I mean the way he died.' Wanda shrugged her thin shoulders elegantly. 'It rather sticks with you, doesn't it, when something so tragic and horrendous happens to one so young?'

'Yes,' Hillary agreed quietly.

'And, like I said, Rowan was the kind of young man who liked to make an impression on others, so he went out of his way to charm me. He was a born entertainer, in many ways. He used to call me Mrs L, and was always over-flirtatious whenever we met. I tried to put a stop to that of course, but he was the sort of boy who needed to be constantly admired and adored. He used to make me laugh, to be honest, he was so transparently needy, whilst at the same time, so full of himself, and full of life. He was obviously going to be a handful for any young woman to take on, and Darla was never the kind of girl who would have a strong enough hand on the reins to keep him in line.'

Hillary nodded. 'From the notes Inspector Gorman made, I got the impression he was something of a Jack-the-lad.'

Wanda nodded. 'Yes, he was. But he was never bad, you know. Just thoughtless and somewhat reckless. He wasn't rotten, like some young people seem to be,' she added, and a flash of pain and bitterness flitted briefly across her face.

Hillary felt her radar give a definite ping. At some point, some young person had caused this woman an awful lot of pain. Could it have been Rowan Thompson? She made a mental note to ask Sam to get a run-down on Wanda Landau's personal history as soon as he could.

'Now, the day he died,' Hillary changed tack gently, 'what can you tell me about that day?'

Wanda Landau visibly straightened her shoulders and became

business-like. 'Well, it was a day just like any other. Except Christmas was nearly upon us, and the young people would be heading off to their family homes soon. I always enjoy the holidays between terms when I have the house to myself,' she admitted, with a wry smile. 'I woke up at my usual time – about eight. I had breakfast, and tidied up, and was getting ready to do some Christmas shopping.'

Wanda took a sip of her tea, without leaving a trace of her plum-coloured lipstick on the rim of the thin china cup, of course, and frowned thoughtfully. 'Something made me go upstairs – what was it…? Oh, yes, it had begun to rain and I wanted to make sure the landing window was shut before I went out. One of them up there was a bit of a fresh-air fiend – I rather think it might have been Mr Hargreaves – and living in the city you have to be so careful of burglars. The amount of break-ins—' Wanda suddenly broke off and flushed guiltily, aware that she might be sounding somewhat critical in front of the police. 'Not that I've ever experienced it myself, of course.'

Hillary smiled. 'It's all right, I understand. Oxford has its fair share of crime, just like any other big city. And you're quite right to be careful. I wish more people were.'

'Yes. Well, I went upstairs to make sure the window was shut – it was, by the way, I remember telling that to Inspector Gorman – when I saw the door to Rowan's room was standing open. There was nothing really unusual in that, but everything seemed very quiet. Usually, with four students in the house, I was used to hearing noise of some kind, so I called out a general sort of 'hello' but no one answered, so I went to shut the door – these old houses tend to be draughty, you know, and in the middle of winter…. Anyway, when I was in the doorway, I sort of looked in and saw him. Well, his legs, mostly. Lying on the floor. I rushed in, I thought he might have fainted – well,' – again Wanda gave a slight blush – 'I thought it more likely that he might be passed out drunk, I'm afraid. Not that I had any real reason to think that – some of the young people I've had here over the years might have a problem with binge drinking, isn't that what they call it? But Rowan, although he might have shown up here a little the worse for wear sometimes, never had to be actually carried in or anything.'

Wanda, after this marathon stint, paused for breath, and smiled weakly. 'Anyway, I saw him lying there. He was covered in red, all across his middle and it was leaking about him on the floor. For a really odd, strange moment – and I don't really know why I thought this – I thought someone had sloshed a tin of red paint over him. Then I saw the scissors on the floor beside him. And he looked so pale, so still. So ... inanimate. It almost didn't look like Rowan at all. Except that it was him, of course. So I backed away and called the police.'

'You didn't touch him?' Hillary asked, although she already knew from the reports that there had been no sign of Mrs Landau's footprints in the blood beside the body.

'Oh, no.' Wanda gave a small, graphic shudder. 'I couldn't.'

'And you never heard anyone come to the house that morning?'

'No.'

'You heard the others leave?'

'Yes – well, I can't say for sure, but I heard female voices in the hall sometime just after I'd had breakfast, which I took to be Marcie and Darla leaving. And a male voice too – I'm not sure which of the men it was, though. I never heard anything more, but there was no one else in the house by the time I found Rowan. Of that I'm sure. You get to know when a house is empty, you see.'

Hillary did.

So at some point that morning, all the students had left. Mrs Landau had heard three of them. Had a fourth stayed behind, and then sneaked out after killing Rowan? Or had one of them sneaked back in?

She took Wanda Landau carefully over it all for a second time, but the landlady had nothing to add to her original statement.

Finally Hillary thanked her and rose. 'We'll probably need to see you again some time in the future. And I'd quite like to see the room Rowan died in at some point. I take it there's someone currently in residence?'

'I'm afraid so. And, of course, there's nothing really to see anymore. Rowan's family had all his things, and it's been entirely redecorated since then.'

Hillary nodded. 'Yes, I expected as much. Well, thank you, Mrs Landau, you've been very helpful.'

Outside, back under the lime trees, Hillary regarded the house thoughtfully.

'Nice woman, guv,' Sam ventured timidly. 'Must have come as a bit of a shock for a lady like that. Finding a body, I mean.'

Hillary nodded. 'So she struck you as being a lady, did she, Sam?' Hillary mused. 'Don't fret,' she added quickly, when the lad looked alarmed, as if he'd done something wrong. 'She struck me that way too. But I get the feeling that life's not exactly been all peaches and cream for our landlady. What's she doing raising her grandson, for a start? When we get back to the office I want you to find out everything you can about Mrs Landau's personal history.'

'You really think her family life is relevant, guv?' Sam asked, surprised. 'I mean, I know the first person to find the body is always looked at closely, but in this case, you don't think the old lady really had anything to do with it, do you?'

Hillary smiled grimly. 'Right now, Sam, everyone who lived in that house when our victim died interests me. And as for what might be relevant and what isn't – until we know all there is to know, we can't possibly tell what might matter and what doesn't. Can we?'

And with that rather sage advice ringing in his ears, Sam followed her across the road and back to the rust-heap of her car.

CHAPTER THREE

PC Tom Warrington tied up the laces on his steel-toe-capped boots and walked back towards the central lobby. He'd been working a stint in admin for several weeks now, since coping with perpetual paperwork was always an unpopular pastime with his colleagues, and he knew that taking it on had earned him some much-needed brownie points with his sergeant. The bastard had never liked him, and since the sarge wouldn't be caught dead in admin, it had the added bonus of keeping him out of Tom's hair.

But even that wasn't the real reason why Tom had applied for the job in records. It simply gave him much-needed access to the information he wanted. But he had to be careful, he knew that.

At twenty-six, he was getting rather old to still be in uniform after nearly eight years in the service, and sometimes that still rankled. He knew that he had the reputation for being something of a loner, and he knew as well that many of his workmates seemed to avoid him. He was sure it was because they were jealous.

Ever since he'd hit puberty, he'd worked out with weights, and his body-building had left him with a formidable physique. Which meant he did more than his fair share when it came to manning the lines at football matches when hooliganism was expected. He was also seconded regularly to help out when extra numbers were called upon for riot-control work. Not that he was complaining about that – he loved it. The adrenaline rush was something else.

As he began to cross the foyer, he noticed that a large gaggle of uniforms, most of them from Traffic, was clustered around the front desk. The second shift had obviously arrived, for a much older man had replaced the desk sergeant of that morning, and there seemed to be a fair amount of raucous ribbing going on. Obviously, the younger element was keen to impart the latest news to the old-timer. Tom's cat-green eyes narrowed in contempt at the gossiping horde, before two words that always caused his heart to leap got his attention, and he veered off towards them.

'And he's sure it was Hillary Greene?' the desk sergeant was saying.

'Straight up,' one of them shot back. 'In the car park, they were.'

'Actually snogging?' the desk sergeant asked, a somewhat sceptical lilt in his voice.

Tom's heartbeat accelerated even further as he came to stand a few feet behind a pair of WPCs.

'And it was definitely her super?' one of the others asked.

'No doubt about it. They'd just had a cosy dinner together in the pub, hadn't they?' was the response.

'Who's this Superintendent Crayle then?' one of the WPCs in front of him asked the woman beside her, and her friend grinned back.

'Dishy Steven? Haven't you seen him yet?'

'No, I've just been transferred from Newport Pagnell. Only been here a week,' the other one responded. 'Good-looking, is he?'

'I wouldn't say no, if he asked.'

'Well, I suppose there's nothing against it,' the desk sergeant handed down his verdict magisterially, causing the WPCs to suddenly pay attention. 'The super's been divorced for years, and Hillary's as free as a bird. Good luck to 'em, I say.'

'But he's younger than her, ain't he, Sarge? You don't reckon he'll be another Danvers then,' someone asked, and there was a general burst of levity.

'Danvers? Who's that?' The newcomer from Newport Pagnell nudged her mate with her elbow.

'He was Hillary Greene's guv'nor when she was still a DI,' her friend explained patiently. 'He was dishy too, but DI Greene wouldn't have him.'

One of the women suddenly spotted Tom standing just behind them and shot him a curious glance. It was the newcomer, and her eyes widened appreciatively as she took in his impressive figure. She liked the dark hair and green eyes too, but before she could make any sort of approach, Tom Warrington turned away abruptly. Her curious friend saw where she was looking and whispered loudly, 'Forget it. He looks buff, but they say he's a bit of a weirdo.'

He knew they were talking about him now, but it barely registered. His hands, however, were clenched so tightly into fists that they were white with the lack of circulation, and his nails dug painfully into his palms. He punched the code into the keypad on the door that would allow him access to the offices beyond, and his teeth ground as he heard another burst of laughter behind him.

An unbecoming flush of rage stained his face as he pushed through the door and into the quietness of the corridor that lay ahead. How dare they laugh at her like that behind her back? A gossiping bunch of stupid old women, the lot of them.

And what they were saying about his Hillary and Steven Crayle couldn't possibly be true. He simply didn't believe it. Everyone knew that Hillary didn't even look at the men she worked with. Danvers was the proof of that. And everyone knew she'd been just good friends with her boss before that. Crayle wouldn't prove to be any different. There was nothing special about *him*, after all. He was nothing but a pansy, a tall, lean streak of wind in his fancy suits. His Hillary wouldn't look twice at a poser like that.

He marched towards the toilets and slipped into the gents. A civilian clerk was at the urinal and nodded at him briefly. Tom slipped into a cubicle, pulled the toilet seat down, and got out a mobile phone.

He had purchased it yesterday – a cheap, pay-as-you-go affair that he'd use for a few more days, before disposing of it and buying another.

Unmarried, unattached, and still living with his parents in a neat semi not far from the station, Tom had very few expenses and could spend most of his pay cheque how he wanted.

Now he keyed in the only number stored in the mobile's memory and began to text. When he'd finished, he checked the screen closely. It wouldn't do to have made a spelling mistake. His Hillary had earned an English literature degree at an unaffiliated Oxford College, and it would be disrespectful not to get everything just right. He'd even read up a book on grammar, so as not to let her down.

But he could see no problems with what he'd written.

MY DARLING HILLARY
WHAT ARE YOU DOING DINING OUT WITH YOUR SUPERIOR OFFICER? YOU KNOW HOW PEOPLE GOSSIP. I KNOW IT CAN'T BE TRUE THAT YOU AND HE KISSED. BUT DON'T MAKE ME JEALOUS, MY LOVE. IT WOULDN'T BE RIGHT. REMAIN FAITHFUL, OR YOU MAY FORCE ME TO DO SOMETHING WE WILL BOTH REGRET. ALL MY LOVE.
YOUR ONE AND ONLY.

With a nod and a press of his thumb, Tom sent the message winging its way to her and cautiously opened the cubicle door. But the other man was gone, and he was on his own. Relieved, Tom Warrington walked to the mirror and met his handsome reflection with a small smile.

He was pleased with the message. It showed the proper amount of love and concern, but it was also scrupulously fair. He'd warned her not to cheat on him, after all – so if anything bad had to happen, it wouldn't be his fault. Not that he was worried.

Hillary was smart, and faithful and all his. Nothing would go wrong this time, he thought determinedly, straightening his tie and washing his hands. Not like with the others. They had just been mistakes. Silly girls, who'd never understood him. Looking back now, he could see that all three of them had been doomed to fail.

Hillary was different. She was in the job, she was more mature and, most importantly of all, she was actually worthy of him. None of the others had been.

But his eyes still glittered with repressed anger, and he felt a sour, ugly taste in the back of his throat. And he knew why. He suddenly wished he could plant a bomb that would blow the whole HQ sky high, because they seemed determined to ruin it all for him. With their stupid gossip and snide, ugly, humdrum lives, they were trying to taint what he and Hillary had together.

Well, he wouldn't let them. But now that they'd planted a seed of doubt, he knew he had to root it out before it could do any serious damage. He had to make sure, just for his own peace of mind.

He thought about the CRT and Hillary's team, looking for a possible weak link.

It didn't take him long to find it.

Hillary returned to the station with Sam after talking to Rowan's landlady, and went straight to the small office shared by Jimmy, Sam and Vivienne. 'Sam, type up your notes and give them to Jimmy for the murder book. Vivienne, any word yet from the Drugs Squad?'

'No dice,' Vivienne said sourly. 'The prat I talked to said it was hardly top priority. The case is donkey's years old, and without the ME giving a clear indication of what the drug might have been, he thought we was having a laugh.'

Hillary sighed heavily. 'OK, leave it to me. I must have an old pal on the squad somewhere who owes me a favour. You can get on to the next thing on your list. And if you're actually serious about joining the service, don't let anyone hear you call another officer a prat. Even if he or she is one.'

Jimmy grinned but didn't look up from the folder he was reading.

Vivienne rolled her eyes at Hillary, but wisely kept her pretty, bright-red-painted mouth firmly shut.

'Sam, who is there on our list of witnesses who still lives locally?'

Sam quickly reached for his notebook. 'Most of them, actually, guv. Well, localish. Darla de Lancie's the nearest. She's just in Botley.'

'Right.' Hillary checked her watch. If the woman was at work, they wouldn't catch her in, but she was willing to risk it. 'We'll take her next.' She hesitated, then glanced reluctantly at the younger girl. 'Vivienne, would you like to come with me on this one?'

Although she was sure that Vivienne wouldn't be with them for much longer, and that she was already bored with the idea of being a policewoman, she still felt obliged to fulfil her unspoken role as mentor with an even hand.

'Sorry, Hillary, I can't. I've got too much on.'

Again Jimmy grinned, but didn't lift his eyes. He knew as well as the others that the only reason the little minx didn't want to leave the office was because she wanted another chance to run across the boss and make yet another play for him. Sooner or later she'd get the message that he just wasn't interested. And then there'd be tantrums!

'OK,' Hillary said quickly, visibly relieved. 'Sam, you stay and do the notes, and get on with the background checks I asked for. Jimmy, fancy getting out of the office?'

'I always do, guv, I always do,' Jimmy reassured her cheerfully.

Seeing as it was lunchtime, they stopped off in the Black Bull for a sandwich and half a pint of shandy, before heading towards the Oxford suburb of Botley.

Darla de Lancie was now Mrs Pitt, and lived in a nice little detached residence in a small cul-de-sac of similar new-builds. Each plot had a driveway with a carport against one wall, and in Darla's small patch of lawn the other side stood a dwarf cherry tree, with spring bulbs planted around it.

Modest, but nevertheless probably still expensive enough, given house prices, Hillary thought, as she walked up the path and rang the doorbell. Darla had obviously done well for herself.

She waited, almost half-expecting her summons to remain unanswered. Even if Mr Pitt had a good job, nowadays most couples needed two incomes just to survive, and she was about to turn away from the door, resigned to having to make an appointment and thus lose the element of surprise, when the door suddenly opened.

The woman who stood there looking at them uncertainly hadn't aged much in the ten years or so since she'd been a student. The petite figure was perhaps a little more rounded, but the riot of red hair, the freckled face and big green eyes were all the same.

Before she could speak, there came the wail of an infant from the depths of the house behind her, and the reason for the slightly thickened waist, as well as the explanation for why they'd found her at home, was made suddenly clear.

'Sorry, can you make this quick?' Darla said, waving a vague hand behind her. 'I don't buy at the door.' Her gaze flickered nervously to Jimmy. 'And I don't want to talk about religion either.'

'Sorry,' Hillary said, holding out her ID card. 'Please, go and see to your child, Mrs Pitt. We can wait outside a bit until you're ready.'

Darla blinked at the information on the card and gave a quick glance around. 'Oh no, that's all right. Please, come in. You're the police?'

'We work for the police, yes,' Hillary corrected her, as they stepped into a small, rather anonymous-looking hall, carpeted throughout in beige. 'We work with the Crime Review Team.

We're currently taking another look at the Rowan Thompson case.'

Darla's freckled face visibly paled. 'Oh. I see. Can I just....' She indicated the stairs to the left, as yet another fretful wail wafted down from upstairs.

'Yes, of course.'

'Please, go on through to the lounge,' Darla said, pointing vaguely towards a half-open door. 'Make yourselves comfortable. Have a seat – I'll make a cup of tea in a minute. Sorry, Terry's teething. I've been trying to settle him down for his afternoon nap.'

She suddenly turned and bolted upstairs, clearly nonplussed and upset by their presence, and Hillary shot Jimmy a quick, speaking look. Careful not to be overheard, they made their way to the lounge and shut the door behind them.

'We've certainly thrown her for a loop,' Jimmy said, glancing around. The lounge was small, and again carpeted in beige throughout. A neutral magnolia wash covered the plastered walls, and a substantial three-piece suite in coffee-coloured hard-wearing cotton took up most of the room. A large-screen television hung on one wall, and a large bunch of rust-coloured chrysanthemums sat in a pot on a windowsill.

'Yes. We're an unwelcome blast from her past all right,' Hillary agreed, taking one of the armchairs and finding it surprisingly comfortable. Jimmy took a seat on the sofa.

Eventually, the noise from upstairs abated, and a few minutes later, Darla joined them. In spite of her promise of tea, none was forthcoming as she somewhat reluctantly took the armchair opposite Hillary.

'So this is about Rowan, you say?' Darla began diffidently. 'I have to say, all of that seems like another lifetime ago now. Uni, and all that. We were all so young.'

She was only in her early thirties now, Hillary thought with amusement tinged with envy. Wait until you're fifty. Still, Darla did look tired, and there were rings around her eyes. No doubt motherhood had made her feel far more mature than her actual years would indicate.

'You got your degree?' Hillary decided to ease her into the interview gently. 'English lit, wasn't it? That's the same degree I took, but I expect the texts were very different.'

'Yes. I'm a teacher now. Well, on maternity leave at the moment. I work at the Forsyte Academy. You may know it?'

Hillary did. It was a private school for girls between the ages of sixteen and eighteen. Its sole purpose was to take the brightest and the best and groom them to Oxbridge standard. Or Durham, at a pinch. No doubt the pay was significant, the work hardly arduous, and the kudos of working there would delight the most snobbish of standards.

'Very nice,' Hillary said, and meant it. 'And your husband?'

'Oh, he works for the *Oxford Times*. A financial correspondent.'

'Does he know about Rowan?' Hillary probed carefully.

Darla jerked a little in her seat. 'No. Well, I mean, not really. He knows I had boyfriends before I met him, of course. Terence is a bit older than me. I met him when his daughter from his first marriage attended the academy. But I never told him about Rowan, I mean, all the trouble.... It just seemed so long ago.'

Hillary nodded. 'Yes, I understand. He's maybe a bit conservative in his outlook, and you saw no reason to go into details?' she guessed, careful to keep her voice non-judgemental.

Darla flushed guiltily. 'Well, there was no reason to. Not really. I mean, we don't know what really happened to Rowan, do we? I mean, no one was ever caught. And it was really nothing to do with me.'

Hillary's eyebrow lifted slightly, but she made no comment, and Darla, as if sensing that her last statement might have sounded, at the very least, disingenuous, again shifted uncomfortably in her seat.

'I just mean that I didn't have anything to do with it, or know what happened, so it was nothing to do with me in that sense,' she expanded on the theme nervously.

Hillary nodded.

'Terence doesn't have to know, does he?' she went on breathlessly. 'His mother is the daughter of a Tory peer, and, well, she's a bit of a dragon about some things. She hates scandal, and fuss, and, well, she's never really liked me. Terence's first wife was the daughter of her old schoolfriend, and they're still very close. She never approved of the divorce, and blames me for it, which is silly, because I hadn't even met him then. She only puts up with me at all because she knows she'd never get to see little Terry if she didn't, but I know she'd just jump on it, if my name gets dragged into the papers again.'

Hillary nodded with every evidence of sympathy. Of course, the Thompson case would have been widely reported in the local press at the time. Supposedly, her husband either hadn't been living in the city at the time, or else had a poor memory for names. She wouldn't be surprised, though, if the mother-in-law from hell hadn't already had a PI check out her son's second new trophy wife, and already knew all about it.

'There's no reason why we would need to speak to your husband, Mrs Pitt,' Hillary said, adding craftily, 'so long as you co-operate fully with us, of course.'

'Oh, I will. Obviously. I mean, I want whoever killed Rowan to get caught. Of course I do,' Darla said quickly.

Scribbling down his notes, Jimmy didn't think that she sounded all that sincere, but then it was understandable. If they solved the case, there'd be a murder trial, and the chances of Darla being able to keep her past a secret from her older, snobby husband would be practically zero.

'All right, then. So, at the time of the murder you and Rowan were an established couple, yes?' Hillary began.

'That's right. We'd met when we took rooms at Wanda's, so we'd been together for a couple of months.'

'Was it serious?'

'Yes. Well, no. I mean,' – Darla took a deep breath, making a visible effort not to ramble – 'I thought at the time it was, but looking back on it now, I could see that it would never have worked out.' She smiled a shade grimly. 'You tend to see things differently at thirty than you did at twenty. More clearly.'

'Yes. But at the time you were in love with him. Or thought you were?' Hillary pressed.

'Yes. But even then, I sort of knew at the back of my mind how he was. Even if I didn't want to admit it to myself.'

'And how was he?' Hillary asked gently.

Darla Pitt looked down at her hands, twisting nervously in her lap, and took another long, slow breath. 'Rowan was one of those men who could tie you in knots. Sometimes he seemed almost like a boy, and could be cheeky and charming and exasperating, all at the same time. And then it was fun. At other times, he could really sweep you off your feet. I mean, really make you feel special. Like this was it. The kind of way that every woman dreams a man will make her feel.' She flushed slightly, and glanced quickly at Jimmy and then away again, her voice lowering confidentially. 'You know – he could be genuinely passionate. Made you feel like you were living in one of the big romances. *Wuthering Heights*, and all that.'

She sighed somewhat wistfully. 'And that was just magical.' Her pretty face suddenly fell. 'And then there were times when he could be like any other man, and be just a little shit,' she added, with more sadness than bitterness. 'Just shabby and ordinary and disappointing. He'd turn from Heathcliffe to just another bloke who'd climb into anyone's knickers, given the chance.'

Hillary nodded. A typical young male, still more adolescent than adult, by the sound of it.

'He hurt you?' she said softly.

Darla shrugged. 'Once or twice. And I know what you're thinking, but I didn't kill him because of that. I couldn't. I wouldn't,' she stressed tensely, rocking a little back and forth on the chair now.

'I understand you used his room to make clothes,' Hillary said, making no comment on her protestations of innocence, but keeping her voice quiet and level.

Darla slowly subsided back against the chair and nodded dully. 'Yes – his was the biggest room. We all four of us applied to the house at around the same time, and it was typical of Rowan that he charmed the old lady into letting him have the biggest room.' She smiled wistfully. 'I liked making my own stuff – I'd always done so, and sort-of had ambitions to be a fashion designer when I was younger, until common sense took over and told me the chances of success in that cut-throat field were pretty low. Which is why I went to Oxford – to have a second fiddle to my bow. Glad I did, now, I can tell you. But back then, I was still really into it, and it was much cheaper than buying real designer gear. And Rowan didn't mind my using his room. And again, I know what you're thinking. The scissors that were used to … to … stab him, were the ones I used to make my outfits, but that didn't mean it had to be me who killed him, did it? I mean, they would have been just lying around in plain sight for anyone to see. I'd been using them the night before, and I hadn't packed the stuff away. I told all this to Inspector Gorman at the time.'

She was becoming more agitated as she rambled on, so Hillary said smoothly, 'Yes, and that's a point well made. I'm here to take a fresh look at things, Mrs Pitt, not to go over the same ground as DI Gorman. Tell me about what you did that morning.'

Darla ran a somewhat shaky hand through her red curls and sighed. 'I went out about nine o'clock that morning, I think. I ran into Marcie on the stairs and we went down together. She was due to take the train back to her parents that afternoon, and had some paperwork to drop off with her tutor. We chatted a bit as we went, then parted company outside on the road. I had some last-minute gifts to get. It was Christmas. I went to Debenhams and bought some silver ear-rings and some perfume. When I came back, the police were already there. At the house. Wanda had found him.'

Hillary nodded. Gorman had, of course, gone over Darla's

alibi, such as it was, meticulously, but the results were inconclusive. It was Christmas, and Debenhams, not surprisingly, had been busy. Neither of the sales staff at the perfume and jewellery counters remembered her specifically, but there was no reason, in the crush of shoppers, why they should. The store's CCTV picked her up a couple of times, proving that she did indeed buy the items she claimed to have done, but that in itself meant nothing. The store was only a few minutes' walk from the house. Darla could have returned to the house unseen and killed Rowan at any time. Or indeed, he might already have been dead when she left.

'When you left the house that morning, did you notice anyone hanging around?'

'No.'

'Was Rowan nervous of anyone? Did he ever say that he was having trouble with one of his women, or the ex-boyfriends of any of the women he'd known?'

Darla smiled grimly. 'Not to me, but then he wouldn't, would he? He always denied seeing other women after we got together, even when it was blindingly obvious that he was. He seemed to think that he could just give me one of his cheeky grins and somehow that would make all the hurt go away, or charm me into making it not matter. He could always make me laugh, too, like it was some kind of medicine. But the truth was, he didn't really care if I liked it or not – me not having exclusive rights to him, I mean. If all else failed, and I called him on it, he'd just shrug.'

She stared down at her hands, and gave a sad, twisted smile. 'You know, I don't think he would have cared if all the women he'd cheated had got together and ganged up on him in one big, hissing fury. He'd just have gone on to the next one with a blithe grin. And as for the boyfriends – forget it. He wouldn't have cared a fig what they thought or felt about it. It was like it was all a big game to him: if they couldn't hang on to their girlfriends, then that was their look-out, you know? If he saw an opportunity to sneak in and raid the hen-house, it was almost like he saw it as his duty to do so. He loved a challenge; he liked taking risks and

FAITH MARTIN

didn't seem to care a toss if he was hurting someone, or might get hurt himself in the process. But he wasn't nasty about it.'

Darla shook her head in frustration. 'It's no good. I just can't quite describe what he was like. He lived by a set a rules that was entirely his own. And if you didn't understand them, or approve of them, or like them, well, that was just tough. But even that isn't quite right. That makes him sound aggressive or utterly selfish – and I don't think he was either of those – not really. He liked people to be happy. He was always happy himself. He seemed to see life as one great big adventure and a bit of a lark. Perhaps he would have grown out of it if....'

Suddenly her pretty, freckled face crumpled, and she began to cry.

Jimmy made a gentle tut-tutting sound, and reached into his jacket for a handkerchief.

Darla waved it away, and reached under a small coffee table for a box of tissues. She extracted one and wiped her eyes, staining them black with her running mascara. 'I'm sorry,' she sniffed.

'Take your time. There's no rush,' Hillary murmured. 'I'm sorry if this upsets you. We won't be much longer.'

'It's fine. I'm fine.' She took a long, wavering breath, and leaned back in the chair again. 'It's just that it suddenly hit me: he'd be the same age as me now. Who knows, he might even be married and have kids, too. Instead he's.... It was all taken away from him, wasn't it? That's what suddenly got to me. And he didn't deserve to have that happen to him – no matter what he might have done.'

'What did the others at the house think of him?' Hillary asked curiously, and sensed Darla's withdrawal immediately.

'Oh, you know. Marcie never really thought about him one way or the other at all, I'm sure. She didn't have much interest in any of us, really. And Dwayne used to encourage him, I think. They used to go out drinking together, and have silly bets, so there was no reason for them to fall out. And Barry was such a nice man – I think he found it hard to fit in – being older and all,

52

and married with a family and working in the building trade and all that. But Rowan never teased him about any of it. Barry was the sort who got on with everyone. I really don't believe any one of us did it. I know Inspector Gorman was obsessed with thinking that it had to be one of us, but I think it was someone else in Rowan's life. They just came to the house, Rowan let them in, and they killed him. Wanda, being in the basement, didn't always know who came and went.'

Darla looked at Hillary with flat, green eyes. 'None of us killed Rowan, of that I'm sure. That's why you people – the police, I mean – never solved the case. Inspector Gorman simply wouldn't look at someone outside of the house. If you want to find out who killed Rowan, that's where you're going to have to look.'

Hillary nodded gravely. 'You might well be right, Mrs Pitt. Thank you for talking to us. We might have to come back at some point with some follow-up questions, but I'll be sure to call ahead first, and make sure that you're alone.'

Darla, who'd obviously been about to object, nodded reluctantly. 'That's fine. I wish you luck, I really do.'

Hillary smiled and rose and followed her outside into the hall.

Back in the car, she sat behind the wheel and looked out thoughtfully at the neat, suburban streets. 'So, what do you think?'

Jimmy shrugged. 'She seems genuine enough. But she's the tense and nervy sort, isn't she?'

'Yes.'

'And if the young lad led her a merry dance, like it seems he did, she might easily have snapped and stabbed him. The emotional types tend to do that.'

'Yes.'

'And her alibi's no good, one way or the other.'

'No.'

Jimmy grinned. 'She stays on the list then, guv.'

'Oh yes, Jimmy. They all stay on the list until we can definitely cross them off it,' she agreed flatly.

*

Vivienne was hungry by the time she made it into the canteen, but didn't care. She'd been listening out for Steven's door to open and close all that morning. She knew he often went upstairs late – just as he had today. Now, as she pushed through the door, she saw him standing in line at the food bar and quickly fell in behind him.

She thought for a moment he was going to turn around and acknowledge her, but when he didn't, she made a great play of reaching out for a tray in the pile nearest to him, letting her hand just brush his arm as she reached past him.

She watched him select a fish and salad option and quickly did the same, although she was not particularly fond of seafood. She ignored the desserts – although if she'd been on her own the chocolate mousse would have been her first port of call, and selected a bottle of mineral water instead.

Vivienne was just a few steps behind him as he stepped out into the main body of the room. She was about to come abreast of him and suggest they find a table together, when he suddenly veered off to the left, and took the last seat available at a table for four. One was a DI from Juvie whom she vaguely recognized, and the other two also had that higher-rank air about them.

A vexed flush flashed across her pretty face as she glanced around forlornly. There were plenty of empty tables this late in the lunchtime stint, so why the hell couldn't he have sat at any one of them?

Just then, she saw a man sitting at a table for two half rise, and smile at her diffidently, indicating the empty chair in front of him with the air of a man who was expecting her to ignore him. He was obviously making a play, which was much more what she was used to, and, feeling slightly mollified, she walked towards him, her eyes assessing him quickly.

He had a really good body, but he was a bit younger than she liked. And he was just a humble PC in uniform, too. Small fry for her. But he had really good hair – thick and dark, and his eyes were really pretty hot. She'd never had a man with green eyes before.

'Hello, I saw the big chief ditch you. The man must be mad,' Tom Warrington said quietly. 'Don't know why you're wasting your time on him. He must need glasses, if you ask me.'

Not bad for a quick, spur-of-the-moment pick-up line, but she didn't like to hear someone criticizing Steven.

Vivienne tossed her head. 'He didn't realize I was behind him, that's all,' she said sharply. 'Otherwise it would have been different.' She set her tray down and held out her hand. 'I'm Vivienne Tyrell.'

Tom grinned and shook her hand. 'Tom Warrington.' He glanced at her healthy-option tray and nodded. At least she knew how to treat her body right. Perhaps this wouldn't have to be so tedious after all.

'You look too young not to be in the same boat as me,' he said, patting his uniform with a wry smile.

'Oh, I'm still a civilian,' Vivienne said. 'Just making my mind up whether or not I want to join up. I work for Superintendent Crayle at the CRT.'

'Wow. I'm impressed,' Tom lied.

Vivienne preened and picked at the unwanted fish on her plate. 'It is pretty cool,' she conceded.

'Good, is he? To work for? Crayle, I mean. My sarge is a right pain in the arse, I can tell you.'

Vivienne smiled smugly. 'He's amazing.'

Tom's green-eyed gaze flickered. Another female who was ga-ga over bloody Crayle. He just couldn't understand what they all saw in him. Suddenly, the need to make contact with Hillary washed over him. To actually feel his arms around her, to hear her voice.

It was dangerous, he knew, but the impulse was almost over-whelming. Soon, he promised himself. Soon.

He forced himself to smile at the girl in front of him, a wide, white-toothed smile. 'So, tell me all about how things are in CRT,' he said.

CHAPTER FOUR

The next morning, Hillary awoke to the sound of a pair of newly arrived chiff-chaffs making their iconic calls in the willow tree opposite her boat. She lay awake for a while, listening to the fragile feathered creatures that had migrated thousands of miles to come to England, and wishing that all that flying had tired the noisy little sods just enough not to call right outside her porthole window.

With a sigh, she rolled out of bed, pulled on an old terry-cloth robe that had seen much better days, and made her way through to the small galley kitchen where she set the coffee pot boiling. She contemplated toast, then decided not to bother, and instead reached for yesterday's *Oxford Times*.

She turned to the financial section, but there was no report in it by Terence Pitt. But then, just how often would a financial correspondent be called upon to write an article? This was Oxford, not London. She wondered if it could be Darla who was the main breadwinner in that family, despite her husband's high-falutin' family connections. She sighed again and drank her coffee, then had a one-and-a-half minute shower and dressed.

By her watch it was nearly 8.35 when she stepped out onto the towpath, and the chiff-chaffs flew off in alarm. She had just a short walk past the rest of her neighbours' narrowboats before the pub car park hove into sight. But as she approached Puff the Tragic Wagon her steps slowly faltered.

What the hell?

Her car was usually a pale-green colour (with creative swirls of rust here and there) but for some reason, her eye kept straying to the colour pink. And red. And yellow. And orange. And white. All of which seemed to be crammed against every window in the car.

For a moment she thought some hooligan had sufferered from a touch of creative originality, and instead of spray-painting foul slogans over the outside, had for some reason gone for a more abstract theme, and confined himself to the windows only in some show of minimalist reticence.

But as she cautiously approached her car, she saw instead that it was literally stuffed full of roses. Bunches and bunches of them. She walked slowly to the driver's side door and looked inside. She couldn't see the foot pedals for red roses and ferns. Carnations, roses and other frothy greenery was piled high on the driver seat, and the passenger seat beside it. The back seat and the rear floor was also submerged by roses and other flowers of every hue that reached, literally, to the ceiling of her car.

Hillary bent down and squinted at the lock of the door handle. Tiny scratches showed where someone had picked the lock.

She stood up again and glanced around. Most of the cars that were left in the car park on a regular basis were gone now, but that was only to be expected. It was a working day after all, and most of the villagers and boat owners had a longer commute than she did, and would have left earlier. She wondered what they'd made of the sight of her rainbow-hued old rustbucket. They'd probably just grinned and thought she'd struck lucky with some romantically minded new partner.

But she'd have to track them down and ask them if they'd seen anything or anyone lurking around. Not that her admirer was likely to have let himself be seen, and there were plenty of hours of darkness once the pub was shut for him to have left his gift unnoticed.

But it had to be done, since you just never knew. The thought of other people knowing she might have a problem wasn't pleasant, however, and she was in no hurry to start questioning her neighbours.

Instead she reached into her bag and called Steven Crayle.

It was answered on the second ring with a curt, 'Crayle.'

'Steven, it's me. Are you at work yet?'

'Just approaching the turn-off. Why?'

'Can you come on down to Thrupp for a few minutes?'

There was a brief moment of silence, and then he said, 'I'll be about five minutes.'

Hillary thanked him, then snapped shut her mobile and stood looking at the floral bouquets inside her car. She tried to tot up the cost of them, but found it almost impossible. All the bouquets were wrapped in the clear plastic cones that came from florists shops, and most had ribbon around them, so they looked professionally done. So it wasn't someone who was a keen gardener who grew their own and thus saved much moolah by making up their own offerings.

And even if the flowers underneath were the cheaper offerings, like chrysanthemums and daisies, saving the roses and carnations for the more visible bouquets on top, she guessed she must have been looking at easily £500-or-so worth of flowers. If not more.

She'd been assuming that her admirer was in the lower-income bracket, but perhaps that wasn't so. But at least she had some place to start now – no florist getting an order this big was likely to forget it. Unless, of course, he'd boxed clever and had simply taken the time to order three or four bunches at different shops around the shire until he had enough for his grand gesture. Just how many florists were there within easy driving range?

And if he paid cash for them, there'd be no paper trail. Would he have the patience to have done that? Hillary was just gloomily contemplating the fact that he probably was when Steven's very nice BMW pulled up beside her.

He slowly climbed out, all lean grace in a silver-grey suit, dark-blue shirt, and electric-blue tie. His black shoes shone in the late April sunlight, and there was the glint of gold at his wrists.

Hillary had an involuntary flashback to the other night, in the pub car park when, well aware of the watching eyes of the voyeur from Traffic, he'd pulled her into an embrace and kissed her.

And very nice it had been too.

He was tall enough to have to stoop just slightly to reach her lips, and he'd smelt of something gorgeous and expensive. It had been a long time since Hillary had been held in any man's arms and his kiss had literally taken her breath away.

No two ways about it, the man knew how to use his lips.

'I take it you're going to be late for work?' Steven asked drily, as he came to stand beside her and look at her over-stuffed car.

'Just a bit,' she agreed just as drolly, and opened the door. Several colourful displays toppled out onto the gravel and landed dramatically at her feet. She gave them a brief nudge with the toe of her sensible, reinforced-capped shoe.

'I've got a mate with a van,' Steven said, already reaching for his mobile. 'He can help you shift them.'

'I'll need to go through them for messages or florists' names and receipts first,' she said. 'After that, he can pick out the best of them for his mum or girlfriend or significant other, and then deliver the rest to some old folks' homes or whatever he likes.'

She walked around the car, checking for any mistake her stalker might have made whilst Steven gave his friend directions. After he hung up, she had circumnavigated the car and was back beside him.

'Anything?' he asked briefly.

'Nothing worth having. There's a faint scuff-mark trail where he's parked his own vehicle, and you can see a clear trackway through the gravel where he's gone to and fro with armloads of flowers, but the gravel's too thick for the mud beneath to take tyre tracks or shoe-marks. No dropped cigarette butts or chewing-gum wrappers or what-have-you, but even if there were, they could have been there for a while, or dropped by anyone. The pub is fairly well used.'

Steven nodded. It was what he'd expected.

'You think he's watching now?'

'He might be,' Hillary agreed mildly, without lifting her head or looking around. It was one of the first things she'd thought of. 'It's human nature to want to stick around and see how well a grand romantic gesture goes down. I dare say right about now I'm supposed to be smiling radiantly, a look of joy on my face, and holding my trembling hand over my fast-beating heart.'

Steven grinned. 'Can't manage the smile of joy, huh?'

'Seems to have escaped me for the moment.'

'If he's watching, don't you think we should do something to make him good and mad?' Steven asked, trying to keep any inflection out of his voice.

Ever since he'd kissed her, he'd found himself reliving the moment at the most inconvenient of times – during budget meetings, driving home, in the shower, and most of all, alone, in bed.

Since his divorce there'd been the odd date or two, of course, but nothing that had really touched him. The sexual encounters had been pleasant enough, naturally, and mutually satisfying, but hardly important.

Now, at the thought that he might be about to kiss her again, he found himself tensing up like an excited schoolboy about to get his first grope. It made him feel both elated and uneasy.

Hillary glanced across at him thoughtfully. He was totally unable to read her expression, and he felt a cold but oddly not at all unpleasant sweat break out on him practically everywhere.

'I suppose we'd better,' she said finally, and stepped towards him.

Steven Crayle obediently took her in his arms and kissed her.

And then again.

And then again.

It was nearly 10.30 by the time Hillary pulled into the Thames Valley HQ car park. Her car, which still smelt better than it had in years, bore traces of the odd detached colourful petal. After she'd parked she walked quickly through the foyer and down into the bowels of the building, where the rabbit warren that housed the CRT was located.

She'd found no receipts amongst the flowers and had made up a list of over fifteen different florists, the names of which had been incorporated in colourful logos on the polythene wrappers.

At some point she was going to have to run up her phone bill contacting them all, but she could already sense it wasn't going to lead anywhere. In these days of the internet and modern technology there were so many ways he could have ordered them electronically without leaving a trace. And if his 'romantic nature' had led him to buying each and every bloom in person, what was the likelihood of a shop assistant remembering him specifically from all the other customers?

'Guv,' Jimmy called, looking up from his desk as she passed by the open door on her way to the stationery cupboard that everyone else euphemistically liked to call her office.

It was the first time he could remember her being late to work and, sensing that she was distracted, assumed that she'd gone somewhere else in relation to the Thompson case before coming into the office. 'Anything for the murder book?'

Hillary shook off thoughts of florists, and shook her head to match. 'No. Neither of the youngsters in?' she asked, seeing he had the small office all to himself.

'No, Sam's got lectures and Vivienne's doing something for the computer nerds,' Jimmy said.

The larger team who used computers to search for crime patterns in the statistics carried out most of the CRT's work. They also had a large liaison team with the forensics department, and such painstaking and detailed work required a lot of manpower. Not surprisingly, they often poached an extra pair of hands from Steven Crayle's investigative team when needed.

So long as they didn't call on her, she didn't care. But she knew the likelihood of that happening was practically zero. Commander Donleavy wanted her doing detective work, not number crunching.

'That's fine. We'd better get on with the next of the witnesses, though. Where's Dwayne Cox hang out nowadays? Darla told us he encouraged Rowan's sexual exploits, remember? He seems the logical one for our victim to have boasted to, or confided in if something had backfired on him.'

'Wouldn't he have told Gorman about it if he had, guv?' Jimmy asked, reaching for his coat.

'Not necessarily. It depends. If he dared or egged Rowan on and involved him in something that later led to him getting killed, he wouldn't be in any hurry to confess to it, would he?'

Jimmy smiled. 'Suppose he wouldn't. And he lives and works in Reading now.'

Thinking of her sweet-smelling car, Hillary said firmly, 'Grab your car keys. We'll take yours.'

Hillary didn't know Reading particularly well, and was happy to let Jimmy both drive and navigate.

'Tell me what he does now?' she said as the urban sprawl began to surround them.

'He works at the Reh-laxe Clinic, guv. I googled it – it's one of these health-spa-cum-retreat-cum-touchy-feely places for the well heeled who are feeling a bit glum.'

Hillary couldn't help but smile at the scarcely hidden disgust behind Jimmy's tone. 'My generation was taught to just bite the bullet and get on with it,' the ex-sergeant continued phlegmatically, letting a boy-driver in a souped up Mazda cut him up at an approaching roundabout. 'Nowadays, it seems if you stub your toe you can suffer from depression and need professional help to get you through the trauma. Always supposing you can pay through the nose for it,' he griped.

Hillary ran briefly through the notes she'd been reading since leaving HQ. 'Cox was in the second year of an experimental psychology course,' she murmured. 'Unless I miss my guess, that's more to do with science and arcane knowledge for the sake of it, than any practical use in the world of psychiatry. Did your googling say exactly what he did at this clinic?'

'Some sort of therapist, I think, guv. I understood about one word in ten of their blog. Too new age for an old-age pensioner like me.'

Hillary grinned. 'He must either have gone on to do another course, or he decided that there was more money to be made in the private sector. You have his address?'

'Yes, guv.'

'We'll go to the workplace first. This time of day, he's not likely to be at home. Let's just hope he can fit us in. If not, perhaps we can sample some of the Reh-Laxe's facilities. Care to submerge yourself in a cold seaweed-and-mud bath, Jimmy?'

Jimmy Jessop gave a very short and pithy answer to that.

Hillary was still savouring it when they pulled up outside a Victorian villa on the outskirts of town, set in a large acreage of flowering cherry trees and neatly mown lawns. A stone terrace ran along the front, complete with a balustrade bearing urns of bright geraniums. As they parked the car and climbed out, she saw that several bath-robed clients were sitting on the terrace in the full sunlight, drinking from glasses that seemed to hold a range of beverages from disgustingly healthy-looking green slime, to gin and tonic.

'Nice work if you can get it,' Jimmy said flatly, sounding not one whit envious.

They entered a black-and-white tiled foyer, and a pretty young woman immediately rose from behind an oak-panelled reception desk, a wide smile plastered onto her face.

'Hello – Mr and Mrs Felix Ottenmeyer?'

Jimmy looked at Hillary, his face a picture of dismay. 'I don't look like a rich Yank, do I, guv?' he asked mock-anxiously.

'No. Perhaps she thinks you're just an eccentric millionaire,' Hillary said consolingly, holding out her ID.

'We were wondering if Dr Dwayne Cox was in, and if so, if he could spare us a few minutes?' Hillary asked pleasantly.

The young woman's face flickered briefly between them, before she smiled, evidently deciding that the way to handle such an unprecedented turn of events was to pretend that they were potential guests.

'Of course, I'll just check. Would you like to take a seat in the conservatory?' She pointed to a set of internal French doors, which led to a green and leafy room beyond, with an original domed glass ceiling. Potted palms, rattan furniture and exotic blooms held sway here, and Jimmy cast a particularly gaudy orchid a suspicious glance.

The room was empty – which was probably why the young lady had so adroitly shunted them into it. It was also quite warm. Hillary slipped off her beige jacket, revealing the cream-and-orange blouse underneath. She took a seat in a wide, circular-backed chair and watched, amused, as Jimmy seated himself gingerly in a similar chair opposite.

He caught her look and grinned self-consciously. 'I'm never convinced that these grass seat things are going to take my weight, guv.'

'I think they're bamboo based – which is supposed to be incredibly strong, given what it is.'

The chair creaked and groaned a little as Jimmy settled back cautiously. He got out his notebook and marked the date and time. As he was finishing doing this, a tall man with near-black hair and blue eyes walked in. He was classically good-looking, and Hillary noticed that his eyes went straight to her, hardly registering Jimmy at all.

A lady's man, in spades, Hillary thought. She didn't rise, but smiled briefly up at him. 'Dr Cox?' she murmured, suddenly amused at the man's name. It seemed so appropriate somehow. 'I'm Hillary Greene, this is Mr Jessop. We work for the Crime Review Team out of Thames Valley Police Headquarters. We're currently taking another look at the Rowan Thompson case, and hoped you wouldn't mind giving us a little of your time. If it's not convenient, we can arrange for a more formal interview,' she added blandly.

Dwayne Cox shook his head and quickly dragged over a chair

to sit next to her. 'No, no, that's fine. My next patient isn't until after two.'

Hillary nodded. Hardly a hectic schedule, then. From the files, she knew that Dwayne Cox came from a strictly working-class background, and had got to Oxford through excellent exam results and the backing of one of the teachers in the under-achieving comprehensive he'd attended.

It was apparent, with one look, that he had very successfully put his humble beginnings very firmly behind him. He was dressed in a suit that even Steven couldn't have faulted, and had obviously found a very good barber for himself somewhere in town. As he leant forward, he looked confident and trustworthy – just the sort of man to help you sort out your problems. And with his good looks, Hillary was willing to bet that the vast majority of his patients were women – probably middle-aged, divorced, lonely and wealthy – all of whom were no doubt only too ready to spill their deepest, darkest secrets, and innermost needs.

She knew from the file that Dwayne Cox was not yet married. He was probably having too much of a good time being single, she realized with a mental smile. And when he was ready to take the plunge – well, in a set-up like this, he'd have his pick of a rich crop. Maybe that was what he was doing working here? Sorting out a cushy future for himself?

'So, after all this time,' Dwayne said quietly, 'I still think about him often, you know. He was so young. At the time we didn't think of ourselves as being particularly young, but now, of course, I find myself realizing that we were. Barely out of our teens.' He shook his head and gave a devastatingly self-deprecating smile that no doubt was used to very good effect on the clinic's clientele.

'What can you tell me about Rowan?' Hillary asked simply.

Dwayne spread his hands in a what-can-you-say kind of gesture. 'Rowan was full of life. He was a bit of a nutter at times, to be honest. Nothing was too outrageous for him to try. He was smart, of course, that goes without saying, and charming when he liked, but he was basically good-natured and good-hearted.'

Hillary nodded. So far, everyone seemed to be singing from the same hymn sheet when it came to their victim's personality. 'We've already spoken to his girlfriend at the time. She said much the same thing,' Hillary agreed.

'Darla? Darling Darla,' Dwayne said softly, and smiled in a show of reminiscence. 'How is she?'

'Married, with a child, good job, nice house, happy,' Hillary said briefly. 'She tells me you and Rowan used to encourage each other to be naughty – egg each other on and so forth. I imagine, reading between the lines, that you must have had a bit of a rivalry going on between you two,' she added craftily.

Dwayne tried to look abashed, and almost pulled it off. 'Like I said – we were young. And yeah, I suppose you could say we had a bit of a thing going – you know, to see who could pull the most. He was one kind of girl-magnet, and I was, so they tell me, another kind.'

'No need to be modest, Dr Cox,' Hillary said drily. 'You are the classic, tall, dark and handsome type. Rowan, as far as I can make out, was the cheeky-chappy, fair-haired, naughty-boy type. Between you, I'm sure you cut quite a swathe through the girls.'

Dwayne sighed. 'It all sounds so cold-blooded and heartless, but really, it never felt that way. And Rowan was fond of Darla in his way. He was just never cut out for monogamy.'

'When he was killed, did you really have no idea who might have done it?' she asked bluntly, wondering if shock tactics might cut through the rather sickening self-aggrandizing that was going on with this vain young man.

'No,' Dwayne said, with seemingly genuine surprise. 'Nobody could have wanted Rowan dead.'

'But by your own admission, he must have left behind him a stream of resentful women and their cheated-on boyfriends.'

'I suppose. But it was nothing that serious. I mean, you have to have a really serious affair to make someone hate you so much that they want to kill you when you break up, right? But Rowan was like a butterfly – a flit here, a sip of nectar there and on to the next flower. And, like I said, he could be charming. You just tended to like the guy. Even when he was indulging in one of his more outrageous stunts.'

'Outrageous, how?' Hillary asked, intrigued.

'Oh you know. Experimentation. Rowan was always hungry for a new sensation – something he hadn't tried before. It was almost as if he knew he was going to die young and wanted to fit everything in whilst he could.'

'You think he'd been receiving threats? He felt afraid for his life?' Hillary asked sharply, and Dwayne quickly back-tracked.

'Oh no, nothing of that kind. I'm just…. It's sort of hard to explain. Rowan was just greedy for life, that was all. He wanted to sample everything, try everything, do something new all the time. Take the Freeling brothers, for example.'

Hillary raised an eyebrow. Dwayne Cox gave a slightly embarrassed smile. 'The Freelings were these brothers who worked at a bicycle hire shop we used to use. Mark was the oldest, Jeff much younger. They were both as gay as gay, and came on to Rowan the moment he first walked into the shop. He was their type, I guess. Anyway, the Freelings took sibling rivalry to the extreme, and each of them wanted to get Rowan between the sheets first. So he played them along a bit, and then, and this is pure Rowan, when he had them worked up to fever pitch, he said he couldn't possibly choose between them, and said he would make a one-night offer only to take them both on at once.'

'And did he?' Hillary asked.

'Oh yes.'

'Was he gay?'

'Not as far as I know. I think he wanted to find out if he might be bisexual. But that's what I mean about him being extreme sometimes. Where angels might fear to tread, he just rushed in.'

Hillary nodded. 'I see.' Now, that sort of attitude was just the kind that could get you killed. 'Tell me about the morning he died,' she said flatly.

Dwayne took a long slow breath. 'Well, I left the house early. It was nearly Christmas, I was in a rush to get all the last-minute things done before heading off home. I wasn't looking forward to it, but what could I do? The family expected me there for the holidays. When I left, I heard someone moving around in Rowan's room, and thought it was either him or Darla. I never saw him or spoke to him, though. When I got back to the house, the police were already there.'

Hillary nodded. Just as he'd described it in his original statement to Gorman. And just like Darla, it might have been true, or it might not. The original team had certainly found witnesses who could put the handsome Dwayne in the various places he'd said he'd been, but again, like Darla, he could have slipped back to the nearby house and killed his friend without anyone being the wiser. None of the sightings of him had made the time-line impossible.

'You saw no one hanging around the house or in the street when you left?'

'Nope.'

'He never complained of being scared of anyone?' she pressed.

'Nope.'

'You haven't thought of anything in all these years that might now seem significant that didn't occur to you at the time?'

'Sorry, no. And believe me, I've been over and over it hundreds of times since then. I know the original detective, Gorman, thought that either Barry or Darla did it, but I think he's way off track there. Darla simply doesn't have it in her, and Barry was one of the most 'got-it-all-together' people I knew.'

'Is that your professional psychological view, Dr Cox?' Hillary asked, a touch ironically.

Dwayne gave that white-toothed self-deprecating grin again. 'For what it's worth, it is. Any psychologist will tell you that the human mind is practically unfathomable at times, and the most we can do is take really good, educated guesses as to what's going on.'

Hillary nodded. 'Well, thank you for your time, Dr Cox. We may need to speak to you again sometime,' she warned.

'Any time, I'd be only too glad to help.'

Hillary nodded, thanked him, and got up. With some difficulty, Jimmy got out of his creaking chair, and they walked outside.

Back at the car, Jimmy relaxed behind the steering wheel.

'Was it only me,' Hillary said, 'or did you get the urge to push the good doctor's smug little face in?'

'From the moment I set eyes on him, guv,' Jimmy reassured her.

'Huh,' Hillary said, glad that she wasn't the only one. 'So, apart from not liking him, what do you think? On the face of it he's got no motive for killing Rowan. So far, everyone seems to agree they were friendly enough. And after meeting him, I think our friend the doctor has, and probably always has had, far too high an opinion of himself to ever have regarded the likes of Rowan as much of a threat.'

'No. I got the feeling they played off each other and were having too much fun to be get seriously jealous of each other,' Jimmy agreed.

'So unless they had some sort of sudden, violent argument, he's not looking like a hot contender,' Hillary mused. 'Did anything else he said strike you as being possibly significant?'

'The bit about the gay blokes was interesting,' Jimmy said at once. 'Not wanting to sound homophobic or anything, perhaps the Freeling brothers didn't like being played. Or sharing.'

Hillary sighed. 'You'd better check them out. And you'd better take Vivienne with you for protection.'

Jimmy, for some reason, seemed to find that highly amusing.

Back in his office, Dwayne Cox reached for the telephone. He had no need to look up the number, since it was one he'd used many times over the years.

'Hey, it's me,' he said cautiously. They never used names, and were always careful about what they said, having evolved, from long practice, a sort of personal code system.

'What's up?' the familiar voice asked just as cautiously in his ear.

'Have you been visited by unfriendlies yet?' he asked.

'Hell, no – I never have. Have you dropped me in it?' the voice asked aggressively.

'Don't be stupid, you know I wouldn't do anything like that,' Dwayne said, slipping almost unnoticed into a professional, soothing tone. 'It was about the boy from Birmingham.'

There was a startled silence on the other end of the line for a few moments, and then, 'What about him? They can't be digging all that up again after all this time.'

'But they are.'

'Shit!'

'Relax,' Dwayne said, still in that soothing, everything-will-be-all-right voice he usually kept for the punters. 'There's nothing they can prove after all this time, you know that.'

A sigh came across the telephone line, then a thoughtful grunt. 'No. I suppose not. But if they've been on to you, it'll only be a matter of time before they get around to me.'

'So what?' Dwayne asked, flipping a pen between his fingers, a thoughtful frown on his handsome face. 'You telling me you can't handle a bit of pressure?'

'Now who's being absurd?'

Dwayne flipped the pen some more. 'Exactly. So no problem, then. We hadn't better meet up for a while – you know, just in case.'

'You don't want any more presents, then?' the voice said flatly.

'Perhaps not just yet. For a while, anyway. Why take risks?' Dwayne pointed out reasonably. 'But when everything's gone back to normal, then so can we. Right?'

The voice on the other end of the line laughed. 'Maybe I'll have found someone else to give my presents to by then.'

Dwayne Cox laughed himself then – a hard, grim chortle that

sounded distinctly unfunny. 'Good luck with that. Mind you don't fall foul of some unfriendly pretending to be in need of a nicely gift-wrapped package, though.'

The warning lay flat and ugly for a moment, spanning the silence in the ether. He let it. Then he said, again in that soft, soothing tone, 'But I think it'll be better to stick with the devil you know, don't you?'

'Fine,' the voice said reluctantly, and suddenly Dwayne was left with the dialling tone sounding in his ear.

Thoughtfully, he hung up and sat in his swivel chair, absently twirling the pen between his fingers.

He didn't like the police coming to his place of work. He didn't like having the past raked over. And he didn't like being threatened by the person on the other end of the line.

Trust Rowan Thompson to still be making trouble, even when he'd been ten years dead.

Suddenly, Dwayne had to laugh. 'Oh, Rowan, you stupid bastard,' he said softly.

CHAPTER FIVE

Tom Warrington cursed early shifts as he glanced morosely at his watch. He'd been hoping to stick around and see Hillary's face when she saw his gift, but he had to keep the dragon who ruled the admin office sweet and hadn't dared to turn up late. It was doubly annoying since she was only a civilian, but she was highly thought of and had been working there for donkey's years, and he knew damned well who his sergeant would believe if she started making complaints about his time-keeping.

But even the dragon couldn't keep him from taking his regulation lunch break, so at just about half past one he wandered out of the boring office and down into the foyer. He hardly ever actually drank any tea or coffee on his breaks, and never ate food from the HQ, since the muck they served in the canteen wasn't fit for a dog. Usually he preferred to grab a sports drink from his locker and wander around outside if it was nice, with some fresh fruit or cereal bars.

Being in records might give him access to the files he needed, but the stuffiness of the office environment made him crave fresh air in his lungs.

He'd just found an impromptu seat on the wooden wall surrounding some rather desultory square flowerbeds that were scattered throughout the parking area, when he noticed Jimmy Jessop's car pull in. His heart lifted at the sight of the woman in the passenger seat. Just a glimpse of the familiar bell shape of dark chestnut hair made his spirits soar. And again he felt a longing to actually feel that hair in his fingers, to smell the scent of her shampoo. Worshipping her from afar was all right, but it was rapidly becoming frustrating. He could feel the familiar momentum building up inside him. He must make flesh-and-blood contact with her soon. The pressure to actually hold her in his arms was so strong it was an almost physical ache.

But the time just didn't feel right quite yet. Not whilst she was in the middle of a case. It wouldn't be right to distract her. Tom nodded to himself, pleased with his own thoughtfulness. Yes, he respected her so much, surely she would appreciate that? But once the case was over – when she'd solved it, as he knew she must, because she always did – then he would reward himself.

Pleased and reassured by this promise to himself, Tom let his mind wander aimlessly.

He knew all of Hillary's team by sight, and was less than impressed with any of them. Jimmy Jessop was all right, he supposed, and being so old and past it, he wasn't any kind of rival to Tom. And from what he'd gleaned here and there, Jessop had been a well-respected sergeant in his day, but he really should have been put out to graze long ago, and never let back in. If his Hillary got into any kind of trouble with a thug, just what kind of back-up would a grey-haired wrinkly like him be to her? She needed someone like himself, young and alert, fit and strong, to protect her.

In his fantasies he always found a way to get assigned to her team, and regularly rescued her from various knife-wielding scumbags.

Vivienne Tyrell was proving useful to him, since he could get her to talk about anything and everything, but she annoyed him with her sickening vanity and her girlish, flirting inanity. It was also very obvious that Vivienne didn't like Hillary, and had no respect for her and her accomplishments. She was a stupid, ungrateful cow and he didn't know how someone like Hillary could stick her. He'd have to be careful not to lose his temper around her, but the urge to shut her complaining mouth and get her out of Hillary's hair for good was something he'd have to be careful to control. At least for a while. Right now, he needed her eyes and ears on what was going on, more than he needed to indulge his own wants.

And as for Sam Pickles – Tom gave an inner snort. He hated Pickles more than anyone, because he had the job Tom craved. Just to be in Hillary's orbit every day was something that he could only dream about, and the fact that Pickles was living the dream, and seemed oblivious to the honour, made him want to chew the walls. Not only that, he was a gormless, lanky git who was more interested in his textbooks than in being a copper.

It made Tom rage at the second-class people she had to work with. Hillary Greene was a star, and everyone knew it. Her solve-rate made Commander Donleavy and the rest of the brass salivate, so he'd heard, and with her gallantry medal, and her reputation for standing by her colleagues, she was in a class of her own. And she was so beautiful. He wasn't going to let Steven Crayle get his damned hands on her.

As he watched her get out of the car, she seemed to Tom to walk like a model. She had real curves, and maturity and grace. His green eyes bore into her back as she headed towards the HQ's main doors. If only she would turn and look his way. She must know he was there; she must have seen him: she noticed everything.

But, of course, she had Jimmy with her, so she couldn't openly acknowledge him. He understood that. He'd seen for himself how everyone in this place just loved to gossip. But he couldn't wait until they could make their love public. Then everyone would know that she was his.

He slowly raised the bottle of sports drink to his lips and took a swallow. He wondered what her narrowboat looked like, bedecked with his flowers. Everywhere she'd look, she would be reminded of him.

He smiled at the thought.

Just then, Steven Crayle pushed through the double glass doors and headed for his BMW. He stopped and looked up, as he heard his name called.

'Superintendent Crayle.'

The voice was female, and totally familiar. He stopped, wondering why he wasn't 'Steven' anymore, then saw that Hillary had Jimmy Jessop with her. He watched them approach, and nodded a greeting.

'I think we should be on first-name terms by now, Hillary, don't you?' he said easily, and just to make the point, nodded towards the older man. 'Jimmy. How are things?'

'Fine, guv, thanks,' Jimmy said. He glanced at Hillary, who smiled. 'Go ahead and write up the Dr Cox interview for the murder book, Jimmy. I'll be in in just a minute.'

Steven shifted his briefcase to his other hand. 'This is the young student killed in Oxford, right?'

'The Rowan Thompson case. Yes, sir, I thought you might like an update,' Hillary said, pausing until Jimmy had entered the building, before turning to look at him properly.

'Thanks for sending your friend over,' she said. 'I was glad to see the back of those damned flowers.'

Steven nodded, looking at her closely. 'Beginning to get on your nerves, is it?' he asked quietly, smiling a little as she stiffened perceptibly.

'It's nothing I can't handle, sir,' she said flatly.

'I never said it was,' Steven took her arm and began to walk her towards his car. 'Relax,' he said quietly, lowering his head a little towards her. 'I wasn't implying that you were about to need the services of a funny farm. But you wouldn't be human if you weren't feeling a little bit tense by now. Having a stalker is one of the most stressful things that can happen to a woman. You don't need me to tell you that.'

'No, sir, I don't,' Hillary agreed deadpan.

'And stop calling me sir,' Steven shot back, just as deadpan. 'A couple of hours ago we were snogging like teenagers, after all.'

Hillary's lips twitched. He had a point.

'So, how is the Thompson case going, anyway?' he asked, rather belatedly, and again Hillary's lips twitched.

They were still walking towards his car, their heads close together, as she briefed him on what she'd done so far. Spoken out loud, it didn't seem like much, but then, he could hardly expect miracles. It was still very early days, and she was still playing catch-up with the earlier investigation.

'So far, I can't see any glaring omissions or mistakes made by the original investigation,' she concluded, knowing that this was one of the CRT's worst scenarios. Nobody liked to make trouble for another team by exposing bad policing. It riled the troops, allowed the press to get their sanctimonious knickers in a twist, and put you on the brass's shit list for years to come.

'Good. You getting any feelings for it yet?' Steven asked curiously.

'Nothing overt, sir. Just putting out feelers, and seeing what sets my spider senses tingling,' she said sardonically.

Steven cast her a quick, puzzled glance, wondered what had put her back up, reviewed the conversation, and held out a placatory hand. 'All right, all right. I wasn't trying to suggest you rely on woman's intuition or anything like that. I just know you've got a good copper's nose for things, that's all.'

Hillary sighed, then nodded. 'Fair enough, guv,' she said. She supposed she was getting a bit tetchy. But she was feeling a bit wrong-footed by this were-they/weren't-they pretend courtship they seemed to have fallen into. It made his every word and gesture open to question and interpretation.

From behind a horse chestnut tree, Tom Warrington watched them closely. Why were they walking so close together? And didn't Crayle know enough to keep his damned hands off her? What right did he have to take her arm like that? Why didn't she shake it off?

He watched them stop by Crayle's sleek car, and his hands tightened on the bottle in his hand as he watched them chatting. They looked friendly, and close, standing together like that.

And was she smiling?

Tom rather thought that she was.

'So, what's your next move?' Steven asked, reaching out to brush away a strand of hair that had fallen across her left eye.

Hillary went still and looked a question at him.

'In case he's watching,' Steven Crayle said softly.

Yeah, Hillary thought. Right. She reached up and rested her fingers against his wrist. Surreptitiously, with two of her fingers, she took his pulse.

It was racing.

Her lips twitched again.

'We'll interview Barry Hargreaves next. Gorman, the original CIO, liked him for it,' she said. 'But then he also liked the girl-friend for it. He just couldn't bring it home to either of them.'

Tom Warrington began to move parallel across the car park, always keeping them in sight, but being careful not to actually turn his head to look their way. He knew any sort of movement of that kind attracted attention. Those who suspected they were being watched tended to get a heightened sensitivity to such gestures.

He was making his way towards his own car at a steady pace. He still had nearly an hour of his lunch break left, and he suddenly badly needed to be somewhere.

'Well, I've got a meeting to get to,' Steven said regretfully, reaching into his jacket pocket for his keys. 'Keep me up to date on everything. And call me, if you need me.'

Hillary nodded thoughtfully. 'I'll do that,' she said, and stood back as he got in the car. She gave a brief salute as he pulled away, then turned, and watched another car pull out across the aisle. She couldn't tell, from the angle, who it was who was driving, but it probably wasn't significant. She'd begun to take note of which cars were behind her nowadays, but surely her stalker wasn't interested in trailing her boss.

She made her way back to the office, deep in thought.

Just how far did Steven think they were going to take this

public courtship thing? At some point, one of them was going to have to come out and admit that all this romantic play-acting for the benefit of her potential watchful stalker was just so much pie-in-the-sky. That, underneath it all, lay a serious attraction that was going to have to be addressed and sorted out, one way or the other.

Which probably meant that it would have to be her. Men were such wusses.

Tom trailed Steven Crayle only so far as the entrance to the HQ, for the superintendent's car turned left, towards Oxford, and he needed to go right.

He drove for barely ten minutes, before turning down a minor single-track lane that dead-ended at a five-barred country gate. He got out quickly and vaulted lithely over the obstacle, all but jogging down a farmer's rutted track towards a small copse in a large field of greening wheat.

Sometimes, the need to visit his special place just overwhelmed him, making it impossible for him to ignore its siren call. Whenever he needed reassurance, or peace, or simply to remember the glorious past, he always came to this spot.

Here there was a small rill and a damp, boggy patch of ground, with a cluster of hazel, hawthorn, and mostly sycamore trees. It made for a perfect escape from prying eyes and nosy parkers. It resembled a small leafy oasis in a sea of wheat, since the farmer didn't have the money or inclination to drain the bog and fell the trees, and nobody ever came here, since there was no public foot-path or right of access.

Tom had discovered it many years ago as a boy, it being within biking distance of a ten-year-old, and was just the sort of place a lonely child could imagine was a den of highwaymen and pirates. He'd even built a rough shelter here, many moons ago, which had long since been reclaimed by the elements. Once or twice the farmer had caught him on the land, but when he'd been a boy, he hadn't minded, and in later years Tom rather thought it pleased the landowner to know that a copper was 'keeping an eye' out for him. Nowadays, the thefts of tractors, combine harvesters, and other expensive farm equipment was sky-high, after all.

Of course, as a boy, he'd had no idea how useful the little copse would be to his future self.

Or to what use he would put it.

But now, as he approached his rather ordinary, rather scrubby little personal kingdom, he felt the healing magic of it wash over him. Here he could leave behind the petty, ugly realities of his humdrum day-to-day existence, and really come alive.

The peace of the copse in the midst of the green fields always soothed him. Birds always sang here, and the little rill in the middle of the dampest patch of ground always shone, even on the dullest of days. On a warm, sunny April day, it looked like a seam of silver, glittering in the dappled shade.

He made his way to one side of the bank, where a single silver birch tree grew. It was still barely twenty feet tall, and looked delicate and lace-like against the more prosaic native species. But then, he'd only planted it here, what, six years ago?

He'd needed something beautiful to honour his ladies, and the tree he'd spotted at Yarnton Nurseries had looked just the thing. The metallic sheen of its trunk and branches seemed to echo the theme of the silver rill. Its romantic, slightly ethereal appearance would, he knew, have pleased all of the ladies here – especially, perhaps, Gillian, who had liked to think of herself as a bit of a gypsy.

'Hello, ladies,' he said softly, as he made his way to the grassy bank, and sat down, a few yards from the tree. 'I know it's been a long time since I visited, but I haven't forgotten you. I'll never do that, you know that.'

Overhead, a pair of nesting robins flittered about in agitation, but Tom barely noticed them.

'I hope you haven't been arguing amongst yourselves,' he admonished, patting the grassy earth beneath him. 'You ladies need to play nice.' He sighed heavily. 'Especially since you might be getting a new friend for company.'

He shivered suddenly, and hunched forward.

He shook his head.

No, that wouldn't really have to happen, would it?

He didn't think so, but then, he'd always thought that before. And he had sensed a new kind of intimacy between his Hillary and that bastard, Steven Crayle. Something new, something that hadn't been there before.

'No,' he said out loud. She wasn't like these others. He glanced around the copse, and then up through the lace-like leaves of the silver birch. Hillary was the one. This time, he'd got it right. He was sure he had.

It couldn't all go wrong again. He wouldn't let it.

But he still felt a suffocating kind of dread clawing at the back of his throat which made him feel vaguely nauseous, and his fingers clawed compulsively at the grassy turf underneath his hand, lodging soil underneath his fingernails.

When Hillary returned to her office from seeing Steven off in the car park, she caught up on her paperwork, which was never designed to put her in a good mood. Then, once that chore was over, she called her contact in Narcotics, and explained the circumstances surrounding her latest cold case. And although he didn't give her the runaround, as his colleague had done with Vivienne, and definitely didn't treat her to the same amount of scorn, the results were pretty much the same.

'The trouble is, Hill,' her old pal told her, 'twelve years ago might have been back in the Stone Age as far as designer drugs are concerned. From what you tell me, your vic had been snorting something pretty recent for the time, probably home-made and brewed up locally. And being Oxford, do you know how many ex-biochem majors there always are just milling around and more than ready and willing to pay the old tuition fees by making up some kind of makeshift buzz?'

'I wouldn't like to hazard a guess,' she said with a shudder.

'Exactly. Whoever made the drug your vic had in his system

was probably only in operation for a couple of years at most, before earning their degree and moving on. Then you've got the problem that it's almost impossible to pin down the exact components from a slight trace from an ME report, and without the "signature" of the drug, there's no way we can compare it with other cases of around the same age. Even then...'

'OK, OK, I get the picture,' Hillary said with a sigh. 'Any chance you can look back in your records from around that time and see if any significant arrests were made? You must have had a few more likely lads and lasses who were probably behind whatever the current craze was. If I can just track down who supplied the gear, it'll give me a starting point at least.'

Her friend snorted derisively. 'Do you know the facts and figures involved here?' he asked with a weary laugh.

Hillary didn't, but had a sinking feeling she was about to find out.

'To begin with, the vast majority of drug designers and peddlers for a close-knit and targeted clientele are never caught in the first place. Very few know who they are, and even less are willing to grass on them if they're caught in possession. And of those pushers we do nab, the crafty sods usually hold such a small amount of gear at any one time, the CPS are reluctant to take up court time by prosecuting them at all. When you factor in plea bargaining and what-have-you, the likelihood of the perp you want even being in the system at all is ... well ... think up a metaphor of your choice.'

Hillary sighed. 'OK. Well, thanks for the time.'

'Hey, Hill, I don't mind, I'm just sorry I can't toss you any crumbs. But if you do stumble across any drugs link in the case, be sure to punt it my way. I could do with a good collar or two. My guv'nor is beginning to look at me a bit sideways, know what I mean?'

Hillary laughed, acknowledged that she did, and hung up. Her boss too was beginning to look at her sideways, but almost certainly not for the same reason as her friend's was. At least, she hoped not. Her pal's guv'nor was built like a brick outhouse and he had a personality to match.

She glanced at her watch, saw it was barely three, and decided it was too early to just do fill-in work until clocking-off time. She was restless to get back out and about and if it meant wandering into unpaid overtime, too bad.

She grabbed her coat and stuck her head into the small communal office just across the way. Her eyes fell on Sam Pickles, who must have finished his afternoon classes at uni early.

'Sam. I'm just going to question one of the original flatmates in the Thompson case. Feel up for it?'

Sam grinned, his freckles standing out against the flush of pleasure that crossed his face. 'Yes, guv.'

'We'll take your car,' she said, pretending not to notice the flash of relief that crept into his expression. 'Get Hargreaves's particulars, and meet me in the car park.'

Hillary knew Swindon only in the vaguest of terms, but they had little difficulty in finding Barry Hargreaves's home address. They were trying his place of residence first, since Vivienne's research had shown that Hargreaves had just very recently been made redundant from his position in a large accountancy firm, and thus was more likely to be at home.

His house turned out to be a fairly new build, in the mock-Tudor style in a cul-de-sac of six similar builds, in a leafy and pleasant suburb of the town. It wasn't her cup of tea, but she could well see why a construction worker of humble origins would have seen it as a definite step up from a council house on an estate.

'Leaving building work to take an Oxford degree certainly paid off for him, didn't it?' Hillary mused, as Sam parked up his precious Mini outside a set of wide wooden gates. A short gravel drive, and the requisite rose garden in front of the big main windows, fronted the house.

'Nice, guv,' Sam agreed.

A tall, thin woman, with greying fair hair swept back in a

ponytail answered the door. She was wearing navy-blue slacks and a white-and-blue striped jumper. She had large, rather boiled-gooseberry pale-grey eyes, and was make-up free.

'Yes?' she asked, a shade peremptorily.

Hillary and Sam showed their IDs, which made the eyes pop just that bit more. 'We're hoping to have a word with Mr Barry Hargreaves. Is he in?'

'Barry? You want to talk to my Barry? Why, what's up? There's nothing funny been going on at the firm, has there?' she asked nervously.

Hillary wondered why Barry Hargreaves's wife should instantly jump to that conclusion. Were there rumours going around about embezzlement? Had her husband left under a cloud? Hillary had assumed that Barry Hargreaves's redundancy had been as a result of the mournful state of the economy and the seemingly never-ending recession, but perhaps there was more to it than that.

'Nothing of that kind, Mrs Hargreaves,' she reassured her quietly. 'Is your husband at home?' she pressed.

'Oh. Oh, yes, you'd better come in, then. Through to the study – first door on the left. Barry's working on his CV again.'

Hillary nodded and followed the woman into a hall rather similar to Darla Pitt's, in that it seemed largely lacking in character and carefully colour-coordinated in neutral shades.

The older woman knocked on a door and looked in nervously. 'Barry, there's some police people here to see you,' she hissed.

Hillary hid a grimace. Although she was slowly getting used to not being a DI anymore, she didn't particularly relish being called 'police people'.

'What? Are you sure?' a baritone voice rumbled back. In answer, his wife simply stepped back and looked at Hillary and Sam.

Hillary went in first.

'Would you like some tea or coffee?' the tall woman asked tentatively.

Hillary smiled and shook her head. 'No, thank you, Mrs Hargreaves, we're fine.'

From behind a small desk with a laptop lying open on top of it, a burly man got to his feet. His hair – what was left of it – was that grizzled steel-grey kind that looked a bit like a scouring pad. His face was round and red, no doubt as a result of years of outdoor work. He was barrel-chested, and had a beer belly, but his eyes were the sort that most people would describe as 'twinkling' and of a startling blue in colour.

'Hello. Police?' he asked, his voice sounding more curious than worried.

Hillary held out her ID, and explained who they were and what they did.

'Cold cases? This'll be about Rowan, then?' Hargreaves said with a nod. 'Just a minute – let me shut this down.' He fiddled with the laptop, saying over his shoulder, 'Please, take a seat and get comfortable. I won't be a mo.'

The study had obviously been a second reception room, and housed two comfortable-looking armchairs, a window seat and a fireplace that had probably never been meant to work.

Hillary chose a chair, whilst Sam went to the window seat and opened his notebook.

'OK, all done,' Barry Hargreaves said, closing the lid of the laptop and moving to the chair opposite Hillary. He cast a quick look at Sam, noting that his words were being taken down, but again, didn't look particularly alarmed about it.

Hillary decided to do some gentle probing first.

'Your wife seemed to think we were here about embezzlement at your former place of work, sir,' she said softly.

Barry looked at her, one of his caterpillar-like, bushy grey eyebrows going up, before he laughed – a deep, rumbling belly-laugh.

'Oh that's just Mary. Don't pay no notice. If worrying or pessimism was an Olympic sport she'd have gold medals lining the walls. When I was laid off, she was convinced there was something sinister behind it. There wasn't, of course – just that I was last in so I was first out when the work started drying up. And, of course, now she's convinced we'll have to sell the house and move back to her mother's or some such. I keep telling her, with my qualifications I'll be employed again by the end of next month, but she won't have it. She's always been the same. I find it best not to argue with her and just let her get on with it. She'll be happy enough and settle down once I've got another job.'

He spoke with a kind of loving exasperation that bespoke many years of patient marriage.

Hillary decided to leave it for now. But she made a mental note to herself to get Vivienne to contact Hargreaves's employers and just make sure that everything was as he'd have them believe.

'So Rowan, huh?' Hargreaves said, leaning forward a little in the chair and letting his big beefy hands fall lankly between his slightly spread knees. 'Been a while since I thought about him, to be honest.'

Hillary looked at the big man thoughtfully. With the other housemates she'd taken a more softly-softly approach. Perhaps now was the time to change tactics a bit.

'You are aware, I'm sure, that the original investigator, Inspector Gorman, regarded you as his chief suspect, Mr Hargreaves?' she said, careful to keep her voice flat and just a touch hard.

'Because of that rumour about the twins, you mean?' Hargreaves surprised her somewhat by immediately taking the bull by the horns. At least there was going to be no beating around the bush here, with coy denials and waffle.

Of all the people living in that house, only Darla – as the injured and put-upon girlfriend – and this man had anything approaching a significant motive. That had been obvious from just a casual reading of Gorman's notes.

'Natasha and Romola, yes,' Hillary agreed. 'They were both fifteen at the time of Rowan's death, I believe?'

'That's right.'

'And they used to come and see you regularly whilst you were at Oxford.'

'Yeah. Well, it's not as if Swindon's at the other end of the world, is it? Not even an hour away by train, and they liked to get away from the eagle eye of their mum and whoop it up around town on their own. Like I said, Mary's a bit of a worrier, and she tended to keep them on a short leash. Coming to see me gave them a much-needed bit of freedom, didn't it?' he pointed out.

Hillary shifted a little on her seat. It all sounded so very reasonable and laid-back. But surely it couldn't be that simple.

'But Inspector Gorman found out that both of the girls had been intimate with the victim,' she pointed out. 'That must have made you angry, Mr Hargreaves. Apart from anything else, that made it statutory rape. Why did you never press charges?'

Barry Hargreaves shook his head. 'No, no, you don't get it. It never happened. Rowan had this reputation, see, as a bit of a … well … what should we say to be polite, like?'

Hillary barely smiled. 'Yes, we've been learning a lot about the victim's personality, sir. I think we can take it for granted that he was something of a sexual athlete and predator.'

'Exactly. I know for a fact he had women of all sorts going in and out of that room of his. And men too, it wouldn't surprise me. Trannies, you name it.'

'So the thought of a man like that taking advantage of your twin girls must have made you see red,' she insisted.

But again Barry Hargreaves shook his head. 'Like I told that Gorman at the time – it didn't happen. I always kept a careful eye on the girls when they came to see me, just because I knew what Rowan was like. Don't get me wrong – he was a nice lad in some ways. Had a good enough sort of heart really, but he was a typical lad. Thinking with his cock – sorry, excuse the language. So I never trusted him as far as I could throw him, see? I made sure he never got his hands on Nat or Rommy, don't you worry. No matter what anybody else thought.'

Hillary looked at Barry Hargreaves thoughtfully. He certainly seemed to believe what he was saying, but Hillary had read the files. Gorman had interviewed several witnesses and friends of Rowan, who had sworn that the murdered man had told them that he'd had both of the Hargreaves twins in a twosome on several occasions.

'That's not the information Inspector Gorman had, sir,' Hillary pointed out, as diplomatically as possible.

Barry smiled. 'No, I don't suppose it was. But people like to talk, don't they? I suppose it made a better story to say that Rowan had seduced the girls, rather than the more boring truth – that he'd lucked out. Who knows, maybe he boasted that he'd bedded them. Or maybe some busybodies saw them out and about and put two and two together and came up with five. Who can say? But *I* know there was nothing in it. I tried to tell Inspector Gorman that, but he didn't seem to hear me.'

Hillary ruminated on that for a bit. Was Hargreaves just blowing so much smoke? Did he, in fact, know that Rowan, that avaricious Romeo, had had his girls, and even now just couldn't bring himself to acknowledge the fact?

Or did he actually believe what he was saying?

Or was he, in fact, right? She couldn't see someone like Rowan admitting defeat. Maybe it had been just idle bragging on his part.

Then again, Barry Hargreaves was nobody's mug. Admitting to knowing that his fifteen-year-old girls had been corrupted by Thompson put him well and truly in the frame when it came to looking for the young man's killer. Given the fact that he lived in the same house, had access to the murder weapon and, like the rest of the house's occupants, didn't really have an alibi put him right up there on the suspect list.

It might make even an innocent man gulp and start stretching the truth a bit when put under questioning.

'Besides, I asked the girls, afterwards, right out, if they'd slept with him. Both denied it. And Romola especially wouldn't lie to her old dad.' Barry grinned. 'Nattie, now she could be a bit tricky, sometimes, I admit. But I know both my girls, and I know when they're telling the truth.'

Hillary barely gave that much of a thought. Since when did teenage girls ever tell their daddies the truth about their sexual shenanigans? She knew she bloody well never had.

'I see. Tell me about the morning Rowan died,' she asked, changing tack slightly.

'Well, like I said at the time. I left about twenty past eight or so. I saw the two girls in the hall – Darla and Marcie. I said a quick hello and we had a brief chat about what we had planned for Christmas – you know, that sort of thing.'

'Right.' Mrs Landau had said she'd heard both female and male voices in the hall that morning, so that fitted.

'I had stuff to do – I needed a quick chat with my tutor so I went to college, then I picked up an artificial Christmas tree to take back to Swindon with me. When I got back to the flat the cops were already there, and Ma Landau was in a bit of a state. That's about it.' He shrugged his powerful shoulders helplessly.

He certainly had the build to overpower a smaller lad like Rowan, Hillary thought. But then, with a sharpened pair of scissors, was that really significant? According to the ME, anyone would have been able to land the killing blow – especially if Rowan had been taken by surprise, as seemed to be the case, given the lack of any defence wounds on the body.

'Did you see anyone hanging around outside when you left?' She went through the by-now familiar list of questions without much expectation of anything useful. Which was just as well.

'No.'

'Did Rowan ever confide to you that someone was making threats against him? Did he seem scared of anybody or anything in particular?'

'Rowan? Good grief, no.'

'Do you have any idea who might have killed him?'

And with this question, finally, she felt something of a nibble. For a brief moment, Barry's easy manner seemed to stiffen just slightly. The blue eyes didn't quite meet hers so openly. He went, just for a fraction of second, rather still. Then he shook his head. 'Sorry, no.'

Hillary knew it would be pointless pressing him now. Once a witness had committed him or herself, they very rarely went back on their story right away. But she'd be back. Barry Hargreaves, of all the housemates so far, interested her the most. But maybe not for the same reasons as he had attracted the attention of the rather two-dimensional-thinking Inspector Gorman.

'Well, if you think of anything else, sir, please call me,' she said, handing him her business card with her name, and the CRT's telephone numbers and email address.

With the fretful Mary hovering nervously in the background, Barry Hargreaves showed them out.

Back in the car, Hillary sat staring thoughtfully ahead as Sam did up his seatbelt.

'When we get back, I'd like you or Vivienne to check into Barry Hargreaves's work history after he left Oxford.'

'Yes, guv.'

'And find me the addresses of his daughters – both of them. I want to have a word with them.'

'Yes, guv.'

'And did you have time yet to do a background check on the landlady, Wanda Landau?'

'It's a bit sad, really. They only had the one child – a girl. I can't remember her name right off, but I've got it all down in a report ready for the murder book. She got involved in drugs at a young age. Her boyfriend was a bad sort, and died of an overdose before their baby was born. Mrs Landau tried everything to help her – paid for rehab any number of times, but it was no good.'

Hillary nodded glumly. 'Let me guess. Prostitution?'

'Yes, guv. She did time for shoplifting and theft as well. Mugged an old lady and broke her leg when she wouldn't let go of her handbag, and she was pulled over onto a pavement. Social services took the kid off her, and Mrs Landau petitioned the courts to take her grandson on and raise him herself. Won, too. Not easy that, considering her age at the time.'

'Good for her,' Hillary said, and meant it. 'And the daughter?'

'Don't know. Went off the radar when she was released from gaol.'

'Which means she's probably dead somewhere. Lying unidentified on a slab, or buried in an anonymous grave, courtesy of whichever borough council she ended up in.'

Sam sighed. 'She might have got off the gear inside and gone straight, guv,' he said.

Hillary said nothing about his *naïveté* but it touched her, none the less, making her smile sadly. 'Yes, maybe. OK. So, what do you make of Mr Hargreaves, Sam?' she asked briskly.

'He seems straight enough.'

'Yes, he does, doesn't he?' she mused.

But she was sure that Hargreaves, if not actively lying to them, was definitely not telling them all that he knew.

As Sam turned the key in the ignition and started the drive back to Oxford, battling against rush hour all the way, she wondered what it was that Hargreaves knew or suspected.

And who it was he was protecting.

CHAPTER SIX

The next morning, at just before 8.30, Tom Warrington leaned forward in his car and checked the scene through the viewfinder of his favourite camera. He had a lot of camera equipment, including a large lens for distance work, but for unobtrusive outings like this one he preferred the little common-or-garden Canon. It was small enough to fit into his jacket pocket if someone spotted him, and yet it had a zoom facility and being digital, recorded good, clear shots.

He was parked in Hillary's preferred area of the car park at Thames Valley HQ, and had an open folder splayed out against the steering wheel. To a casual observer, he looked like someone catching up quickly on some paperwork before venturing inside. It also allowed him to keep the camera out of sight between his knees in the steering well when not in use.

Just before a quarter to nine he saw her car pull up and park a few spaces down. He frowned, as right behind her, a familiar saloon car also hove into view.

Crayle. It almost looked as if they'd come together, but he knew that couldn't be right. Hillary's boat in Thrupp meant she came in via a different route than Crayle, who had a house on the other side of the town.

It had to be a coincidence that they arrived at the same time.

He waited very carefully, making sure that neither of them was looking his way, before taking out the camera and taking photographs. He already had some good shots of Hillary taken with his long-range telephoto lens, but he preferred getting the closer shots. It felt more personal, somehow. More intimate. He liked her to know that he was always close, always watching over her.

Today, she was wearing a pair of black slacks, with a cream, black and mint-green blouse, and a matching mint-green jacket. The cool, classic colours complemented perfectly her dark russet hair. She hardly ever wore jewellery, he'd noticed, and she was wearing only her usual, plain, black-strapped watch today. Her make-up was minimal – but then, she didn't need it. Her classical bone structure would make her beautiful, even when she was eighty.

She was class, through and through, Tom thought with pride, as he took another illicit snap and watched her turn and wait for the approach of Superintendent Crayle.

Her face looked thoughtful, composed and wary, as it usually did, but he didn't like the way she smiled as the tall, elegant man approached her.

'Hello, what's up?' she asked, as he reached her. 'Why the rendezvous?'

He'd called her that morning, asking her to wait for his car on the Oxford road just this side of the turn off, and then to follow her in.

'I just thought it would be a good idea for us to start showing up at the same time a couple of times a week,' Steven said, reaching out and offering to take her briefcase.

'Oh, the desk sergeant,' Hillary said wisely. Through the big glass-fronted double doors in the foyer, the desk sergeants always had a good view of the car park and the various comings and goings. They liked to be in the know, and it added to their kudos of being the all-seeing, all-knowing heartbeat of the station house. And it wouldn't take the eagle-eyed sods long to start noticing how Hillary and her boss were starting to arrive – albeit in separate cars – on each other's heels.

'Good thinking,' she agreed with a smile, and handed over the briefcase to his waiting hand. 'But isn't that pushing it a little too far?' she asked, nodding down at her case. 'Gallantry of that kind went out with the fax machine.'

Steven smiled. 'Well, we're not exactly trying to be subtle, are we?' he pointed out. 'And just in case your friend is watching, we want to be sure he gets the message.'

In his car, Tom Warrington lowered the camera back under the steering wheel. He didn't want to take any photographs of his Hillary now that *he* was in the frame.

He watched, morosely, as the smarmy superintendent took Hillary's briefcase from her and they walked together into the building.

He should be the one carrying her case for her, of course. It wasn't fair. She shouldn't have let Crayle take it. He sighed heavily. Why did they always make it so difficult?

He could see that the text messages weren't going to be enough to remind Hillary that she belonged to him now. He was going to have to think of something else. Something more worthy of her. After all, flowers and cards and texts were so predictable. He had to be original. To think up something unique and creative. She was Hillary Greene, the station-house legend. The best damned detective on the force. The smartest, the bravest. The best. He needed to think of something to engage her attention, to entice her out to play with him, to remind her that he was always thinking of her. Something unique to Hillary that would warm her heart but engage her spirit and mind as well.

He'd have to think about it. What did she like doing? What would please her? What would make her remember him, her true love, when the likes of the handsome, elegant distractions like Steven Crayle came her way, tempting her to stray?

With a sigh, Tom put away the camera and the folder and traipsed in to do his stint at the coal mine. He would ask Vivienne Tyrell out to dinner tonight, and see what she knew about Hillary's current case. That way, he might be able to predict her movements, and maybe even arrange to 'accidentally' bump into her somehow.

She would like that.

*

Back inside his office, Steven Crayle paced about restlessly. He had a hard ache between his shoulder blades that was part tension and part unease. All throughout his conversation with Hillary in the car park he'd felt a bit jittery, as if he could sense hostile eyes watching him.

But the car park had been full of people coming and going, and cars parked with people in them having the first cigarette of the morning before entering the no-smoking zone of the office, or catching up on paperwork. There'd been groups of people, some in plain clothes, some in uniform, coming off night shift and chattering away, and a regular stream of people coming in, some of them looking at Hillary and himself, some of them not.

It had been impossible to pinpoint exactly where the trouble was. And maybe it was only the situation beginning to tell on his nerves anyway. Maybe there'd been nothing wrong at all. But if he was feeling this antsy, what the hell must Hillary be feeling like?

And yet, nobody would know there was anything wrong to look at her. None of her team was aware that she was under stress, of that he was sure. And so far, he hadn't reported the situation any higher either – although if things did start to pop off, he'd have to tell Commander Donleavy. Although he and Hillary hadn't discussed it yet, there was a tacit agreement between them that they wouldn't bring the brass into this unless it became absolutely necessary.

He sighed and went to his desk, but only to swing restlessly from side to side on his chair as he did so.

He didn't like to think of Hillary alone on that boat at night, for one thing. Although there were other boats moored up and down from her, it just felt so isolated. And the *Mollern*, whilst charming, was so restricted. If her stalker got inside, where could she run or hide? She wouldn't even have much room in which to put up a decent fight.

Perhaps he should start staying the night? He was sure the seating arrangements in narrowboats could be transformed into single beds, so there'd be room. And it would certainly help their fake romance along if her neighbours saw him as a regular presence on the boat and started spreading it around.

The trouble was, he just couldn't see Hillary going for it. She valued her independence too much.

Besides, he wasn't sure that he wanted to be that close to her either – not on a regular basis. She was beginning to seriously get under his skin. He could recognize the signs. Already her welfare meant far more to him than that of a boss's natural worry for a member of his team.

There was only one solution that he could think of: he reached for his phone and pressed two digits, giving him an internal line, and then pressed another two digits. He listened to the brief burring on the other end, and then tensed as the summons was answered.

'Jessop,' the voice said simply.

'Jimmy, it's Steven. Can you spare me a few minutes?'

'Sir.'

The line went dead. Steven smiled. The ex-sergeant might be a man of few words and no social charm, but Steven had no doubt that he was reliable and, just as importantly, could be counted on to keep his mouth shut.

A moment later, he heard the knock on the door. 'Come in.'

Jimmy Jessop looked worryingly old as he stepped through the door, but his eyes were wary and alert, and he walked like a man at least a decade younger than his grey hair and baggy face would indicate.

'Jimmy, sit down.'

The superintendent waited until the older man was seated, then carefully marshalled his thoughts.

'Jimmy, a situation has arisen that needs some delicate handling. And by that, I mean discreet handling. Off the record.'

Jimmy Jessop blinked and looked even more wary. Steven

smiled a shade grimly. 'Don't worry – it's nothing bent.' He wasn't sure that he liked it that Jimmy was still so unsure of him that he didn't know he played things strictly straight. 'It's Hillary,' he carried on, seeing the surprise in the older man's eyes. 'She's picked up a stalker.'

Briefly but leaving nothing out, Steven brought him up to date on the situation so far.

When he'd finished, Jimmy nodded slowly. Several people had approached him in the last two days who wanted to pump him for information on the Crayle/Greene romance, and he'd laughingly denied it.

Now, at least, it made sense.

'And you're sure it's one of us?' he asked glumly.

'Someone working at HQ, yes. We think it more likely than not,' Steven said.

'I think you're right,' Jimmy agreed reluctantly. 'And if Hillary thinks he's probably done this kind of thing before, she's almost certainly right, guv. She usually is.'

Steven nodded. Jimmy was obviously another Hillary Greene fan, which didn't surprise him. The whole station was a Hillary Greene fan. In fact, he realized with a not-exactly amused inner smile, he was becoming one himself, wasn't he?

'You want me to see if I can find other victims of her stalker?' Jimmy asked. The CRT records were the best there were, and if there was a serial stalker around, especially one who operated on their patch and right under their noses, the boffins and number-crunchers should be able to winkle out the names of other victims.

'We've thought of that, but asking for official help makes it an official problem, and we're not ready to do that yet,' Steven said. 'No, what worries me more is that in trying to make our pal jealous, we might just force his hand too far. And Hillary's alone on that boat at night. It makes me nervous.'

'Ah. Got you,' Jimmy said at once.

'Of course, I can't just order some uniforms to keep obbo. It would be all over HQ by the next morning, and besides, I don't have the budget for it. And again, it would make it official.'

Jimmy nodded. 'Don't worry, guv, I know what you need. I've got three or four pals from the old days who are bored stiff with fishing, or hanging out in their allotment sheds. A bit of night-time obbo will relieve the boredom. And it's nearly May now, so it's not as if we'll freeze our balls off. And, besides, they'd do it for Hillary Greene even if we were up to our necks in snow.'

'I haven't told her I'm bringing you in on this, Jimmy, and I don't intend to. Her instinct will be to keep you all out of it. So whenever you take your turn watching her, be sure she doesn't catch you at it. And that goes for your pals, too. She's sharp, don't forget, and she's already on the alert, looking out for chummy, so you'll all have to be extra careful.'

Jimmy Jessop smiled grimly. 'I know she's smart as a whip all right, guv. Don't worry – me and my mates might be old, but we've got plenty of experience under our belts. She won't know we're there.' He only hoped he was right. Just how embarrassing would it be if his guv'nor nabbed one of his mates, thinking he was her stalker? He'd never hear the end of it – from either of them.

'Good. I want you to both look out for her, and see if you can spot anybody tailing her. Check the faces around her and see if you can spot one that you see more often then you would expect to. Oh hell, you know the drill – I don't have to spell it out.'

'Yes, guv. I take it you don't want us to apprehend?'

'Hell, no. If you get a lead on someone, trail them, get a picture if you can, any details, but leave well alone. Well, unless there's any clear and present danger to Hillary, naturally.'

'Got it, guv,' Jimmy said. 'We'll start tonight.'

'Good. Oh, and Jimmy, don't forget: he's broken in to her car, her locker and her boat. If you can find enough mates to help, it might be useful if they keep watch on her property when she's not around. Unless he changes his MO, we might just be able to catch him in the act.'

Jimmy nodded. 'Good idea.'

Once outside the office, he began making a mental list of his pals best suited to the job. They had to be fairly fit, and still fairly young. Well, the right side of seventy, anyway.

And they had to know how to handle themselves without making a mess of it. Because they'd have to be tooled up – there was no way around it. Stalking tended to be a young man's game, so chummy would already have an advantage over them.

But there were ways and means of evening the odds. Hammers, a weighty length of chain, even a good old-fashioned police baton. The choice of weapon would be down to individual choice. He himself had always preferred a stout hazel stick with a nobby end that had been soaked over and over again in a handed-down family recipe, until it had the density and weight of iron.

In her office, and oblivious to the arrangements that were being made to watch over her, Hillary checked through the murder book. It was well stuffed with the most recent and up-to-date facts and interview notes, but it didn't provide much by way of inspiration.

Cold cases were annoying because there was little chance of the status quo changing through sheer momentum. Working a current case, you never knew when the phone might ring with new information coming in from forensics, or the uniforms doing house to house. You had the option of choices: going to the press with an appeal for information, for instance, or maybe staging a reconstruction in the hope of jogging someone's memory. And you had the added bonus of pressure – both on yourself, and on the perp. Pressure, she knew, was a sometimes badly needed spur to egg on the SIO in charge to up their game. Likewise, it put pressure on the guilty. They dreaded the ring of the telephone, and jumped at the peal of the doorbell. Not knowing how the investigation was going but fearing the worst very often did a copper's job for them, so that when you got around to questioning them, you could tell by the state of their nerves that you were on to a winner.

But there was none of that with a cold case. In a cold case, all sense of urgency and pressure had evaporated. And time had a way of making everyone feel safe. Motivation was never something that needed to be cultivated on a current case.

Hillary sighed and closed the murder book with a snap. All she could do was plug on, re-covering old, cold ground, and trying to keep her mind focused.

Her admirer, and the growing absurdity of her situation with regards to her relationship with Steven Crayle, were distractions that she could really do without right now.

She got up, grabbed her bag, and stepped across the corridor. Jimmy was nowhere in sight, but Sam Pickles looked up hopefully as she stuck her head through the doorway.

'Marcie Franks?' she said, her voice making it a question.

'Down in the Smoke, guv.'

Hillary sighed. She was not a big fan of London, which probably put her in the minority. 'Does the budget stretch to letting the train take the strain?'

Sam grinned. 'Doubt it, guv, but I don't mind driving.'

Hillary smiled grimly. 'Just as well, Sam,' she said. 'Grab your keys.'

Luckily, the rather sci-fi-looking laboratory where Marcie Franks worked as a researcher was on the right side of London for them, so they only got lost twice. The nearest car park gobbled up coins like it was expecting a famine, and even though paying for the privilege, they still had to park at the top of a multi-storey sans roof. Luckily, the weather was still mild and sunny.

'What exactly does this company of hers – Futech Corps, is it? – do?' Hillary asked curiously, as they walked to the lifts and rode down in graffiti-decorated elegance.

'All sorts, guv. Mostly stuff for the beauty industry, whatever that means.'

'Perfume, face paint and moisturizers, I expect,' Hillary said. She herself seldom wore perfume and had never yet resorted to anti-wrinkle cream. Come to think of it, she went shopping for make-up about once in a blue moon as well. Whoever paid Marcie Franks's salary, they certainly didn't get rich on what Hillary Greene spent on their products.

'No medical research at all?' she asked curiously, thinking of the designer drug angle. What had her pal in Narcotics said? Oxford was rife with chemistry and biochemistry graduates coming up with ways to pay their tuition fees?

'Marcie Franks was reading biochemistry, right?' she asked.

'Yes. But she was one of those who did a double degree. She also has a second in chemistry. And later a third degree in physiological sciences from Cambridge.'

'Hmm. Sounds like a bit of a perpetual student to me,' Hillary mused. 'Either that, or she had a specific reason for wanting to hang around universities for a while.'

'Guv?'

'Never mind. Just thinking out loud. So, apart from moving to London and getting a high-paying job in the beauty industry, just what else has she been up to? Married? Kids?'

'No. She bought a nice flat in a swanky area though, three years ago, when the prices began to fall. Now they're starting to rise a bit again, she's probably sitting on a gold mine.'

'So she's financially savvy as well as having brains,' Hillary mused. 'The two don't always go hand in hand,' she pontificated, as they walked the busy streets of the nation's capital towards the high-rise modern monstrosity where Futech Corps hung its corporate hat.

Inside, the reception foyer was all glass bricks and modern sculpture, with a large board on one wall listing the businesses within. Futech Corps had the entire fourth floor to itself.

'Nice,' Hillary mused a few moments later, as the lift disgorged them into a gold, black and turquoise-accented room. Large posters of beautiful women wearing black lipstick, or glow-in-the-dark mascara or whatever, lined the walls. A large vase of white gladioli sat on a reception desk, where another beautiful woman rose to greet them.

She looked politely puzzled.

Hillary held out her ID.

She looked even more puzzled. 'You have an appointment, Mrs Greene?'

Hillary sighed. 'We'd like to speak to one of your researchers, Dr Marcie Franks?'

The woman sat back down and tapped a few keys on her keyboard. 'Doctor Franks is currently working in lab fifteen. I'll call ahead and let them know to expect you. It may take a little while – I'm not sure what the protocols are for Dr Franks's work.'

Hillary thanked her and listened to the directions they were given. When they'd turned the first of many corridors, into what would be one of many other corridors, Sam muttered a trifle uneasily, 'Protocols? You mean like wearing suits with helmets, like spacemen? Doors that have inner doors and vacuum-cleaned what-not? There aren't any superbugs being grown in here, are there, guv?'

'I doubt it. Not unless freckle remover has been designated a bio hazard,' Hillary said sardonically. 'Relax. They're more worried about industrial espionage than Ebola in this place, take my word for it.'

Sam grinned, and began to relax.

Even so, Marcie Franks took twenty-five minutes to find them in a small waiting-room where they'd been parked by the guardian of laboratory fifteen, a fifty-something woman who'd been wearing more make-up on her face than Hillary would have applied in a month.

'Jennifer said you were the police?' Marcie Franks said, coming into the small, gold-and-white-painted room, decorated with slightly smaller posters of women's painted nails. She was wearing the requisite white lab coat, over black trousers.

Hillary once again showed her ID.

Marcie Franks was about five feet ten, skinny and had very long brown hair currently tied up and back in a chignon. She had wide, brown, rather bovine eyes and wore not a scrap of make-up. She checked both Hillary's and Sam's cards thoroughly. 'So you're civilians, not actually police officers?' she clarified sharply.

'Yes. We work for the Crime Review Team – we take a new look at cold cases.'

'Ah.' Marcie took a seat in one of the gold velour-clad chairs. 'This is about Rowan, then.'

'Yes.'

'New evidence has come to light?'

'I'm afraid I really can't discuss that, Miss Franks,' Hillary said. 'Doctor or Ms.'

'Ms Franks. What can you tell me about Rowan?'

Marcie Franks glanced at her watch and frowned. 'You want to do this now? I mean, I'm at work. I thought you were here to make an appointment or something.'

'We can always do this at Thames Valley Police Station, Ms Franks,' Hillary said smoothly. 'I just thought it would make your life easier if we came to you, and made this interview more of a personal chat. But some people prefer to stick to formalities.'

For a moment, Hillary wondered if Ms Franks was going to call her bluff. She was very well aware that she did, in fact, have no powers whatsoever to ask Marcie Franks to go to Kidlington HQ for a formal interview.

'Well, I can't be too long,' the other woman said reluctantly.

'I could always have a word with your supervisor, Ms Franks, and explain the situation,' Hillary offered mildly.

A low, dull flush suddenly swept across Marcie Franks's thin face. 'I don't have a supervisor, Mrs Greene,' she responded stiffly. 'I'm head of my department.'

Hillary smiled. 'Perfect. Then you can dictate your own hours?'

Marcie smiled. Or rather, she showed her teeth. '*Touché*, Mrs Greene.' She managed an unconvincing laugh before briskly admitting defeat and finally settling down to business. 'So,

Rowan. What can I tell you about him? Well, he was an undiscerning, randy little shit, to be frank. He got by on charm and luck.'

'You didn't like him?' Hillary said, making it a question.

Marcie sighed. 'Yes and no. I didn't not like him. He was basically harmless, but he could be very annoying.'

'He tried to come on to you? Made a pest of himself?'

'Not likely. He knew it wouldn't wash with me. But he did … well, pester a friend of mine. A close friend.'

'His name, please?'

'Her name was Sally Jenkins,' Marcie said flatly.

Hillary nodded. 'You and she were close? This was around the time that Rowan was killed?'

'Yes. She was reading jurisprudence at St Ed's. She was going to go into chambers in Cambridge when she'd graduated. Her family heads a firm of solicitors there – has done for generations.'

'It was serious between you?'

'We were going to set up home together in Cambridge,' Marcie admitted, before her eyes narrowed. 'It didn't quite work out that way, as it happens,' she added tightly.

'Because of Rowan?'

'Not exactly. But he certainly didn't help matters.'

'He pestered her, you said.'

'Yes.'

'How exactly?' Hillary pressed.

'Oh, you had to know Rowan to understand that. He found us a challenge, you see. Two lesbians, we were a bit like a red rag to a bull. He wanted to 'see what it was like' to bed us. Of course, I gave him a flea in his ear,' – she showed her teeth again – 'or rather, to be more accurate, a well-placed knee in the groin. So he turned his attention to Sally. She, alas, was more vulnerable,' she said with a sigh, looking down at her spread hands.

Hillary noticed that her nails had a distinct lack of varnish on them. Whatever they paid her, Dr Franks, or Ms Franks, didn't seem inclined to spend her salary on the company products.

'Vulnerable? In what way?' Hillary asked, pricking up her ears.

'She was more conventional. Her family sort-of knew about her leanings, but were hoping she'd grow out of it – like it was some sort of phase she was going through. And Sally wanted to please them, obviously.' Marcie Franks gave another unconvincing laugh. 'Don't get me wrong – we were happy together, but I was always aware that she found it much harder to cope with the lifestyle than I did. If anyone ever gave me grief, I simply gave it right back to them in spades,' Marcie said, her voice as hard as the nails on the posters around them now. 'But Sally felt each and every slur and took the prejudice personally. It made life for her very difficult and much harder than it needed to be.'

'She was thin-skinned, in fact?' Hillary said quietly.

'Yes. And Rowan didn't help matters any – always playing on that and trying to undermine her. Sally hadn't really had a boyfriend before, and Rowan kept promising her that it was better with men, that he'd show her, and all that guff. And of course, Sally wanted to believe it. Like her parents, I think she was half-hoping he might 'cure' her.'

Hillary nodded. There wasn't really any delicate way to ask what she had to ask next, so she simply got it over with.

'And did she sleep with him?'

'I don't know,' Marcie admitted frankly. 'I don't think she did. But it made things between us tense, as you can imagine. In the end, she couldn't even visit me at Ma Landau's without Rowan trying on the charm. So I always had to go to her digs. She had housemates who were very carefully politically correct about our relationship, which in some ways was even more trying than out-and-out gay bashing.'

'Not a very good environment for romance, then,' Hillary said drily.

This time, Marcie's smile was a little more sincere. 'Let's just say it wasn't ideal.'

Now Hillary could make sense of Marcie Franks's rather over-achieving academic career. After graduating from Oxford, she'd gone to Cambridge more as a way to follow her love, than to do another degree – which had probably turned out to be an unnecessary one.

Had it been worthwhile? Or had Sally Jenkins's parents tried to put a stop to their relationship? Or had Sally herself decided to call it quits?

'Are you still together?'

'Hardly. I've been living with my partner Jane Dailey for nearly five years now. She's an interior designer.'

'It sounds to me like you had a reason for wanting to see Rowan Thompson dead, Ms Franks. And I know from reading the original notes that you never mentioned any of this to DI Gorman – the inspector in charge of the case at the time.'

'I wouldn't have told that insensitive clod anything,' Marcie Franks shot back defensively, another dull, ugly flush suffusing her face. 'And I'd hardly call that sufficient grounds for murder, Mrs Greene. Rowan was a nuisance and a pest, but that's all.'

Hillary let that hang in the air for a moment, then decided to let it pass.

'What can you remember about the morning Rowan died?'

'I met Darla on the stairs that morning, and we had a quick word. I think Barry Hargreaves came down and left around the same time. As far as I knew, Rowan was still in bed. He always was a late riser. Both he and Dwayne were lazy sods. I went to my college, did some last-minute work, did a bit of shopping, and was, I think, the last one back at the house. By which point, the police were there. And before you ask, no, I didn't see anyone suspicious hanging around; no, I never knew of any enemies Rowan might have had, and no, I don't know who killed him.'

Hillary showed her own teeth. 'Thank you for your time, Ms Franks. We may need to speak to you again.'

Marcie sighed heavily, but made no comment. Instead, she rose and left them without another word.

When she'd gone, she heard Sam let out a long, low breath. Hillary smiled across at him. 'All right, Sam?'

'Guv. I don't think she looked at me once while she was here,' he said, more in relief than irritation.

'I don't think you count, in Ms Franks's world, Sam.'

'You gave her as good as you got, guv,' Sam said with admiration.

Hillary grunted. She wasn't so sure about that. In fact, if Ms Franks had called her 'Mrs Greene' one more time, Hillary might have taken very voluble exception.

The trouble was, now that she was no longer DI Greene, she *was* Mrs Greene. And the only thing she could do about that was revert to her maiden name.

Which would make her a Miss.

Abruptly, Hillary gave a short bark of laughter. Sam smiled uncertainly.

'Well, the ice queen has a motive, guv. No matter what she says,' Sam said with growing eagerness, 'I think Rowan Thompson put the kibosh on her relationship with Sally. And no matter what she says, I think she knows the two of them slept together. And she did keep quiet about it at the time.'

'Oh, she's a new lead all right,' Hillary agreed. 'When we get back, be sure to add your notes to the murder book right away.'

'Yes, guv.'

'And find me a current address for Sally Jenkins.'

Sam grinned. 'Yes, guv.'

Once back out on the streets, however, and traipsing back to the multi-storey car park, Hillary wondered why Marcie Franks should have been quite so forthcoming. After all, there hadn't been any sniff of a motive for her in Gorman's original investigation. So why had she put herself on the police radar by volunteering so much information now?

For some reason, Hillary was uneasily reminded about gift horses. But did she need to seek out the Greek bearing gifts, or did she need to check out the equine dental equipment?

*

Dwayne Cox took the train to London and, knowing the city well, had no trouble finding the Cosy Fox café in Camden. Taking a seat and ordering the vegetarian option, he people-watched for a while and flirted half-heartedly with the waitress, until Marcie could join him.

When she arrived, he smiled across the table at her grimly. Wordlessly she drew out her chair and slumped down.

'You look like something no self-respecting cat would even dream of dragging in,' he said. 'For pity's sake, why don't you put on some make-up, or get a decent haircut at least?'

'I don't doll myself up to flatter the likes of you,' Marcie shot back with a cool smile. 'Just like I don't wear high heels or thongs, or anything else that the male sex would like to see us women neutered with.'

'Huh?'

'High heels are bad for the spine. They force women onto their toes, hobbling their movement and damaging their physiology, just for the sake of making it look as if we have longer legs, thus reinforcing the doll-like image you have of us. And as for thongs – please.'

Marcie suddenly grinned ferociously, and Dwayne laughed.

'Good to see you, Marce. So what's up?' he asked.

'I've had the filth in. Just like you said I would. A rather tasty redhead, with a string-bean satellite in tow.'

Dwayne nodded. 'What did you tell them?'

'Nothing they didn't already know, or could easily find out.'

'So why do you want to meet now?'

'I just thought we should clear the air a bit. Make sure we're both clear on what's at stake,' she said flatly.

Dwayne speared a piece of asparagus and chewed on it thoughtfully.

'You didn't wait to order, then?' Marcie said sardonically and, catching the waitress's eye, ordered the same vegetarian option and a cup of herbal tea.

'I thought we'd already decided to lie low for a bit,' he pointed out. 'You didn't need to drag me here just to ram home that message.'

'Yes. But I know you. You've always got an angle. Besides, you like to have your cake and eat it too,' Marcie said flatly.

'Meaning?'

'Meaning, you won't be happy to have Rowan's case opened again, and having the police sniffing around will make you doubly nervous. You like to think you're one of the Wild Bunch, but you like to feel safe, Dwayne. You always have.'

'Again, meaning?'

'If you thought you could feed me to the cops to save your own worthless hide, you'd do it in a nano-second. I just want to make sure that you realize that wouldn't be a good idea, that's all.'

Dwayne smiled. 'You worry too much.' And she knew him so well, damn her. 'Besides, it's not as if either one of us has to worry. We didn't kill Rowan. Right?' he asked, spearing a sautéed piece of aubergine and looking at her closely.

'Well I certainly didn't,' Marcie agreed coolly. 'Did you?'

'Nope.'

Marcie nodded. Just then the waitress brought her dish, and for a few minutes they ate in silence.

'I did just wonder though,' Dwayne said at last. 'That last, er, present I sold to Rowan. You didn't spice it up a bit too much, did you?'

Marcie smiled grimly. 'Aren't you forgetting something?' And when Dwayne looked at her questioningly, she smiled that wide, humourless smile again. 'It was a pair of scissors that did for our little Rowan.'

Dwayne nodded. 'Yes. I know. But what if he was feeling somewhat, shall we say, incapacitated at the time?'

Marcie sighed and sipped her tea. 'Just what have you been fantasizing about now? Why would I want to help someone else bump off the annoying little sex-maniac? Now, when you do want the next delivery?'

'Not for a while,' Dwayne said quickly, suddenly looking

alarmed. 'Not until the police have finished nosing around. I thought all that was settled.'

Marcie suddenly laughed. 'I know, and I agree. I just wanted to see the look of fear on your face. You really are a spineless little shit, Dwayne.'

Dwayne smelt the acrid scent of sweat seeping out from his armpits and swore softly under his breath. Amused, Marcie continued to eat, then added slyly, 'But aren't you worried that all your neurotic little bunnies will desert you when their candyman suddenly loses his sweetness?'

Dwayne grunted. 'You always were a first-class bitch, Marcie.'

'And don't you forget it,' Ms Franks said shortly.

CHAPTER SEVEN

The next day, with Vivienne Tyrell still being 'too busy' to accompany her with work on the Thompson case, Hillary collected Jimmy from the HQ and, in a still distinctly floral-scented Puff the Tragic Wagon, headed north, for the outskirts of England's second biggest city.

Brum, as the locals called Birmingham, was relatively unfamiliar territory to Hillary, but not to Jimmy Jessop.

'The missus came from Kingstanding way. We used to take regular trips up see her family when her mum was still alive. And to do some shopping, naturally,' he drawled.

'Oh, naturally,' Hillary agreed, indicating to overtake a trundling lorry containing something that needed a warning diamond panel on the back of it. She gave it a wide berth.

'Reckon I know my way around the Bull Ring better than most,' Jimmy continued ruminating. 'Mind you, it's been some years now since I was up there. So with the way they're building on anything that doesn't move these days, I dare say I won't recognize a bloody thing,' he muttered darkly, staring out at the passing scenery.

May was nearly upon them, and although the day was so far overcast, the hedgerows were white with hawthorn blossom and the roadside verges frothy with cow parsley.

'What can you tell me about Solihull, then?' she asked. 'Rowan's parents still live there, according to the latest updates.'

'Posh area, or so my missus always said. Although that could mean anything, mind you, from millionaires' mansions to four-bed semis. My wife's family made church mice look like Richard Branson, bless 'em, so anything that wasn't the slums was posh to her.'

Hillary nodded. 'So long as you can point me in the general direction, I won't complain,' she promised.

In the end, the childhood home of Rowan Thompson was relatively easy to find. As they climbed out of the car and looked around, the road reminded Hillary of those to be found around north Oxford. Cherry trees, some still flowering, were the norm, with fair-sized gardens fronting fair-sized houses.

'Posh enough,' she said thoughtfully. 'The Thompsons had three children, right?' she asked, although she didn't really need reminding. She'd read up on their file before heading home yesterday.

'Right. One son now lives in Australia, where he manages a sheep farm the size of Wales. The daughter married something well-heeled in publishing,' Jimmy confirmed.

'I'm impressed you remembered it all.'

'Don't be, guv. When I dealt out the background checks I handled most of the Thompson family myself.'

'No skeletons in the family closet that you could find?'

'Not so's you'd notice.'

'Any sibling rivalry I need to know about?'

'Don't think so. Rowan was the youngest – he and his sister seemed to get on, and the elder son was older by some years and was mostly grown up and fledged before our vic could have got too many complexes over who Mummy loved best.'

'Do I detect an edge of cynicism in your voice, Jimmy?' Hillary asked with a grin, as he opened one side of a pair of black wrought-iron gates and let her precede him up a short gravelled driveway.

'Who, me, guv?'

They were expected of course, since Hillary had made a very discreet phone call to them on being handed the case, setting up this initial interview.

The door was opened by a woman in her sixties, who was doing everything possible to appear to be a woman in her forties, and mostly succeeding. A very good and no doubt expensive facelift could only just be discerned by the barest of faint pale lines just behind neat ears. The earlobes were adorned with a gold and emerald set of studs. Hair that nature would have rendered silver by now was instead coloured ash-blonde, and shaped in a becoming, rather sixties-style geometric cut, that gave the impression of retro-youth.

She was dressed in a white trouser suit, with a russet-coloured blouse and chunky, gold jewellery.

'Mrs Thompson?' Hillary said, and held out her ID.

Rowan's mother was roughly Hillary's own height, but was much leaner, which gave her a rather straight-up-and-down boyish figure that spoke of many hours in a gym, probably with the services of a personal trainer thrown in.

'Yes, Amanda Thompson. Please come in.' Her voice had the pronounced regional twang that only a life-time native of Birmingham could achieve. 'Go on straight through – my husband's waiting in the lounge. He took the day off work – and if you knew how much of a workaholic he is…. Well!' She shrugged her thin shoulders and led them through to a large, wooden-floored lounge area.

Hillary had never been a fan of minimalism and to her the white-painted room seemed bare and unwelcoming. But her attention was quickly fixed on the man rising from a black leather chair.

He looked a much older version of his son Rowan. Not particularly tall, with salt-and-pepper hair and big, wide-open brown eyes. When he smiled and held out his hand, Hillary had an overwhelming sense of the man's charm.

'John Thompson. How do you do.' His own accent came from further north somewhere – Newcastle maybe.

'John, this is Hillary Greene and … er … sorry….' She looked at Jimmy helplessly, who quickly gave his own name and selected a chrome and black leather hard chair that was tucked away against one wall. There he took out his notebook and somehow, in that minimalist expanse, almost managed to disappear. It was quite some feat, and Hillary, at least, could appreciate it for the gift it was.

'Please, sit down, er….' John Thompson hesitated a moment, her lack of recognizable rank clearly throwing him a little.

'Please, call me Hillary,' she said quickly. 'I used to be detective inspector before joining the CRT. But I think it's easier if we're all on first name terms. As I told your wife on the phone, I'm in charge of taking another look at your son's case, so please feel free to call me anytime, or ask me any questions that you want to.' She wouldn't necessarily answer them, she added a silent, mental rider, but she'd at least keep them in the loop as much as she could.

John Thompson nodded and waited until his wife was seated on a matching black leather settee before resuming his own seat.

'Firstly, let me add my condolences on the loss of your son. I know it's been many years, but I also know that's totally irrelevant,' Hillary eased into the interview carefully. 'I take it you'd like a quick overview of what's been happening?' she added.

Amanda Thompson made a compulsive, jerky movement, but said nothing. Out of the corner of her eye, Hillary could see her chewing on her bottom lip in a nervous habit that she seemed unaware of.

She kept her focus on John, who nodded briefly. 'That would be appreciated, yes,' he agreed simply.

'Well, so far it's very early days, but I've spoken to Rowan's landlady at the time of your son's death, as well as all those who shared rooms in the house with him at the time.'

'Inspector Gorman seemed convinced it was one of those living at the address who was responsible for our son's death,' John said, the lift in his voice at the end of the sentence making it more of a question than a statement.

'I agree they're a top priority, but I'm also looking outside that circle as well,' Hillary said, keeping her comments truthful, but broad enough to not give much away. Although she could understand and respect a victim's family wanting to be kept up to date, it was not her job to be specific.

Especially since, for all she knew, Rowan's killer might be in the room with her right now.

Although Gorman had found no trace of any member of the Thompson family being in Oxford on the day Rowan died, Mrs Thompson's non-existent alibi consisted of being home alone while her husband was at work. But John Thompson had worked in an environment where it would have been easy for him to slip away for a few hours unnoticed. So neither of them was ruled out yet, even though Gorman's initial investigation had shown no major rifts or problems in the Thompson family unit.

But Hillary, as was every copper, was well aware that statistics showed that most murder victims were killed by family and friends, and just because you couldn't find a problem in those nearest and dearest to your victim didn't mean it didn't exist.

'Your son ... Rowan, touched a wide range of people, and the motive for his death might not lay in the house where he was lodging,' Hillary said, choosing her words carefully.

John Thompson smiled at her briefly. 'You needn't pussyfoot around us,' he said, casting a quick eye at his still-silent wife. 'We know that Rowan was what my granny would euphemistically call a bit of a scamp. Especially with the women.'

Hillary nodded, and shot a quick glance of her own at the dead boy's mother.

She was still chewing nervously on her lower lip. Her hands, clenched in her lap, bore many rings – mostly in gold, diamonds, and emeralds. Hillary doubted she found much comfort in all the expensive bling, though.

Her son might have been dead for more than a decade, but she had the feeling that for Amanda Thompson, time had tended to stand still. Was that what her pursuit of perpetual youth was all about? If she could somehow stop the time from passing, her son might yet still be young and alive as well somewhere? She was no psychologist, but she wouldn't have bet against it.

'Has anyone approached you during the past years since Rowan's death?' she asked gently. 'Old friends, perhaps, wanting to talk, or asking for a little keepsake? Something that didn't seem to mean much at the time, but now strikes you as odd?' she asked quietly.

She had always had the sense that Rowan's death had been impetuous and deeply felt. Whatever had motivated the killer had come from the heart and the wellspring of human emotions, not from a cool and calculating mind. And killers of that ilk sometimes obsessed about the act itself, or could simply not let go of the victim. They felt this need to remain close by, seeking out contact with the victim's family and friends, and often tried to insert themselves into their victim's now-defunct life.

But both Amanda and John Thompson were shaking their heads. 'No. We had the usual sympathy cards, and telephone calls. But no one ever approached us.'

'And the last time you saw Rowan?'

'Our anniversary in October.' John again answered the question. 'He came down to spend the weekend. Gave us a silver-engraved ice bucket.'

'We still have it,' Amanda said, then looked startled at the sound of her own voice.

'Did he appear different in any way? Nervous or pensive? Maybe quieter than usual?' she pressed.

'Not Rowan,' John said, with that smile that could charm a snake from its basking rock. 'He was as full of himself, and of life, as ever.'

'You knew his girlfriend, Darla?'

'She was only the latest in a long line, I'm afraid,' John said. 'Rowan mentioned she liked making clothes, and she was going to make him some sort of outfit for Christmas. He thought it was funny – he said he'd probably look like a bad Adam Ant wannabe, but he'd wear whatever it was, if only for a laugh.'

'He didn't mean to be cruel,' Amanda Thompson said, with anger in her voice, and her husband shot her a worried look.

'I didn't mean to imply that he was, sweetheart,' he said. 'But we both know he didn't always think before he spoke. Or acted.'

Hillary thought that both of the Thompsons probably understood all their children better than most. But in the end, what good had it done either of them?

'So, as far as you know, Rowan was acting and feeling as normal the last time you saw him?'

'Yes. We told all this to Inspector Gorman,' John Thompson said.

'I know. I'm sorry if it seems to you that we're just going over the same old ground,' Hillary apologized. 'Did your other son or daughter visit Rowan at Oxford at all?'

'No. Rex was already in Australia by then, and Therese was always too caught up in trying to be a fashion model to ever leave London. Luckily, she grew out of that after a couple of years of catalogue work,' John said with a wry smile.

'Is there anything you want to ask me?' Hillary asked simply, hoping there wasn't.

'Will you get them?' Amanda Thompson said abruptly, her voice hard and sharp. And Hillary noticed a small red splash of colour on her bottom lip that owed nothing to lipstick.

Amanda Thompson had drawn blood. Her own.

'I'll do everything I can, Mrs Thompson,' Hillary said.

And meant it.

Outside, Jimmy Jessop stretched shoulders that felt tight with tension and let out a long, heartfelt breath.

Hillary knew how he felt.

'All the years I've worked, it's always the families that get to you,' he said. 'I thought working cold cases might mean that the years in between would make it easier. For them, and for me. But it doesn't work that way,' he said, somewhat ungrammatically, but Hillary knew instantly what he meant.

'Think she drinks?' Hillary asked abruptly. She felt no need to elaborate, and sure enough, Jimmy's response was almost immediate.

'The hubby thinks so. Did you clock the way he kept an eye on her?'

Hillary sighed, and walked back to her ancient but obliging car. They drove back to Oxford in silence.

It was nearing lunchtime, so Hillary dropped Jimmy outside the Black Bull for a pie and a pint, before driving the few hundred yards back to HQ. After talking to the Thompsons she herself had no appetite.

She walked with her head down and a thoughtful frown on her face, and jogged down the wide concrete steps into the basement where the CRT hung its hat, her mind still on Rowan Thompson.

Just what had he done to earn him that pair of scissors in his gut? Was it really a case of one sexual conquest too far? Or one outrageous stunt that someone, somewhere, had been unable to forgive? It seemed, on the face of it, to be the most likely explanation. The drugs angle was too tenuous, and there certainly couldn't be any monetary motive. Although his parents had plenty, he himself had been a debt-ridden student. And yet…. The jealous boyfriend or the disgruntled sexual partner just didn't ring true to her for some reason. There was nothing she could put her finger on, and she certainly wouldn't voice the thought out loud to anybody else on her team without something solid to back it up with. But she knew from experience that, a mere hunch or not, it didn't pay to ignore her instincts. But it was hard to pin down exactly where the problem lay.

The whole thing just wasn't … meaty enough. To stick a pair of scissors into someone, face to face … that spoke of something … desperate. Something big. A spat due to boy-girl, or boy-boy, or boy-twosomes just didn't seem to have enough weight behind it to make sense.

And yet what else was there?

She walked into her stationery cupboard, determined once

more to read through every scrap of paper in the Thompson case in search of a sniff of anything more substantial than mere sexual peccadillo, and found instead a wooden cross lying on her desk.

She froze momentarily in the doorway, and then glanced behind her. Which was absurd, of course. The basement was a rabbit warren of corridors and little offices. And whoever had left her latest 'gift' was long gone.

Cautiously, wearily, she tossed her handbag into the space under her kneehole desk and walked forward.

The cross wasn't big – about twelve inches tall by five or six inches across, and was evidently hand-carved from some sort of native wood. She was no expert, but it could have been ash. Or hazel, maybe. No doubt there'd be an expert somewhere who could tell her what it was, and maybe even the area where it had been cut from. Although what good that would do her, she wasn't sure.

The bottom of the cross had been whittled into a sharp stake – like someone out to give a vampire a bad time.

She reached into the pocket of her jacket and drew out a pair of thin latex gloves. It was an old habit, carrying them around with her, since her work at the CRT made them largely unnecessary now.

But she was glad of them as she picked up the cross and inspected it closely. In the crossbar section, on the horizontal bar that joined the vertical shaft, a hot poker had been used to carve the letters JOY.

Hillary slowly sat down and stared at the cross thoughtfully.

This, she could see at once, was different.

No more roses.

Or chocolates.

Or Valentine cards.

Or text messages.

This felt like the next level to a very different game.

Briefly, she wondered if the cross could have been left by anyone other than her stalker, but quickly dismissed it. Likewise, it could have no bearing on the Thompson case.

No. This was him.

So. What exactly was this wooden cross supposed to tell her? This cross with a lethal spike on the end?

Well, the cross was symbolically a religious symbol, of course, but she didn't think her stalker was a man of God. Or interested in His edicts.

The cross was a symbol of death too. Wooden crosses marked graves.

And the word JOY.

The death of joy?

Was her charade with Steven Crayle paying off? Had her stalker finally heard the rumours about her and Steven? Perhaps seen them together? Was this meant to tell her that she had killed his joy by being unfaithful?

Maybe. A bit tenuous, though?

Gingerly, through the rubber of the thin glove, she touched one finger to the tip. It was sharp. Very sharp.

The cross obviously represented a lethal weapon. A killing weapon.

Kill joy.

She was being a killjoy perhaps? Hillary had to laugh a little at that. So her stalker had a sense of irony, maybe.

Then she felt a cold hand suddenly grip the back of her neck, making her swallow hard. Or maybe it meant something else entirely.

She got up on legs that felt just a little bit rubbery themselves, and reached into the lower left-hand drawer for an evidence bag, and dropped the cross inside. Not that she expected to get any fingerprints from it, of course. She doubted the wood would take them well, even if her stalker had been so stupid as to forget to wear gloves himself when handling it.

Locking it in the bottom drawer of her desk, she then walked down to the main computer room.

Sergeant Handley saw her first, and raised an eyebrow. He knew Hillary as Steven Crayle's chief investigator, and as such, she rarely put an appearance in with the statisticians and the number crunchers.

'Hillary,' he said curiously, as she approached his desk.

'Sarge,' she said briskly. 'Can you do me a favour when you've got time? Can you ask your babies' – she indicated the busily working computers all around her – 'to cough up the name of any woman with the first name of Joy who reported having picked up a stalker within the last ten years? Or any woman with the same first name who was reported missing, or has come up dead in suspicious circumstances, again in the last ten years?'

'This for Superintendent Crayle?' Handley asked sharply.

Hillary smiled briefly. 'Of course.' She could lie with the best of them. The truth was, she wasn't going to take this to Steven until she had to. Especially since she might be on the wrong track entirely.

No woman liked to look stupid in front of her boss. Especially one who was making her libidinous hormones jump through hoops.

'OK. It shouldn't take too long,' Handley agreed, losing interest. 'Luckily Joy's not a very common first name.'

Hillary thanked him and left.

Natasha Hargreaves worked for a large PR firm in the Smoke, but luck was for once on their side. When Hillary telephoned her work number, she was informed by a very helpful assistant that Miss Hargreaves was actually in Henley-on-Thames for the day. She was there, apparently, checking out a venue for an advertising campaign for an unpopular politician, who was trying again to be flavour of the month.

The very helpful young lady then gave her directions to a large country club on the river Thames, which made Sam's eyes widen as they pulled up to the entrance to the car park.

The country club had once obviously been a large house for a Victorian gentleman and his very extended family. It had gables and turrets, dormer and round windows, bits here and bobs there, even a bit of gingerbread trim. It should have looked like something of an architectural dog's dinner, but, in that magical way that some buildings have, managed to look quirky and charming instead.

In the car-park, there were an awful lot of Mercedes, and Jaguars and others of their ilk. Hillary hoped the unpopular politician wasn't hoping to reach out to the 'common' man by having a photo opportunity here.

The country club had its own golf course (of course), plus tennis courts and the usual array of spa extras. And being in Henley, it naturally had a flotilla of boats at the bottom of a perfectly manicured lawn. Not to mention some expensive and nifty little water craft for those who liked to mess about on the water in style and comfort.

'Very nice,' Hillary said sardonically, as Sam parked in a space with a Ferrari on the left and a BMW convertible on the right. His sporty little Mini somehow managed to look jaunty and undaunted by the foreign competition. 'I wonder what they'd do if I chugged my narrowboat up here and moored on their jetty?'

Sam grinned, somewhat nervously, since he wasn't actually sure if she was joking or not.

They found Natasha Hargreaves by the simple expedient of asking the first person they saw wearing the acorn and crown motif of the country club on the navy-blue T-shirt of their uniform. He was twenty-something, looked as if he'd been carved from oak, and was already sun-browned. And if the muscles in his upper torso were anything to go by he would probably be rowing for his country in the next Olympics.

'Oh, the PR people – they're all in the bar,' he grinned. 'Go around the side there, past the big conservatory and take the next door in. The hospitality suite is right in front of you.'

They thanked him and followed his instructions. Inside, Hillary had no difficulty in pinpointing the regulars, who were mostly scattered about in armchairs, dressed in tennis whites and quaffing gin and tonics. Over by the bar area, however, were a small gaggle of business-suited men and women who seemed to be hanging onto the words of a white-haired man with the red-veined nose of a serious drinker.

'I've seen him somewhere before, guv,' Sam said uncertainly.

Hillary smiled. 'Nice to see our student body is still socially aware enough to recognize an MP when it sees one, Sam,' she said. 'Let's not go in mob-handed. Natasha's working, and it won't put her in a good mood for talking to us if we go in flashing our Old Bill IDs and making her boss wonder what's up.'

As she was speaking, Hillary was taking one of her cards from her bag, and wrote a few brief words on it and it handed it over to Sam.

'See the tall brunette, beside the bald-headed bloke? Unless I miss my guess, that must be her. The other two women with them are too old. Hand her this and then go to the bar and stand me a pint. Since you're driving, you can stick to orange juice.'

'Thanks, guv,' Sam said, with a grin of his own. Hillary nodded. It was nice to see the youngster was starting to relax a little more around her now.

She looked around, saw a quiet spot in one corner, and went over to it slowly and sat down. As she looked up, she was just in time to see Natasha glance down and read with a puzzled frown the short message on the card that Sam had just handed to her.

She looked around the room and saw Hillary half-raise her hand in acknowledgement, then she whispered something to the bald-headed man beside her and walked over.

As she did so, Sam came up beside her, two glasses in his hands, and followed her to the table.

'Miss Hargreaves?' Hillary showed her ID. 'Would you like a drink?'

'No, thanks. I still have one untouched somewhere. Police? Are you the same people who spoke to Dad? He said you were looking into Rowan's case again.'

Natasha was one of those tall, willowy women with long hair and oval faces who looked like they should be modelling for a pre-Raphaelite painting. She was wearing a short, dark-blue skirt and matching tightly fitted jacket with a discreet red pin-stripe, and a plain white blouse. She wore black tights and a neat black shoe with a modest heel.

She sat down in a single folding movement that kept her knees together and left her posture almost as rigid as that of a Victorian lady in tight corsets.

'Yes. Your father was very helpful,' Hillary acknowledged. 'I just have a few follow-up questions for you. I won't be long, I know you're working.'

Natasha cast a quick look over at the bar and gave a brief smile. 'Don't worry. I'm pretty low in the pecking order for this account. I'm only along to make up the numbers.'

And provide eye candy, Hillary thought cynically and silently.

'So, what on earth can I do for you?' Natasha asked brightly. 'I can barely remember Rowan.'

Hillary sipped at her pint and nodded. Somehow she doubted the veracity of that statement.

'You and your twin sister used to regularly visit your dad in Oxford, back when he was getting his degree, or so he told us?'

'Yes, that's right. But me and Rommy spent most of our time in town though, shopping or hanging out at a burger place we liked.'

'But you went to the house in Kebler Road from time to time. To your father's room there?'

'Oh sure.' Natasha began to fidget with her watch, a small discreet affair with a black leather band.

'And you met Rowan?'

'Yes.'

'How old were you at the time?'

'We were both fifteen. We were sixteen and a half when Dad got his degree. He was so proud of himself. Of course, it had a good effect on us, really, because both Rommy and me went on to uni ourselves. Until then, neither of us had really thought about it.'

Hillary smiled. 'From what I've been learning about Rowan, he must have made quite an impact on a fifteen-year-old girl. From his photographs, you could tell he was a good-looking boy.'

'Sure, if you like that sort of thing. I prefer the David Tennant type myself,' she smiled widely. 'You know – tall, dark and dishy. But Rommy liked the blond cheeky-little-boy type more.'

Hillary nodded. 'So he flirted with her, did he?'

'Oh, all the time. But we never took him seriously. Even at that age, we knew he was just being over-the-top with us. You know, kissing our hands, putting on a funny French accent, playing the clown. He did that sort of thing really well, but it wasn't anything serious.'

Again Hillary took another sip from her glass. 'Did you know that Inspector Gorman – he was the officer in charge of the original murder case – discovered a rumour going around that Rowan had slept with a pair of young identical twins? *A deux*, as it were.'

Natasha Hargreaves's classically beautiful face wrinkled up in a brief flash of disgust. 'Ugh! That sounds so tacky, doesn't it? But what can I say?' She spread her well-manicured hands in a graphic gesture. Her nails, Hillary noticed, were coated in clear varnish. 'It wasn't us. But it was just the sort of thing Rowan would probably make up and boast about, if you ask me. Probably more as a lark than anything else.'

'So you never slept with him yourself?'

'Good grief, no.'

'What about your sister?'

Natasha opened her mouth, but no sound came out. Instead a thoughtful look settled down between her dark, plucked brows. 'You know, I was going to say "no way" without even thinking about it, but I can't really be sure, can I? Even though we're identical in looks, we definitely don't think the same – we never have.

Rommy may have slept with him. She was always more adventurous than I was. And I have to admit, she grew up faster than I did, in many ways. So she might have done. But I still rather doubt it.'

Natasha opened her eyes wide in a 'see-how-painfully-honest-I'm-being-with-you' look.

Hillary smiled her appreciation. And ploughed on. 'How did your father react to Rowan flirting with you?'

Natasha smiled and again waved her expressive hands in the air. 'Oh, you have to know Dad. He didn't really like it, but he didn't go all Raging Bull about it. He warned us both what Rowan was like, said how much he trusted us girls to be sensible, and then made damned sure that whenever we came to the house we were never left alone with him. Rommy thought it was hysterically funny the way Dad guarded us.'

'And how did Rowan react to this?'

'Oh, he played it up to the hilt. Made out he was this big bad-wolf Lothario who would have to go to outrageous lengths to circumnavigate the ever-observant Victorian-attitude father. You know, in clever Oxford academic-speak. It was all very gratifying and ego-massaging for a fifteen-year-old.'

'But it didn't go to your head?'

'Oh, no.'

'He never got you into bed?'

'Oh, no.'

Hillary nodded and sipped some more of her pint. 'Did you ever hear him admit to being afraid of anyone?'

'Rowan? Definitely not. He was fearless.'

Hillary sighed. 'Well, thank you, Miss Hargreaves. And sorry to have had to take you away from your work.'

'Oh think nothing of it. I doubt Geoffrey's even aware I've been gone,' Natasha said with a small laugh, and with another graceful unfolding, stood up in one lithe movement, turned, and walked away.

Sam finished his orange juice rapidly as Hillary drank up.

Outside, the clouds were finally beginning to roll away, and a cheerful blackbird sang loudly from one of the old cedar trees lining the gravel drive.

'So what do you think of her story, Sam?' Hillary asked, as they made their way back to the little Mini.

'A beautiful girl, guv. Way out of my league, mind,' he added ruefully. 'Her sort wouldn't give the likes of me a second look. What do you think?' he asked curiously.

Hillary Greene smiled wisely. 'I think that woman wouldn't know the truth if it bit her on the backside,' she said simply.

When she got back to HQ, a note was waiting on her desk from Sergeant Handley. It was short and to the point.

No woman named Joy reported missing in the last ten years.
No woman named Joy dead in suspicious circumstances, ditto.
No woman named Joy reported a stalker, ditto.

Hillary leaned back in her desk and let out a long slow breath. She hadn't realized, until then, just how very tense she'd been.

Ah well.

She rose, stretched, and reached for the pile of paperwork on her desk.

Time to re-read every scrap of paper once again in the Thompson case. With a sigh for the eyestrain that would inevitably follow, Hillary opened the first file.

CHAPTER EIGHT

Jimmy glanced at his watch, and saw that there was still a good two hours left until clocking-off time. He knew that Hillary was closeted in her office re-reading every scrap of paper on the case, but he was so tired of doing his own paperwork that he checked his to-do list in an effort to find something better.

So far, he'd ticked off several items, and had currently reached the entry marked 'The Freeling Brothers – check circs.' Of course – these were the two brothers who'd competed for and slept with their victim. He grinned, remembering Hillary's advice to take Vivienne Tyrell with him for protection when he went to talk to them. As if anybody, a pair of gay brothers or anyone else, would look twice at him, let alone make so much as a pass!

But it would be good experience for Sam.

'Doing anything, youngster?' Jimmy asked, standing up and reaching for his coat.

Sam looked up from the laptop in front of him, his eyes sharpening with interest when he saw that the older man was getting ready to go out. Although he loved working for the CRT, and was definitely going to join the police as soon as he could after getting his degree, like nearly everyone else he preferred to be out and about and away from the office. Doing actual police work, instead of babysitting computer programs and staying on top of the seemingly never-ending stream of boring office routine was what he'd actually signed up for.

Not that he was complaining or anything. He might still be as green as a cabbage and wet behind the ears, as nearly everyone he ran across at HQ often told him, but even he could appreciate that having Hillary Greene for a boss was like winning the jackpot.

Superintendent Crayle made a good commander, of course, but for on-the-spot training he knew that he'd learned more about the job in the few weeks since Hillary Greene had joined the team, than he had in all the months that had gone before.

Jimmy, too, knew his stuff, of course.

'Where we going, Sarge?' he asked eagerly, as he followed the old man up the stairs and into the light of the afternoon. He often felt like a mole emerging into unfamiliar daylight after a few too many hours down in the basement.

'We're going to see a pair of gay brothers about an orgy,' Jimmy said, deadpan.

'Oh,' Sam said. Was the sarge joking?

No, he realized, some half an hour later, as they walked into a bicycle shop in the suburb of Botley, the sarge hadn't been joking.

He'd read the murder book every day, of course, and the sign outside the shop telling tourists and students alike that bicycles could be hired by the month had triggered his memory.

'These are the two that Rowan Thompson slept with, right?' he asked, as Jimmy pushed open the door of the shop and they both heard the old-fashioned bell ring overhead.

'Right. By the name of Mark and Jeff,' Jimmy said, without having to refer to his notes.

Inside, a range of racing bicycles lined the walls, amid some rather more mundane machines. A few of them even hung suspended from wall brackets. There were even some really old models in the shop window. One old bone-shaker, Jimmy was sure, was a dead ringer for the first grown-up bike his Dad had bought him, back in the late fifties.

'I can see you're a man of taste,' a voice said behind him, and Jimmy quickly turned. The man in front of him looked to be a very well-preserved fifty-something, with dyed black hair, big blue eyes that looked disconcertingly wide-eyed and innocent, and a slim build. His eyes kept straying from Jimmy to Sam, who was shifting a shade uncomfortably from foot to foot and beginning to go a dull red.

'Mr Freeling?'

'Yes, I'm Mark Freeling. Let me guess – you used to have a bike like that one when you were a young stripling,' he said, indicating the red-painted model that Jimmy had been eyeing up.

Jimmy smiled. 'A real bone-shaker, yes. I'm surprised you still deal in them now,' he said, looking at another, even older, black-painted relic, complete with what looked like its original wicker basket fastened in front on the handlebars.

'Oh, those are mainly for the dons who like to play the part,' Mark Freeling said, rolling his big blue eyes in mock-despair. 'What can you do? They like to play up to the tourists, and cycling around in full regalia on a machine you or I wouldn't be seen dead riding is part of the thrill for the old dears.'

Jimmy pulled out his ID, and although the blue eyes flickered slightly, Mark Freeling didn't look particularly put out to find a member of the constabulary in his establishment, even a retired, civilian version of the same, as Jimmy's ID clearly indicated.

'Is your brother Jeffrey here, sir?' Jimmy asked. 'It would just save me some time and some leg work if I could have a little chat with both of you together.'

'Oh yes, he's around somewhere. Just a mo. Jeff! JEFF!' he yelled, making Sam jump nervously.

The two customers in the shop, two young lads who were arguing over the best mountain bike, momentarily paused in their bickering. But they only gave the shop owner a mild look of annoyance before getting back to discussing which was, and definitely wasn't, the best time to change gear when going down Mount Snowdon in a blizzard.

A moment later, a younger version of Mark Freeling emerged from a door at the rear, where, no doubt, they kept their office. He was slightly taller than his brother, slightly leaner, slightly better-looking and appeared to be a good decade younger.

He could well believe that the Freeling brothers regularly competed and argued over everything. Including a prize like Rowan Thompson.

'What are you shrieking about?' Jeff Freeling asked in a disgruntled voice that didn't seem to match the speculative look in his eyes as they went from Jimmy, and then fastened speculatively on the tall, tender redheaded youngster behind.

'Hello there,' Jeff said, clearly addressing Sam.

Sam went a brighter shade of red.

'I saw him first,' Mark said, purely out of habit, Jimmy was sure, because he then went on with barely a breath, 'These two gentlemen are with the police. We haven't been doing anything naughty recently, have we?' And he shot his brother a fulminating look.

'No, we haven't,' Jeff shot back. 'We check the stolen bikes register regularly, and record all serial numbers religiously.'

Sam knew that bicycle theft in Oxford was something of an epidemic, and said shortly, 'This isn't about stolen property, sir. We're working on a murder inquiry.'

He'd always wanted to say something like that, but the moment he'd done so, he instantly wondered if he'd overstepped the mark. He gave Jimmy a quick, anxious look, but the older man didn't seem that put out.

The Freeling brothers, on the other hand, started to twitter like a pair of disturbed starlings. Quickly they ushered the two of them back into the office, and ordered a morose, middle-aged woman who was working on a computer to go and mind the shop.

She went with a huge, put-upon sigh.

'Who's been murdered? Was it a gay bashing?' Mark asked at once. 'Oh, can I get you a coffee or anything?'

'No, thank you. We work for the Crime Review Team. We're taking another look at the Rowan Thompson case, sir,' Jimmy explained patiently.

'Oh, for goodness sake, why didn't you say!' Jeff said. 'Please, take a seat. Poor Rowan.'

There was a general bustle as all four men found various seats in the small office. Mark sighed heavily. 'He was a wonderful boy, Rowan. A bit of a bastard, mind you, but lovely.'

'How was he a bastard, sir?' Jimmy asked, glancing at Sam to make sure that he was taking notes.

He was.

'Oh well, you had to know Rowan to know that,' Jeff said, and then said, 'What?' as his older sibling snorted at him.

'Well, they *didn't* know him, did they?' Mark said scornfully. 'That's why they're asking. Let me tell you, Rowan was something of a sexual gymnast, Officer. He could not only bend and cavort his own body, but he could twist and manipulate anyone around him. Young, old, male, female, one at a time, two at a go or even a group – he was up for it. He was really quite spectacular, wasn't he, Jeff?'

Sam, busily scribbling, went even redder.

Jimmy pretended not to notice.

'We have witnesses who claim that he, er, mucked you and your brother about. Is that true?' he asked, his eyes on Mark.

'Oh, he had us jumping through hoops like trained poodles, didn't he, Jeff? I tell you, sometimes I thought I'd wandered into Crufts by mistake. I'm only surprised he didn't make us go 'woof' and sit up and beg.'

Jimmy did his best not to grin. 'I see. It must have created bad feeling at the time?'

'Oh, yes. Well, no. Well, sort of yes and no,' Mark said, and this time it was his younger brother who snorted in scorn.

'Now who's the one not making sense?' he drawled. 'See, Officer, it was like this. Rowan came in one glorious afternoon to hire a bike for the term. I served him first, and we got chatting, and I knew that I was on to a winner straight away, let me tell you. Anyway, we go out for drinks, but nothing doing. Sort-of blowing hot and cold, like he couldn't make up his mind. Well, all right, I thought, I don't mind a bit of teasing. But when he comes back to the shop the next day to collect his bike, *someone'* – here the younger man shot daggers at his older brother – 'tried to muscle in. Well, this confused poor Rowan. Or so I thought.'

Mark snorted inelegantly. 'Of course, he knew just what he was doing, playing us off against one another.'

'Anyway, in the end, just when we thought neither one of us was going to bag him,' Jeff said, and took a breath, 'he just ups and says that he can't choose between us, so he'll take us both!' Mark put in, and then laughed. 'And that was Rowan.'

Sam scribbled furiously and went a very interesting shade of cerise, Jimmy thought.

'I see. And this happened …?' he probed delicately.

'Oh, just the once,' Mark said, with obvious bitter regret.

'More's the pity,' his brother chipped in. 'It was lovely.'

'This must have made you angry?' Jimmy said curiously.

'Oh, as hornets,' Jeff agreed at once.

'JEFF!' his brother shrieked.

'What?'

'Don't you see, the man thinks we killed him? And you go around saying we were mad at him.'

Jeff turned his big blue eyes Jimmy's way. 'Oh, but we didn't kill Rowan,' he said. 'Why on earth would we do that?'

'Perhaps you wanted him back? You went to his house to ask him to come back to you – er, either one of you. Or both,' Jimmy said, floundering suddenly.

'Oh, no, we wouldn't do that,' Mark said. 'We made the frat oath, see.'

Jeff nodded seriously.

'Frat oath?' Jimmy repeated blankly. Somehow, this interview was beginning to get away from him.

'Yes. Ever since we were kids, we've always fought like cat and dog,' Mark explained. 'Mostly we enjoyed it really, and it didn't mean much. I mean, it never really hurt, or was meant to hurt, you see. But sometimes, it could get out of hand, and then it wasn't fun anymore, so whenever we realized things were getting too heavy for one of us, we'd agree to settle our differences with a fraternal oath. If I was going insane because he would keep using my favourite razor, for instance, I'd scream at him, "Frat-oath. No more." And he'd know I was serious, and not use the razor again.'

'I see,' Jimmy said faintly.

'So when we both got all hot and bothered about Rowan, and very nearly went bald pulling each other's hair out, we both did the frat-oath thing and promised not to see him again,' Jeff said. 'Either one of us. On pain of death.'

Both brothers turned their big baby blues Jimmy's way. 'So you see,' Mark said.

'We never went near Rowan after that,' Jeff said.

'So it couldn't have been one of us,' Mark said.

'You see?' Jeff said.

Jimmy took a deep breath. 'OK,' he said. 'I think that'll be all for now.'

Sam slapped his notebook shut at the speed of light and shot to his feet. Jimmy, wisely not wanting to be stampeded, stood well to one side and let the youngster leave first.

Once outside, Sam stood by the car, watching Jimmy approach. He had, Jimmy was glad to note, turned back to a paler pink colour.

'Bloody hell, Sarge, were they having us on or what?' he asked indignantly.

Jimmy had to grin. 'I'm not sure, son. But I'm telling you this, if the guv wants that precious pair reinterviewed, she can do it herself.'

Hillary's next interview, however, was already set up with Romola Perkins, formerly Hargreaves. She had relocated to Bristol, and for once, Vivienne had been in the office, and had been happy enough to get out of town for what remained of the rest of the day. She was less than happy to have to take Hillary's car, however, and even less than happy not to be allowed to drive.

Romola had gone into the acting profession, according to her updated background check, but this consisted more of am-dram than RADA. Now comfortably married to an advertising executive, she lived in a nice little detached place in Clifton, with a quite spectacular view of the famous bridge.

Vivienne navigated with surprising accuracy, and they made good time in the light-early-afternoon traffic.

When they arrived, Vivienne got out and looked around with the bright enquiring eye of a blackbird spotting a worm. She was dressed in black leggings, with a leopard-print top, and carried a knock-off black leather bag that was pretending to be Prada.

'This isn't too bad,' Vivienne said, then added with searing scorn 'for suburbia.'

Hillary nodded. It wasn't bad at all. Mr Perkins, she thought, must be seriously high-up on the pecking order in the advertising firm.

'I called ahead, so she should be in,' Hillary said, walking up a set of garden steps towards the house, which, like its neighbours, had been built on a ferocious angle on a steep hill. Cleverly terraced gardens frothed with spring colour, and the dull roar of the perpetual traffic in the city spread out below and beyond was almost drowned out by the drone of buzzing insects.

Hillary paused by one prominent flower bed nearest the steps, where a small information placard had been set up, for the edification of the Perkins family visitors.

THIS FLOWER BED HAS BEEN PLANTED WITH NATIVE PLANTS, RICH IN NECTAR AND POLLEN TO HELP FEED AND PRESERVE OUR BEES AND OTHER POLLINATING INSECTS. PLEASE PLANT BIODIVERSELY.

Hillary nodded. 'Quite right too,' she said.

Vivienne merely read it and snorted.

Hillary sighed. If the fate of Britain's wildlife rested solely with people like her young assistant, the entire human race might just as well book its own funeral now, she mused.

'So who is this again?' Vivienne hissed, as Hillary rang the doorbell.

'One of Barry Hargreaves's twin daughters, alleged to have had an inappropriate sexual relationship at the age of fifteen, with the murder victim, Rowan Thompson,' Hillary intoned patiently. 'Have you read the murder book lately?' She turned, caught Vivienne's pansy-brown eyes, sighed, and said, 'Have you read the murder book *at all?*'

Vivienne was saved from having to answer that by the opening of the door. 'Hello? You're the people from Thames Valley Police?'

Romola Perkins was indeed the identical twin of Natasha. Here was the same long dark hair, the same Pre-Raphaelite, beautiful oval face and tall, erect figure. But Romola's make-up was far more slick and professional, her clothes much more colourful and expensive. She wore not only a wedding ring but diamonds on her fingers and in her ears. She was also just a little bit more curvaceous – probably as a result of having borne two children. She did indeed seem far more grown-up and mature than her twin, who had seemed to Hillary to be only playing at being a businesswoman.

'Yes. I'm Hillary Greene, an ex-detective inspector from Thames Valley, and this is Vivienne Tyrell.' She showed her ID, but Romola Perkins was already turning away, and ushering them through.

Inside, there was not a hint of neutral beige or safe pastels. Instead, everywhere Hillary looked she could see the mark of an up-to-the-minute designer, from the big bold pieces of bright pottery that passed as sculpture set on their own plinths, to the double-backed butterfly rattan chairs in the conservatory, to the seriously Scandinavian furniture and African rugs.

Romola showed them into a large open-plan living area where one entire wall was glass. The view it gave of the Clifton Suspension Bridge made it look almost unreal – as if they'd walked onto a film set, and the view was actually a video stills shot lit up on a white sheet.

'Wow,' Vivienne whispered softly and approvingly beside her. 'Now this is the way to *live*.'

'Tea or coffee? Or would you rather have mineral water?' Romola asked, looking from Hillary to Vivienne and back again. 'Please, have a seat.' She indicated a nest of white leather chairs, created around a conversation circle that consisted of a weirdly shaped, sci-fi-looking white plastic coffee table and an orchid.

'Not for us, thank you, Mrs Perkins.'

'Oh, please call me Rommy. Everyone does.'

Hillary nodded. 'You've spoken to your sister Natasha?' she asked, feeling her way in carefully. She was not sure, yet, how close the twins were. Or weren't.

'Yes, she phoned almost right after you'd spoken to her.'

Well, that answered that, Hillary mused. 'You're close, then?' she confirmed.

'Oh, yes. Well, sort of. I mean, we live a fair way apart, so we don't see each other as often as we would like. But that's what webcam is for, isn't it? She tells me you caught up with her when she was on a job at Henley?'

'That's right,' Hillary said. 'I hope her boss didn't mind. She didn't seem that worried about it, but maybe she was just being polite.'

'Oh, no, it was fine,' Romola said vaguely, and crossed her legs elegantly. 'So, Rowan's case is being looked at again, is it? I'm glad. It's always rankled that nobody was ever brought to book for what happened to him.'

'You were fond of him, then?'

'Of course I was. We all were – Dad, Tasha and me.'

Hillary nodded. 'If you've spoken to your sister, then you already know most of what I'm about to ask you.'

Romola nodded gravely and seemed to straighten her shoulders. Hillary wondered if she was practising her acting now. 'Yes. I think so,' she said simply.

'The original senior investigating officer uncovered a rumour, shall we say, that Rowan had claimed to have slept with a pair of underage identical twins,' Hillary kept her voice flat and even. Beside her she could see Vivienne glance curiously at the other woman, no doubt interested to see how she was reacting to this opening gambit. 'Your sister Natasha claimed that it couldn't have been you or herself. Is that true?'

Romola smiled a shade grimly. 'Partly.'

'Care to explain that?'

Romola sighed. 'Well, *I did* sleep with Rowan – a few times, actually. But Tasha didn't.'

Hillary let that sit for a minute, whilst Vivienne made a note in her notebook.

At least the girl was making the effort to record the interview, Hillary thought, supposing she should be grateful for that at least. Even so, she'd rely on her own memory as well. She had a feeling that Vivienne's notes might be rather too edited to be of any real use.

'How old were you at the time?' she asked.

'Nearly sixteen.'

'So legally, he was committing statutory rape?' Hillary pointed out.

'I suppose so,' Romola shrugged one elegant shoulder graphically. ' I'm not a lawyer.'

'Did it seem to worry him?' Hillary asked curiously.

Romola laughed. 'Not him.'

'Did your father know about this?'

'Good lord, no. I didn't tell Daddy.'

'How about your sister?' Hillary pressed.

'She might have guessed.'

'Would she have been jealous?'

Romola thought about the question for a moment, then sighed. 'Maybe. Tasha could be a bit jealous of me at times.'

Hillary nodded. Then leaned forward a little in her chair. 'Mrs Perkins, I don't think you're being perfectly honest with me,' she said softly.

The other woman stiffened, but remained silent.

Hillary slowly leant back again in her chair. 'I think that Rowan did, in fact, sleep with both you and your twin sister. Whether separately, that is, on separate occasions or in a threesome, I'm not quite sure. Or perhaps he did both. You see' – Hillary glanced casually around the stunning room – 'from what I've been learning about Rowan, he wouldn't have been able to resist you. Not only were you his house-mate's daughters, you were twins, and not only twins, but identical twins. Add in the fact that you were beautiful and underage – well, the challenge to his sexuality would have been irresistible for him.'

Romola sighed slowly. 'Natasha, working for a PR firm, is very wary about garnering any bad publicity to herself, as you might expect,' she said, changing the subject slightly. But Hillary followed the reasons for it effortlessly.

'Yes,' Hillary agreed, 'I can see how she might be.'

'She's seen too many people, and not just celebrities, get torn apart by a media frenzy to ever risk putting herself in the position where she herself might be fodder for the press. So, even if she *had* slept with Rowan, even if we *both* had slept with him, she'd never admit it, because if you catch his killer, and it comes to court, the chances are it will all come out.'

Hillary met the other woman's steady gaze and nodded, letting her know that she was following the unwritten subtext. 'I can see that.'

'And, of course, *even if* what you said is true, I would never admit it either, because I have a very happy marriage, and wouldn't want to do anything to put that in jeopardy.'

Hillary nodded slowly. 'But *just supposing* that it was true,' she began, willing to go along with Romola Perkins's game for now, 'do you think your father would have known about it.'

Romola's eyes flickered for an instant, before she slowly, unwillingly, began to smile. 'Now that, if I may say so, is a very leading question. Of course I'm never going to say "yes", because if I do, it automatically gives my father a motive for murder. And if I say "no, of course he didn't" aren't you automatically going to think I'm lying anyway- just to protect him?'

Hillary shrugged. 'At this moment, Mrs Perkins, I suspect absolutely everybody equally. Including you, your sister, your father, and all of Rowan's housemates, his girlfriend and, indeed, his family. So what I need are plain and simple facts. Let me ask you this: do you think your father killed Rowan?'

'Bloody hell! No, of course I don't,' Romola said, suddenly looking properly animated for the first time. 'Dad wouldn't do that.'

'Then the truth can't hurt him, can it?' Hillary said simply.

Romola laughed, but the look in her eyes was as hard as the black granite plinths on which her great pottery sculptures rested. 'Do I look that naive, Inspector Greene?'

Hillary spread her hands helplessly. 'OK. Did Rowan ever confide in you that he was worried about anyone? Anyone making a nuisance of themselves, threatening him, hassling him?'

'No. Rowan just breezed through life without a care in the world,' Romola said, a shade wistfully – a shade resentfully, Hillary thought.

'And you have no idea who might have killed him?' she pressed. 'Now that all this time has passed, and you've grown up yourself, and can look back on that time with an adult's eye, and an adult's experience, has anything struck you as odd now, that didn't really register at the time?'

'No, not really.'

Hillary nodded. 'All right, Mrs Perkins. Thank you for your time.'

Romola looked relieved and rose to show them out.

But on the drive back to Oxford, Hillary knew that another talk with Barry Hargeaves was now a top priority.

Tom Warrington had first seen the notice for the police picnic that was to be held at the weekend several days ago. Now, as he passed it on the way out of HQ, he didn't give it a second glance. The picnics were held three or four times a year, and were supposed to encourage friends and families of police officers to get together at a local park. Somebody set up a barbecue, and most brought picnic baskets of their own, and although booze was supposed to be off limits, a lot of people showed up with either cans of beer or bottles of wine – depending on the rank and the level of alcohol dependence.

It was also an unofficial opportunity for the lower orders to network with the brass, and although Tom had gone to one or two to begin with, he now avoided them like poison. Nobody bothered to talk to you, and you just ended up feeling like a tosser.

As he sailed out on that Friday evening, with the weekend looming free ahead of him, his thoughts were far away from such petty offerings. Instead, he was going to devote the entire weekend to Hillary.

He knew that she must have got his latest love token by now, and no doubt her agile, clever mind was already at work on it.

Tom was very proud of his latest gambit. As he got into his car and drove towards the house he still shared with his parents, he found himself grinning.

He knew that the cards and flowers were all very well, but she was quite right not to be overly impressed with them. The wooden cross, he was sure, would have pleased her far more. It would have given her something to think about and investigate. Given her a chance to do what she did best.

Had she figured it out yet? He laughed, a delighted little chuckle, as he thought of her handling the cross, that wonderfully quick, copper's brain of hers going through all the permutations. And, of course, there was always the chance that she might realize its actual meaning.

And then she'd be on his track, just like she was on the track of whoever had killed Rowan Thompson.

The thought sent delicious shivers down his spine.

Vivienne Tyrell was proving a useful source of information, and he had a fair idea of the case Hillary was currently working on: a murder case that was over ten years old and unsolved even at the time of its execution would be more than most officers could handle, but he knew that his Hillary would close it.

And the thought of her then turning all that energy and attention to himself made him break out in a light sweat all over.

Now, he couldn't understand why he hadn't thought of it right at the start. It was his gift to her. And, inevitably, when it led her right to him, he'd be waiting for her, and they could celebrate properly.

He would have to find and rent a place of his own, of course. There was no way they could consummate their relationship properly in his bedroom at home, with his old mum and dad downstairs in the kitchen!

Pulling into the nearest newsagent's, Tom brought a selection of local papers and, sitting happily behind the wheel, took a pen from the dashboard and began to circle places for rent.

Hillary Greene drove back from Bristol and, it being past clocking-off time anyway, dropped Vivienne at a roundabout near Oxford, where she could catch a bus home.

As she drove towards HQ, she contemplated passing it by herself and heading straight back to Thrupp and her boat, but found herself indicating to turn into the car park in front of HQ anyway. Once a workaholic, always a workaholic, she guessed.

She parked Puff and glanced at her watch. Jimmy and Sam would almost certainly have left, but she wanted to get her interview notes into the murder book so that, first thing Monday, they'd be there and available.

She walked into a quiet lobby, gave the desk sergeant a vague greeting, and trotted towards the stairs leading down into the depths.

'There's no overtime for civvies, you know,' the desk sergeant said with a knowing grin, glancing at the face of the plastic clock on the wall.

Hillary, without turning her head, carried on walking but held

142

up her hand with a single-finger salute that had the desk sergeant chortling.

She went to her stationery cupboard, and quickly typed up her notes. She was just slipping them into the murder book folder in the small office the rest of the team used, when she realized she had left the wooden cross in the evidence bag in the bottom drawer of her desk. Knowing it would be better to remove it, just in case prying eyes found it and wondered what it meant, she quickly went back to retrieve it. She was just picking it up when her eyes fell on the three-lettered message on it.

JOY.

For a moment, her mind had played a trick on her, for she'd half-expected to see the initials R.I.P. on it instead. That was the usual three-lettered message on such a funereal thing, after all.

She shrugged, tossed it into her bag, and stepped through the office door. She'd just closed the door behind her and was walking down the corridor, when suddenly she felt her steps slowing.

Something was clanging away urgently in the back of her head.

What?

Initials.

R.I.P. Initials.

'Oh, shit,' Hillary said softly. How could she have failed to spot that?

She back-tracked just a few steps and walked into the main computer room. She expected it to be as empty as her own small kingdom, but here there were still several people working away at the constantly busy machines, and in one corner Sergeant Handley looked up at her surprised.

'Didn't you get my message?' he asked, as she approached. 'There were no hits of any kind for a woman named Joy,' he said.

'Yes I know, thanks. My fault, I should have thought of it before,' Hillary said, smiling ingratiatingly, 'but could you do the same checks, but this time using the initials J, O and Y. As in J for Jenny, O for Oona, and Y for, say, Young, or whatever?'

Handley made a quick note. 'Sure. That shouldn't take long either. As a set of initials, they don't sound too common. Having Y for a surname isn't anywhere near as bad as having a W or a C for instance.'

'Great,' Hillary said, not really caring about the semantics. 'It'll probably come to nothing as well, but I just need to make sure.'

'No problem,' Handley said vaguely. 'But you won't get any answers till Monday morning, mind.'

'Monday's fine,' Hillary said, and, giving a wave of thanks, stepped back out into the corridor.

It wasn't until she was in the lobby and on her way out that she heard her name being called.

She recognized the voice at once of course, and seeing the desk sergeant's head come up, like a hound spotting a fox's brush disappearing down a hole, made sure she put on a dazzling smile as she turned around.

Steven Crayle was just trotting up the last of the steps leading from the basement. He was dressed in a dark-blue suit, and his tall, lean, elegant frame moved with an athletic ripple that made her throat go dry.

Damn, but he was buff.

'S…Steven,' she said, managing to transfer the word from 'sir' to his forename just in time. She gave a quick movement of her eyes to her left as he approached, and knew from the way he made his smile become very warm indeed that he'd clocked the nosy desk sergeant too.

'Glad to catch you,' he said, somehow managing to make the statement sound suggestive.

Hillary's eyes narrowed. 'Always a pleasure,' she drawled back.

Steven's lips twitched. 'I was just wondering if you wanted to go to the picnic tomorrow.'

Hillary looked at him blankly.

'The police picnic, in the park?' he said. 'You know, they hold them all the time. You go, have a burnt burger, sip stewed tea from a thermos, play some footie with the uniforms and pretend you're all having a good time.'

'Oh right, those,' Hillary said. She'd always thought they were strictly for the desperate-to-please. She'd never been to one in her life.

'Let me guess. You've never been to one,' Steven said, and grinned as her eyes narrowed even further in warning. 'I don't blame you. I wouldn't go either, except that there's an unspoken rule that some of us have to go to at least one once a year. I thought you might like to join me, and we can be miserable together. Who knows, maybe we could go on somewhere else afterwards?'

The desk sergeant was, by now, almost hanging over his countertop to make sure he didn't miss a single word.

Hillary smiled warmly. 'I'd like that,' she said, 'Steven.'

She even managed to make her voice sound husky.

Honor Blackman, eat your heart out, she thought. And saw one of Steven Crayle's dark velvet-brown eyes close in a brief wink.

CHAPTER NINE

The first Saturday in May dawned brightly, with a red flush in the sky that Hillary saw in all its glory, thanks to the noisy birds in the willow tree. She got out of bed, had her usual blink-and-you'd-miss-it shower and tried to remember if red skies in the morning were supposed to give shepherds a smile or a frown.

Since it felt way too early in the day for dredging up childhood nursery rhymes from memory, and given that she was about to embark on an English picnic in spring, she simply dressed for rain.

She was no mug.

The park where the police picnics were held wasn't far from where her boat was moored, and did in fact overlook the Oxford canal. She contemplated giving the *Mollern* a short run and arriving in style, but decided it was hardly worth the effort.

She decided to walk instead, and set out with an hour to spare. The chiff-chaffs heckled her as she passed, and she mumbled a dire warning at them about the likelihood of their getting her toasted breadcrumb leftovers from now on. They didn't look all that worried, it had to be said, but anyone overhearing her would have understood at once that it didn't look promising for the feathered contingent.

As she walked through the streets, she couldn't remember whether Kidlington was still officially the biggest village in Britain or whether it had lost its crown to some other pretender.

Or even if anything had come of the campaign set in motion a while ago to officially recognize it as a town. Considering that she'd lived there more or less throughout her working life, her ignorance should have made her ashamed, but it didn't.

When she entered the park, it was immediately clear where the second of the four annual Thames Valley Police Picnics had set up camp, since there was already an impromptu rugby match taking place, with the hooligans from Traffic doing something dire to the prima donnas from the Fraud Squad.

Hillary winced as someone hit the grassy turf with a bone-breaking thud and a breathless squawk.

Wooden tables, the kind with fixed wooden benches attached to them, were already filling up with the wives and – to a lesser extent – the husbands of serving officers, and their assorted kids. On the benches were the makings of hot dogs and burgers, and a variety of home-made cakes.

Every year, she vaguely remembered someone telling her, a member of the top brass was elected to scorch the meat, but even so, she was rather surprised to see the silver-haired figure of Commander Marcus Donleavy in the act of lighting a barbecue.

For the first time ever she realized that she was seeing him out of his own 'uniform' of grey suit and impeccable tie, for he was wearing instead a pristine-looking pair of denim jeans with a razor-sharp crease. And only the commander, Hillary thought, hiding a grin, would be able to get jeans with a crease. He'd teamed this sartorial phenomenon with a mint-green short-sleeved shirt and was wearing some sort of lightweight canvas shoes of the same colour.

She detoured past the screaming kids (and the screaming members of the Fraud Squad out on the playing field) and headed over to the barbecue area.

As she did so, she noticed Steven's car pull into the parking area. Like him, it was dark, racy and sexy as hell, whilst somehow remaining sober and respectable.

She was still smiling over that particular thought when Marcus Donleavy saw her approaching and waved her over with a smile.

She herself was, for once, wearing a summery dress instead of her usual more austere skirt-and-jacket combo. Reaching just below her knees, it was an attractive empire-line affair with a powder-blue, white and lemon floral pattern. Over it she wore a lightweight white mackintosh. Knee-high white leather boots completed the outfit. Marcus Donleavy watched her approach with a speculative glance.

Could the rumours that had been reaching his ears about Hillary Greene and Steven Crayle actually be true? He wouldn't have predicted it, but nothing, nowadays, ever surprised him.

'Hello, did you know you're a dead ringer for one of my detectives?' Marcus said, the moment she was within earshot. 'If I didn't know better I could have sworn that DI Hillary Greene was gracing us with her presence. But, since I know for a fact that she's never deigned to attend one of these plebeian affairs before—'

'Morning, sir,' Hillary said shortly, cutting across his sarcasm.

'It speaks.'

Hillary wondered how much licence her new status as a civilian gave her when it came to insubordination. After all, Marcus was no longer, strictly speaking, her superior officer. And after working so hard to get her back into harness, he wasn't likely to fire her easily. So perhaps today was the day when her long-held dream of giving Donleavy a hard time could come true.

She met his level, grey-eyed gaze, and thought again.

She was definitely no mug.

'So what does bring you here, Hillary?' he asked, genuinely curious.

Hillary shrugged. 'I was invited.'

When she said no more he typically got right down to business. Social occasion or not, he never turned off. It was something Hillary understood, because she was the same.

'So, how's the latest case going?' the commander asked briskly.

'I take it Steven's got you on something else, now that you've closed your first cold case? And by the way, congratulations on that. We're all well impressed.'

'Thank you, sir. And yes, I'm currently working on the Thompson case.'

'A murder file, is it?' Marcus asked sharply, and nodded, satisfied, when Hillary agreed that it was. She gave him a quick but comprehensive précis, and by the time she was finished, she could sense someone coming up behind her.

Her hormones – ever helpful little things that they were – instantly let her know who it was. She could feel him behind her, his superior height casting just a faint shadow over her, which made her shiver slightly.

'Sir,' Steven said, nodding at Donleavy. 'Did I hear Hillary filling you in on the Thompson case?'

'You did.' Marcus began to neatly load the barbecue with rows and rows of sausages. They instantly began to spit and sizzle and all three of them took a few cautious steps backwards.

'Hillary, you look lovely,' Steven said, conscious of the contingent of nosy wives over by a bench who were eyeing them speculatively. Every one of them knew who the commander was, of course, since all of them had an eye to their husband's chances of promotion and knew who you had to schmooze up to at affairs such as this one. And most of them knew Hillary either by sight or reputation.

'Thank you,' Hillary said, glancing across at him.

Like Marcus, he was also dressed casually in jeans, this time of a more washed and natural appearance, and he'd teamed them with a plain white shirt, unbuttoned at the top. She could just see the beginnings of a few dark, curly chest hairs in the V-shaped length under his throat, and swallowed hard.

Donleavy, in the act of turning over the first of the blackening sausages, shot them a quick, sharp, gimlet glance.

'Did you bring any wine?' Steven asked, before holding up a bottle of Chablis for her inspection.

'Very nice. I brought chocolate,' she said. Actually, she should have said she'd *meant* to bring chocolate, but had forgotten to.

'Well, that's the two staples of any picnic sorted, then,' Steven laughed. He nodded at Marcus. 'Sir,' he said, then held out his hand.

Hillary, without so much as blinking, reached out and took it. It felt surprisingly right and natural to do so and, as they walked away to a quiet, unclaimed bench, it felt surprisingly good when they swung their hands together in motion with their walking, like two schoolkids off on their first adventure.

Marcus Donleavy watched them go, and then suddenly realized his sausages were burning. Even over the acrid smoke, he could hear the gossip beginning to heat up all around him too.

So the stories about Steven and Hillary were true. Marcus had to admit that not only had he not seen it coming, he was not at all sure how he felt about it. When he'd caught the first faint whiffs on the rumour mill of a dalliance between them, his first instinct had been to give it very little credence. But now they might just as well have taken out an advert and put it in the paper.

Already he could see a sergeant from Juvie, who was the unpaid photographer for the police newsletter, taking snapshots of the pair as they sat and drank wine, their heads bent close together.

Marcus sighed and hoped it wouldn't end in disaster. Now that he'd finally got Hillary safely back in the fold and working for the CRT the last thing he wanted was for her to get distracted.

Perhaps he should give some thought to promoting Crayle away from the basement and to a chief superintendency somewhere else?

Over at the bench, Hillary leaned forward and rested her elbows on the table. It brought her head closer to his.

'Have you got anything new from him?' Steven asked quietly, aware of the watching eyes and the listening ears all around them.

Hillary understood what he was asking at once and hesitated. She should really tell him about the cross now, but decided to wait until Handley got back to her on Monday morning. That way she'd have something worthwhile to report. Besides, although she didn't really give voice to the thought, she was feeling more and more reluctant to let anything spoil her day.

She was enjoying herself, sipping wine and having his undivided attention. And it suddenly felt as if it had been a very long time indeed since she had enjoyed herself.

'No more text messages or flowers,' she temporized, not exactly lying but skirting the truth just a tad. 'So, now that we've officially become an item,' she said, looking around with a wry smile, 'how do you fancy having a day out on the boat? It's a nice day, we can have a gentle cruise a couple of miles north – as far as the boatyard at Lower Heyford, anyway. It's a pretty stretch of canal up that way. We could buy some strawberries.'

And finally stop pussy-footing around, she added silently.

When she looked up at him, it was obvious he'd picked up on her unspoken addendum, because his brown eyes were going a slightly darker colour.

The impact of them gave her a very pleasant kick in the stomach.

'Hell, yes,' he said simply.

When they got up and walked away together, neither of them noticed or cared that they were being avidly watched.

When Sam went in to work on Monday morning, he found both Jimmy and Hillary Greene in ahead of him. It irked him slightly, since, at just gone 8.30, he'd assumed he'd be first in, and the warm glow of having achieved the moral high ground was denied him.

Jimmy was sitting behind his side of the desk, and Hillary was half-sitting, half-leaning on the other side of the desk, her bag still slung over her shoulder, so obviously she hadn't been there long enough to have gone through to her own tiny office. It made him feel a bit better.

He smiled, however, when Jimmy glanced at his watch, and grinned up at him. 'Eager, ain't you?' the old ex-sergeant said approvingly.

Sam shrugged modestly.

'Right then, Sam, since you're so on the ball, have you got anything to report?' Hillary asked, catching Jimmy's amused eye. She knew as well as he did how it never hurt to encourage the tyros.

Sam quickly booted up his computer in search of something to give her. Jimmy thought he looked a bit like a red setter eager to give his mistress a chewy toy to play with.

'Jimmy and me interviewed the Freeling brothers, guv,' Sam began.

'I've already been briefed by Jimmy on that,' Hillary said with a grin. 'From what I've heard, you should both be claiming danger money.'

Jimmy croaked out a gruff laugh. 'Either that, or claim compensation for stress.'

'Right. Well, I've done that background check on Mrs Landau that you asked for,' Sam said, a bit disappointed not to be the one to relate the perils of the bike shop.

'The landlady?' Jimmy said, sounding interested. 'You interested in her, guv?'

'Not particularly. I just felt, when we interviewed her, that some youngster had given her a hard time. Sam thought it was probably her daughter who was the culprit. Apparently she had a kid then went off the rails, leaving her mother to raise the grandson on her own. Did you manage to find out anything more, Sam?'

Sam nodded, and quickly re-read his notes from the computer file out loud.

'Melinda Stephanie Landau, only daughter of Wanda Landau. She started getting in trouble when she was in her mid-teens,' Sam read rapidly, 'and then convictions for shop-lifting, affray and prostitution. She had a baby boy when she was nineteen, but the father's name is not listed. Social services were on her case right from the start, guv – although the baby wasn't born already addicted.'

Hillary let out a long slow breath. 'Small mercies,' she muttered darkly.

'Right. Melinda had the baby taken away from her when it was four months old, she went into rehab, got the child back, but was arrested a few months after that for possession. Wanda Landau started petitioning the court for custody of her grandson from that time on. Although technically the baby remained in 'the home of the mother' it was the house in Kebler Road, so Mrs Landau was the one who was actually looking after the baby anyway.'

Sam paused for breath, and read silently for a few minutes, then nodded. 'I had a hard time getting any files from social services, but I did manage to track down one of the social workers who was willing to chat a bit, off the record, like. Seems the grandmother was the primary care-giver more or less from day one, and since Melinda lived with her mother, the courts were more inclined to leave the baby *in situ* than might otherwise have been the case. Then, when the kid was three and a half, Melinda just took off. From the reports at the time, it seems likely that she left with one Malcolm William Purdy, a known drug dealer, who had to scarper PDQ over some sort of turf war with a rival dealer.'

Again Sam paused for breath.

'It took Mrs Landau nearly three years, all told, to be allowed legal status as the child's guardian. She wanted to adopt, but was deemed too old, but by then the boy regarded her as his mother and was well settled, and the social services were happy with their investigations into Wanda Landau's fitness to be the principal carer.'

'Couldn't have been easy, though,' Jimmy spoke for the first time. 'Her age was against her for a start.'

Hillary nodded. 'But she was financially secure, had no criminal record, and was obviously able and willing to take the boy on. Have you had any luck tracking down Melinda?' Hillary asked, getting to the point.

Jimmy's eyes narrowed at her sudden brisk tone. 'You think she might be a suspect, guv?'

Hillary shrugged, unwilling to have to call it one way or the other. 'It doesn't seem likely, no, but longer shots than this have paid off before. Say Melinda comes back and is rejected by her son, who probably wouldn't want to know her. But she sticks around and sees all the students living in what she thinks of as her house, getting on well with her old mum, maybe even being befriended by her son, and you never know how she might react. Junkies aren't known for their powers of reasonable thinking. Wild mood swings, jealous rages, you never know how it might go down.'

Jimmy nodded thoughtfully. 'And from what you said, the old girl seemed to speak fondly of Rowan. He could have been a particular pet of hers. In which case, the daughter might have come to see him as a usurper. Maybe, in her own eyes, he'd taken her place, and needed to be hefted out of the nest to make room so that she could fly back to it.'

Hillary nodded. 'We know from his character that he made it a habit to be charming. And he was the sort who liked his life to be good and easy, so keeping the landlady sweet would be an obvious step. If the dispossessed daughter was lurking around, and saw her mother giving some maternal affection to Rowan....' Hillary sighed and rubbed her chin thoughtfully. 'Oh, hell, who am I kidding? That's so thin it wouldn't even make gruel.'

Jimmy laughed. 'Besides, the chances are, if Melinda had been on the scene, someone would have seen her, or mentioned her presence.'

'Any reports of Melinda Landau hanging around in Inspector Gorman's investigation?' Sam asked curiously.

'No, but I doubt if he'd have been looking for her,' Hillary said. 'And Wanda Landau herself certainly never mentioned her. But then, if Melinda *had* been on the scene at the time, you couldn't expect the girl's mother to just drop her in it. Wanda would have known that her daughter would become a likely suspect. Any junkie at a murder scene is bound to come under suspicion.'

'Well, she wouldn't have mentioned it anyway, would she, guv?' Jimmy pointed out reasonably. 'What with the social services sniffing around, seeing how fit she was to bring up the lad, the last thing she'd want to admit was that her junkie daughter was back on the scene.'

Hillary nodded. 'And Wanda did say that she'd been due a visit from someone from the social shortly after Rowan died. Damn, that must have been tricky for her.'

Jimmy nodded. 'A murder in your home is hardly the kind of thing you'd want, is it, when you're trying to convince the authorities that you're up to taking on a kid. She must have been shitting bricks, the poor old soul.'

Hillary shook her head. 'Sam, anything in your notes from the social about how they viewed Rowan Thompson's murder in relation to Wanda's petition to raise her grandson?'

Sam quickly scanned the notes. 'Well, they liaised with Gorman's sergeant, guv. But, of course, the case was never solved, and Mrs Landau was only ever referred to as a witness. They seemed to be more concerned about the psychological effects on the boy of having someone killed in his own home. He had a few sessions with a child psychiatrist who declared it hadn't affected him much at all. Apparently, he barely knew Rowan Thompson, and since he and his grandmother live, by all accounts, a more or less separate life in the basement, and the murder took place upstairs, in a room he'd never even visited, it didn't seem to upset him too much.'

'Kids can be tough little buggers,' Jimmy said approvingly.

'That must have been a relief for Wanda,' Hillary said. 'If the boy had taken it hard, they'd have removed him from the house pretty quick.'

'Right,' Sam agreed. 'But as it is, it looks as though they just dragged their feet for a bit, seeing if anything was going to break in the case, but when it didn't, Mrs Landau pressed her petition, and in the end it was granted.'

'Must have given her some sleepless nights, though,' Hillary said with feeling. 'In a way, Wanda was very nearly a victim too.'

'So, where does that leave us?' Jimmy asked, and Hillary sighed grimly.

'No further forward, as far as I can see. Mrs Landau was one of the few people in that house who not only didn't have a motive for wanting Rowan dead, but actually suffered as a result of his killing. She could have lost her grandson over it. Still, Sam, I want you to keep on the Melinda aspect of it anyway, and see if you can track her down. Try the rehab clinics, and coroner's offices. And marriages. I'd like to know what became of her, just so I can rule her out. I don't like loose ends, even tenuous ones.'

'Guv.'

'Right. I'd better get on.'

'Have a nice weekend, guv?' Jimmy asked innocently, as Hillary started towards the door. It was all over the station about her and Crayle leaving the police picnic together. And although he knew it was all a set-up, Hillary didn't know that he knew, and in the normal course of things, he'd be teasing her about it.

'Lovely, thanks,' Hillary said. And meant it.

It had been a very nice weekend indeed.

Very nice.

When she got back to her office, though, the first thing that she saw was the message from Sergeant Handley.

And her good mood vanished. With a vengeance. Because Handley's beloved computers had found JOY. Or rather, they'd found a woman by the name of Judith Olivia Yelland, who had been reported missing by her friend nearly five years ago.

Hillary read the stark facts and sucked in a long slow breath.

OK. So a woman with the initials of JOY had been reported missing. It didn't do to jump to conclusions, she knew, but already she could feel a cold, serpentine feeling snaking up her spine, and she put her hand up to the back of her neck to rub her suddenly chilled skin.

She forced herself to sit down and wait for her heartbeat to slow back to normal, and for the sick feeling in the pit of her stomach to settle. It took a few minutes. Then she booted up her own computer, typed in her password and authorization, and logged on to the MisPer records that it allowed her to access.

Slowly, she read the brief.

Judith Yelland had been twenty-five years of age when she was reported missing by her friend Ruth Coombs, with whom she shared a small maisonette in the market town of Bicester.

Judith's photograph showed that she was a pretty woman with long blonde hair and big brown eyes. Her friend had said she was smallish, about five feet five or so, and was friendly and sociable without being flighty. She'd had a regularly boyfriend for nearly three years, but that relationship had petered out, amicably, a year or so before. Judy liked to exercise and took regular karate lessons in the Bicester Sports Centre as a way of keeping fit and for self-protection. She'd recently been seeing a married man, Christopher Deakin.

She felt she needed it, as she'd confided to her friend that someone was sending her anonymous text messages and flowers.

Hillary felt the hairs on the back of her neck start to rise again, but forced herself to carry on reading doggedly.

According to Ruth, Judy wasn't particularly close to her family, as they'd had an unspecified falling out when she was in her late teens, and the breech had never been fully healed. Ruth had never caught sight of her friend's stalker for herself, although Judy had been convinced on several occasions that she had been followed home from work. She had worked in a shoe shop in Sheep Street, in the town centre.

As far as Hillary could see, very little follow-up had been done, since Ruth also told the constable in MisPer that Judy had been talking more and more recently about moving away from the area to shake off her unwanted admirer, and also to start a new life generally. The relationship with her current boyfriend had left her feeling vaguely dissatisfied with her life in general, and she'd also admitted to being 'fed-up' with her 'go-nowhere' job.

The MisPer office was of the opinion that it was more than likely that Judith Yelland had simply relocated, and had done so in such a way as to make it hard for anyone to find her. This made sense, Hillary supposed, if she was trying to shake off a stalker. But Ruth had insistently pointed out that Judy hadn't put in her notice at work or collected the wages that would have been owing to her, hadn't packed her bags, and hadn't left any kind of goodbye note for her flatmate either.

Hillary checked to see if MisPer had checked with Judith Yelland's bank, and found out that they had. She had just the one current account, with a modest balance of just over £800 in it. She had not closed her account or notified them of a change of address and, at the time of the missing person's report being filed, there had been no recent or unusual activity on her account.

So she had not drawn out a large lump sum in cash, which is what most people would do if they'd decided to leave for fresh pastures.

And Ruth was also insistent that Judy was unlikely to leave all her clothes behind – she had one or two expensive outfits that she really liked, for instance. And although she tended to wear a lot of good-quality jewellery, and could easily have sold or pawned these articles for ready cash if need be, Ruth was sure that her friend would have told her she was leaving, at the very least. 'She wouldn't have wanted me to worry' was what she'd insisted to the MisPer officer at the time.

But reading between the lines of the original officer's report, Hillary could tell that he thought Ruth Coombs had been of a rather overbearing nature, and that he wouldn't be at all surprised if the missing girl had left without bothering to inform her. He'd gained the impression that Ruth could be bossy, and that she herself might be part of the reason why Judith Yelland had wanted to start afresh in a new life somewhere.

They had done all the usual checks with local hospitals, but she hadn't met with any accident that had been reported. Likewise her details were circulated to the YWCA, the Sally Army, and other women's refuges, without any result.

For the next hour or so, Hillary let her fingers do the walking, and talked on the telephone to several people, some of whom were helpful, and others who needed some gentle persuasion. But at the end of it all, the picture was clear: if Judith Yelland had got a job somewhere else, she was not paying any taxes.

If she was using a bank account, it was not her old account, which had not been accessed by Judith or anyone else in the five years that she'd been gone.

If she'd been ill, she hadn't been registered with any other GP surgery, and her own doctors had no record of her attending their clinic since she was reported missing. Likewise, her dentist hadn't seen her in five years either, but if she'd registered as a private patient elsewhere, there was no way that Hillary on her own, and using her own humble computer, could find out where and with whom.

She hadn't married, or registered a birth, nor had she changed her name by deed poll. There was no record of her death or burial.

Judith Olivia Yelland, whether of her own volition or not, had succeeded in vanishing.

Hillary printed off all the relevant data, and placed it in a file. Then, retrieving the bagged-up wooden cross, she walked, poker-faced, down the corridor to Steven Crayle's office.

She knocked, waited for his summons, and walked in.

He looked up at her from his desk and smiled at her warmly. And the weekend they'd just spent together was suddenly in the room with them.

Her heartbeat picked up a notch.

Steven got up from his desk and walked towards her.

'Everything all right?' he asked softly, and she nodded, because she knew what he was asking.

Was everything all right between them now? It was, as far as she was concerned. They'd had a nice time, with no strings attached. And she was not about to start trying to attach strings now.

After leaving the picnic they'd gone back to Thrupp, where she'd cast *Mollern* off her mooring and, at a sedate 3 m.p.h., they had glided northwards along the khaki-coloured water. Amid much laughter and bank-banging, she'd taught him how to navigate the canal, and then use a lock, and then turn the boat. When it grew dark, they'd moored up miles from anywhere beneath some willow trees, and then spent the night together in her narrow bed.

It had been good.

Very good, in fact.

The next morning, she'd taught him the trick of the two-minute shower in very cramped and hilarious conditions that had, nevertheless, had its interesting moments.

A frugal breakfast, and back behind the tiller, until they'd pulled up at The Rock of Gibraltar pub on the canal, where they'd had Sunday lunch, and a stroll in the nearby woods, that were just beginning to lose the blue haze of the fading bluebells.

Back on the boat, and a more leisurely bout in her tiny bed, then on to Thrupp. When he'd left her, just as it was getting dark yesterday evening, they'd been relaxed, but largely uncommunicative.

It was as if neither of them had wanted to discuss what had happened, or put a label on it, or attach a timetable to it, or in anyway do anything that might jinx it. It had, for the both of them, been like an episode out of place, a time just for them, and one that didn't really touch the sides of the life that they lived from day to day.

So now, here they were, back in the real world, and he was asking if she had any regrets, or worries.

And the answer to that was no.

She saw him smile and nod, then held up her hands. She wasn't aware of it, but her face had gone remote and blank.

Instantly, he felt himself tense. He looked at her offerings. 'What's this?'

She showed him the bag first. 'I found it on my desk last Friday.' Briefly, she described what it was, then what she'd asked Handley to find out. She handed him the paperwork in silence, then paced his office quietly as he sat behind his desk and read it.

From time to time, her eyes wandered over his face. During the weekend, he hadn't been able to shave, and when he'd left her, he'd had the beginnings of a stubble. Now he was clean-shaven and she could just pick out the tangy citrus tone of his aftershave. His hair had been washed that morning and looked soft. She felt once again the impulse that she'd been able to indulge during their weekend together, to run her fingers through the dark, thick strands at his temples.

She carried on pacing, unable to settle her mind, which kept jumping from thoughts about the fate of Judith Yelland, to a desire to sit on Steven Crayle's lap and kiss him, to the increasingly nagging feeling that she should know who had killed Rowan Thompson and why, if only she could force herself from all the other distractions crowding in on her and think clearly.

She became aware that Steven had finished reading and was watching her. She didn't know how to feel about the look of concern in his eyes. On a personal level, it gave her a warm, gooey feeling inside. What woman didn't like it when a new lover showed his emotions?

On a professional level, she wanted to tell him crisply that she could take care of herself. On a gut-feeling copper's level, she wanted him to give her the Judith Yelland case.

'You think her stalker and yours are the same?' Steven asked eventually.

'Possibly.'

'And that – what – Judith Yelland has been murdered?'

'Possibly.'

'It all depends on whether the word JOY is a coincidence or not,' Steven pointed out. 'You could have misunderstood the message he was sending you. And Judith Yelland could be alive and well somewhere, having started over.'

'Possibly.'

'Stop saying possibly.'

Hillary smiled. 'Sorry. Sir.'

'And don't call me sir either. Not after the last few days we've just spent together.'

Hillary smiled again.

Then slowly, both their smiles faded. 'So what do we do about this?' she asked, nodding down at the wooden cross and the Judith Yelland file in front of him.

Steven sighed. 'We'll have to go to Donleavy,' he said reluctantly. 'Before this, we could have made a case that we were keeping your admirer to ourselves because we wanted to keep a lid on it and solve it in-house, so to speak. But this changes the game entirely.'

Hillary nodded without enthusiasm. 'Yes, I know.'

But would the commander let her investigate Judith Yelland's disappearance? Even if she could, quite legitimately, claim that it came under her territory now, since it was, technically, a cold case.

'Damn,' she said, with feeling.

Steven Crayle then did something that none of her previous bosses had ever done before. He stood up and held out his arms, and said softly, 'Come here.'

And Hillary found herself doing something she'd told herself she would never, ever do again.

She went, and let herself be held in a man's arms and was comforted.

CHAPTER TEN

When she left Steven, she popped her head into the shared office, and saw that Sam was the only one in.

'Sam, have you had a chance to check out Barry Hargreaves's redundancy situation yet? Remember, I thought his wife seemed a little off about it, and I wondered if there was anything dodgy going on there?'

Sam was already nodding. 'Yes, guv, I did, but his boss told me it was strictly on the up and up. He quoted the economic crisis as being the main factor for them having to cut back, and Hargreaves had the least time in, so was due the least redundancy, which was why it made sense to give him the elbow first. He seemed quite satisfied with his work and everything.'

'You did a background check on the company, right?' Hillary said, pleased when he nodded. Good, the lad was learning, she thought. 'Did anything smell off?'

'No, guv, not so I could tell. They're a mid-level, mid-range accountancy firm, fairly well respected, been in business under one name or another for nearly eighty years. Mind you, they are still a private company, so public records aren't as good as if they had shareholders to answer to.'

'Right. So no whiff of financial hanky-panky?'

'Not that I could find out. They don't take on the really big clients, but cater more to the smaller and family-operated businesses. Which means, I guess, that it would be harder for them to cheat than if they had some really big clients, whose left hand didn't know what the right was doing, if you see what I mean.'

'OK. And did the boss of the firm seem to have any beef against Hargreaves?'

'No. I got the feeling they got on all right together. But he was definitely curious as to why I was asking, like, and kept hinting that he'd like to know why the police were interested in him. But I think that was down to natural caution, more than anything else. He was worried in case anything might reflect badly on his firm, if something was in the air. I told him that it was just a matter of routine on a matter unrelated to his work record. I hope that's OK. I didn't like to drop Hargreaves in it, guv. He'll be relying on them for his references and stuff.'

Hillary nodded in approval at his thoughtfulness. 'Good. I'm going to re-interview him in light of what his daughters have told us. Want to come along?'

Sam grinned. 'Need you ask?'

If Barry Hargreaves was surprised to see her back, it didn't show on his face when he answered the door to them. He was dressed casually in rather baggy trousers and a thick-knit jumper.

'Hello. Come on in, I was just about to put the kettle on. The wife's out.'

He showed them through to a bright, cheerful, yellow and powder-blue kitchen. It was fitted out with modern-looking stainless-steel fixtures, sink and work surfaces. The big ex-construction worker looked oddly out of place in the setting, but he made tea and coffee happily enough, and set them down on a breakfast bar, where Hillary and Sam drew up stools.

'More questions about Rowan, then?' Hargreaves asked resignedly, making himself comfortable on a stool of his own and taking a sip of tea.

'Yes, sir. We've had a chance now to talk to your girls,' Hillary said, and saw the way the older man tensed slightly. Now, was that a father's natural protectiveness towards his offspring, or something else? It was hard to tell, Hillary mused.

'Oh? I wish you hadn't had to bother them,' he said, a shade coldly.

'I understand that, sir, but this is still a murder inquiry,' Hillary pointed out firmly. 'Just because it happened a number of years ago doesn't make it any less important.'

Hargreaves had the grace to look a little abashed, and stared down into his mug of tea and heaved a sigh. 'No, of course it doesn't. Sorry, you're quite right. Ask away.'

'One of your daughters categorically denied ever having had any kind of personal relationship with Rowan Thompson,' Hillary said, choosing her words carefully. She didn't want to mention which daughter had done so. She wanted to see just how well he knew the girls and, by being ambiguous, try and get an idea of just how much he actually knew about what had gone on back in 2001.

The oldest of Rowan Thompson's housemates looked at her with a wry smile. 'Meaning, by innuendo, that one of them *did* say that she'd slept with the randy little sod, I take it? Which in turn would imply that I had a reason to stick a knife into him?'

Hargreaves tilted his slightly whiskered chin at a challenging angle, but his eyes looked annoyed. 'Sorry, but I still don't believe that either one of the twins had anything to do with him. If it was Natasha who told you she had, you have to take it with a pinch of salt. Tasha likes to dramatize things sometimes.'

Interesting, Hillary thought. He'd got it the wrong way around.

'And yet it's Romola who does the acting,' she pointed out mildly, taking a sip of her own coffee. 'A leading light in am dram, isn't she?'

Barry Hargreaves let out a reluctant chuckle, and his tensed shoulders slumped just a bit. 'That's right. And yet, for all that nonsense, Rommy's actually the sensible one out of that pair. She's married well, and she's got a good head on her shoulders. She's got kiddies and is now thoroughly settled, praise be! No, it's Tasha that I worry about.'

'Did you worry about her when she was fifteen?' Hillary asked quickly.

Hargreaves both bridled and looked suddenly wary, at the same time. 'Of course.'

'From what I've learned about Rowan, fifteen-year-old identical twins would have been irresistible.'

'So you keep harping on! Look, I told you before, and I'll say it again now if you like, I made sure that he didn't get his mitts on them,' Hargreaves said flatly.

'And if I told you that one of your daughters admitted to me in interview that he had "got his mitts" on them?' she asked, again in that calm and neutral voice as she looked at him levelly.

Hargreaves shrugged. 'What can I do about it now? Nowadays, you're lucky if your thirteen-year-old daughters know enough about birth control not to come home pregnant. I had a mate of mine, when I worked construction, who had a girl the same age as mine who used to drive her to and from her boyfriend's house, last thing at night, and pick her up first thing the next morning. He reckoned she was in more danger when she was walking home, than she was, tucked up in bed with him. He made sure she took precautions, made sure they both had regular VD check-ups and what not. He'd met and sort-of approved of the lad concerned, and had the attitude that if he kicked up a fuss, she'd only do it anyway, and maybe get into even more trouble.'

Hargreaves sighed and took another mouthful of tea. 'And who's to say he's not right?'

Hillary nodded slowly. 'A very enlightened attitude, I'm sure,' she agreed, with a trace of irony. 'Are you saying you share that view?'

Again Hargreaves sighed. 'Not particularly. But this was all a long time ago.'

'Someone killed Rowan,' Hillary said flatly.

'Granted. But it wasn't me.'

And with that, Hillary had to be content.

Back in the car outside, Sam buckled up, watching his boss closely. 'Do you think he did it, guv?' he asked curiously.

Hillary hid a smile. Who did Sam think she was? The Delphi oracle? Still, his faith in her was rather touching.

'Maybe,' she hedged.

'He seemed like a good father to me. You know, like he really cared about his girls. And understood them, too,' Sam carried on.

'Yes,' Hillary agreed. And yet, Hargreaves had got it wrong about which daughter had confessed to having sex with the victim. Unless it had been a double bluff, and he'd known all along that Rommy would be the most likely one to be truthful. In which case, did he know that both of them had succumbed to Rowan's charms? And if so…. Was he trying to protect them?

Or maybe just one of them?

What if Barry Hargreaves knew his daughters very well indeed?

'Suppose you had an identical brother, Sam. He looked exactly like you, and you both fancied the same girl. How would you feel about it?'

Sam looked uncomfortable at being put on the spot. 'I'm not sure. Identical twins are supposed to be close, right? I mean like super-close, can sense when one of them's in trouble, even if they're hundreds of miles apart, right?'

'So they say,' Hillary agreed sceptically. But into her mind's eye came a picture of the business-suited Tasha, and the eco-aware Romola. She hadn't had the impression, when interviewing them, that they'd been particularly close. But perhaps they'd grown apart in the adult years. As fifteen-year-olds, perhaps they'd been inseparable. And able to read each other's mind.

'In which case, I don't know that a girl could cause that much trouble,' Sam said, somewhat naively. 'Although, I suppose, the opposite could be true. I mean, it's a classic sort of thing, right, guv? Siblings torn apart by jealousy.'

Hillary nodded. 'Classic. Yes,' she agreed thoughtfully. If Tasha *had* bedded Rowan first, and then discovered that Romola was also sleeping with him, or vice versa, could that provoke a rage strong enough to end in killing?

Perhaps.

And maybe Hargreaves knew or guessed, and was covering for them by denying it had ever happened.

But what if both twins had been in Rowan's bed in a *ménage à trois*? One would suppose that that scenario spoke of mutual consent and willingness to share and share alike.

But was that really feasible where volatile teenagers were concerned?

Hillary sighed.

'The problem after all this time is getting proof,' she said shortly. 'Hargreaves can plead ignorance as much as he likes, and as much as I'm sure in my own mind that that's just so much tripe, I haven't got a cat in hell's chance of proving it now, after all this time.'

Sam, not knowing what to say, simply sat in silent sympathy.

With a grunt, Hillary turned the ignition key. Puff gave a tragic cough and went quiet.

Hillary stared out of the windscreen at the bonnet in front of her. 'Don't you bloody dare,' she told it quietly. 'I am definitely not in the mood for this.'

She turned the ignition again, and her wagon purred as sweetly as a pussy cat. In the passenger seat, Sam Pickles managed to keep a straight face.

Hillary was quite impressed.

That night, Simon Riggs arrived in Thrupp at just gone ten o'clock. He'd put his fishing gear in the back of the boot of his station wagon, telling his long-suffering wife of more years than he could ever remember, that he was going night fishing. And since he had, in the past, won the odd angling cup or two for carp, which were best caught, he always maintained, by moonlight, she hadn't been suspicious. In fact, he rather thought she was relieved, since she claimed he snored like a trooper, and was probably looking forward to a good night's undisturbed sleep on her own.

Since Simon was seventy-two, had a tricky back, and had never been much of a one for the ladies, even in his youth, the thought that he might be lying to her had never crossed her mind. And if she'd known he'd brought night-vision binoculars with him so that he could spy on a lady, the old dear would have swallowed her dentures in shock.

But that night, ex-Sergeant Simon Riggs settled down in his car, parked just outside The Boat pub in Thrupp, and did just that. Or rather, to be more accurate, he divided his attention between Hillary Greene's narrowboat and her car. Of the lady herself, there was neither sight nor sound, and he guessed that she had probably already turned in for the night.

Jimmy Jessop and Riggs had shared a patrol car back when Z-Cars had still been on the telly – or so it seemed – and they'd kept in touch over the years, even when they'd been stationed at different nicks.

So when Jimmy had called around explaining what was up and what he'd needed, Simon had been only too happy to oblige by taking on a few night shifts. He'd worked for a couple of years out of HQ, and knew Hillary Greene mostly by sight and reputation only, and had been more than interested to hear what his old mate had had to say about working at the CRT, and for the famous Hillary Greene.

He could tell Jimmy was getting on well with her, and rated her as much as the likes of Donleavy and the other brass did. Which was recommendation enough for Simon.

He didn't like stalkers, or any of the kind who liked to prey on women. Rapists and granny-bashers had always been high-up on his personal shit-list. And the thought of one them stalking one of their own had set his blood boiling. That alone provided incentive enough.

Besides, as he'd confided to Jimmy, he was bored enough to be up for some unpaid obbo work, if only for the sake of nostalgia.

Now, he settled down quite happily. It was a warmish night, and he'd dressed comfortably in thermals and two layers of jerseys. He had his thermos of tea with him, and was escaping from the house and the missus for a night or two. What more could a man ask for?

Now all he had to do was stay awake. A doddle, for an old hand like him, he thought confidently.

It was an owl, of all things, that woke him up. A little owl, or screech owl, as his old man had called them – for good reason. He found himself suddenly jerking upright against the steering wheel, and he cast a quick, guilty look around as the owl's strident racket echoed around the dark countryside.

The car park was now more or less empty. He'd stayed awake long enough to see the pub shut up shop and the customers leave. That left just a few vehicles which, like Hillary's old VW, belonged to residents of boats who had permanent moorings.

Now he glanced down at his watch, glad of the luminous dial. It was nearly 1 a.m.

He rubbed his face and, by the light of a nearly full moon, poured himself a cup of tea. He checked on Hillary Greene's narrowboat. Jimmy had told him it was called the *Mollern*, and, picked out in his night-vision binoculars, it looked calm and peaceful. Funny sort of place for a former DI to live, he thought.

Then he remembered that it had been the only place she could afford when she was divorcing that bent waste of space, Ronnie Greene. Obviously she must have got a taste for living on the canal, since he was sure she could have found a house to rent by now, if she'd been of a mind to.

A mate of his who owned a boat had told him that once you'd lived on one, you didn't want to live on anything else. Addictive they were, he'd said.

Simon couldn't see it himself.

He grimaced at the stewed, lukewarm taste of the tea, but drained his plastic cup anyway, then decided he needed to make room for it and quietly stepped out of his car. In one far corner of the car park he found a convenient tree and relieved himself. Not easy, with a large police truncheon tucked down into the small of your back.

Being a modest man, he'd chosen a spot well out of sight of the car park and any possible eyes that might have caught sight of him from the few scattered cottages that overlooked the canal.

He wasn't sure what made him stand slightly behind the tree after he'd finished and check the car park again with his binoculars before going back to the car. Perhaps it was sheer luck, or maybe it was the result of a once-acquired, never-lost, copper's instinct.

But he was glad he did.

At first sweep, nothing seemed to be out of place. Then, a sense of movement had him swinging his binoculars back again to a particular patch of dense shadow. Had something moved? Maybe a branch, swaying slightly? But there wasn't much of a breeze.

And then a figure stepped out of the shadows and approached the old Volkswagen Golf, which was parked at the far end of the tarmac area, nearest the entrance to the towpath.

Simon felt his heartbeats rack up a notch and that old tingle of excitement rush through his bloodstream. He'd almost forgotten how good that sudden surge of adrenaline could feel. Yes! Got you, you bastard, he thought.

But Simon now had a problem. He'd gone to take his leak well away from his car, and hadn't thought to bring his mobile phone with him. So he couldn't ring Jimmy for backup.

Plus, it was still a bright full moon, and there was little cover in the open expanse of the tarmac-covered car park. Worse still, he now found himself at the far and opposite corner of where he needed to be. Which meant he'd have to do a long circumnavigation of the car park, picking his way through the trees and the back gardens that bordered the area, in order to get to Hillary's car.

Swallowing a growing sense of misgiving, Simon Riggs slipped back behind his tree and stepped further back into the shadow of the trees. There he paused to let his eyes adjust and get his natural night-vision back. He'd been using the binoculars looped around his neck, but now he needed to use his own eyes.

He let the binoculars fall back to his chest, and set off slowly and quietly.

In the back of his mind, the cold hard voice of reason was insistently calling a warning. He was over seventy. His wife was waiting at home for him, blissfully ignorant, and thinking he was safely out on a river bank somewhere, catching carp. Jimmy had told him that the man they wanted could be dangerous. He had no backup coming. And his back was beginning to hurt, due to the tension.

Against that, he was damned if he was going to let the creep get away, not now that he'd finally stuck his neck into the trap.

Simon stopped, aware of a small, grating, metallic click, over to his right, where he knew the car was.

The stalker had popped the lock on the Volkswagen.

He moved off again, slowly, even more carefully now that he was edging closer.

The screech owl chose that moment to call again, making him nearly jump out of his skin. He had to smile. How many times had he seen something like that happen on a film – usually one of those hammy old horror movies, and, laughed at the cliché? Now he swore softly at the owl under his breath and carried on.

He took his time – the last thing he wanted to do was fall victim to yet another cliché by standing on a broken twig or branch, and frightening off chummy.

A few minutes later, and he was at the right end of the car park at last. Cautiously, picking a spot in the densest patch of shadow he could find, he raised the binoculars again and took another look.

His copper's eyes noticed everything.

The suspect was bent down at the driver's door, which made guessing his height difficult, especially in the dark, but he didn't look overly tall. About five feet ten or so, Simon reckoned.

He looked bulky, and solidly built, but again it was hard to tell in the dark, especially since he was dressed from top to toe in black. Black denims, Simon guessed, and a black anorak of some kind. And black leather gloves.

He couldn't see his face.

Briefly, Simon contemplated his options. If he waited, chummy might turn around, and let Simon get a good look at him. On the other hand, he might leave at any moment, in which case, he needed to get closer if he was to be in with a chance of making an arrest.

Silently, Simon Riggs stepped back into the shadows and carried on inching closer. He came to an old tumble-down wall, probably backing on to one of Thrupp's cottages, and needed to climb over it in order to carry on. He didn't like losing sight of the perp, but he had no choice. He was still not close enough to be sure of apprehending him, if his presence was spotted. His tricky back meant that he couldn't run as fast as he once could.

He climbed the low wall as quietly as he could, and emerged back onto the fringe of the car park within three minutes, at a rough estimation. He should now be within a few yards of Hillary Greene's parked car.

He felt the muscles in his legs and arms tense in preparation for sudden, physical effort. His heart rattled in his chest, and Simon Riggs tried to convince himself it had more to do with an ex-copper's excitement than an old man's fear.

Taking a deep, steady breath, he picked his spot, raised the binoculars, and checked one last time. If the perp had his back to him still, he'd rush out fast and give him a good whack with the old truncheon that he now transferred comfortingly into his right hand.

If the perp had turned around…. Well, then they'd see.

The old Volkswagen sprang into view. It was totally alone. The front driver's door was shut. It looked untouched.

'Shit,' Simon Riggs said. His binoculars quickly swung around, and he was just in time to catch sight of the perp disappearing into the road entrance at the pub.

Even from that distance, and in the dark, Simon Riggs could tell that the man moved fast and well. He had the look of a strong, fit man about him.

Simon pretended not to feel the relief that swept over him, and moved instead to Hillary Greene's car. He checked the door. It was locked again.

He didn't have a torch, so he couldn't look inside. Torches were a strict no-brainer for night-time obbo. A villain could spot a moron using a torch from miles off.

Feeling gloomy now, and with a growing sense of failure, Simon Riggs returned to his car, and reached for his mobile, which was sitting on the front dashboard. And regardless of the fact that it was now 1.30 in the morning he rang his pal Jimmy Jessop to report the sad tale of his cock-up.

Jimmy listened, sympathized and reassured his old mate that he'd done all that could be expected of him. Nobody, he said sharply, expected Simon to take on the perp single-handed. And at least the stalker hadn't attacked Hillary or tried to gain access to the boat, which was the main thing. Simon happily agreed to spend the rest of the night on obbo, although both of the old-timers doubted that the stalker would be back.

After hanging up, Jimmy called Steven Crayle.

'Any chance of there being any worthwhile forensics on the car?' was the first question Steven asked. Despite being woken in the middle of the night, he sounded alert and calm.

'No, sir, Simon reckoned he was wearing black leather gloves.'

'And he didn't see what the perp had been doing inside the car?'

'No, guv, no torch. I could ring him back and ask him to check. But if Hillary's awake, she might spot someone hanging around. And I don't think Simon can cope with any more action tonight.'

'No. Best to leave it. I'll ring her first thing in the morning and give her a head's-up about what she might find in the car. I'll also send a techie over first thing to see what he can get from it anyway. You never know your luck.'

'Right, guv,' Jimmy said. He didn't bother to ask if Crayle would go over there himself first thing in the morning, just to be with her when she found whatever 'present' the perp had left for her.

They could both guess how well she would take to being baby-sat.

The phone woke her before the birds had the chance to do so. Back when she'd been a full DI, getting an early morning summons hadn't been unheard of, but she'd grown used to her lie-ins.

But as she rolled over in her bed, squinting at her watch in the dawn light, she felt her pulse rate pick up a pace, as she reached for her mobile.

'Greene,' she said flatly.

'Hillary, Steven.'

Hillary thrust back the covers and swung her legs over the side of the bed. 'Sir?' she said cautiously. This didn't have the feel of a lover's solicitous enquiry.

'I've got a confession to make,' Steven began.

He's married, was her first instinctive thought. Which was quickly quashed. No way would he have been able to keep secret a second marriage – not from the nosy gossip-mongers at HQ.

'Oh?' she said cautiously.

'Since you came to me with the cross, I asked Jimmy if he and a few friends could keep an eye on you and your property at night. Last night, we had a near-miss.'

Briefly he explained what had happened. When he finished, there was a brief silence.

'You mad at me?' he asked.

Hillary thought about it, then sighed. 'No. I'd have done the same if one of my team had the same problem. I wish you'd told me, though.'

'Well, I'm telling you now,' Steven pointed out, a smile in his voice. 'I've got a fingerprints man on the way over there now. I don't suppose he'll come up with much, though. Get some kit off him and bag up the evidence and bring it in with you. I haven't gone to Donleavy yet, and I still want to keep this under the radar as much as possible. The dabs man owes me a favour, and he knows how to keep his mouth shut.'

'I hope Jimmy's pal does too,' Hillary said sourly.

'He assures me all his old pals know to keep schtum.'

'I'll get dressed and go see what's out there,' she said flatly. Then added in a softer tone, 'I'll call you back in a bit. Thanks.'

She dressed in a warm pair of black slacks and a cream polo-neck jumper. It was still chilly first thing in the morning, and she felt in need of some added warmth.

The towpath was quiet, as she'd expected. Nobody was up at this hour except for herself and Jimmy's pal. Wherever he'd hidden himself.

As she approached the car park, she saw a car pull away, and guessed that Jimmy had been told she was up and about and had warned his pal to scarper. That was fine with her. Whatever the stalker had left, she didn't want the whole world and his granny knowing about it.

Puff was parked just where she'd left him. A pale mint green, with just a few rusting patches for added character, he looked harmless. Of course, the likelihood of a bomb being planted inside him was remote in the extreme. They had no evidence that her stalker was an explosives expert, and even if he had been, she doubted that the perp would have had time to install it in a place where she wouldn't immediately see it. And according to the report that Jimmy's pal had given he could only have been in the car a few minutes at most.

Even so, she felt a cold hard fist clench in her stomach as she drew closer to her car. She took a few deep breaths.

She stepped up to the driver's side door and looked in.

And there, on the front driver's seat, was another cross – a duplicate of the one she'd found on her desk. Made of the same wood, it looked like, and carved into a point, it was the same size, and had three black initials poker-burned into the cross section.

Only this time the initials were MJV.

Another missing girl.

Another possible murder victim?

Just how many crosses, and how many sets of initials could there be?

'Oh, shit,' Hillary said softly.

It was gone nine by the time she pulled into the HQ car park, since the techie had taken his time and had been more than thorough. He'd taken plenty of samples from the car, hair, fibres and prints, but he and she were both pretty much convinced that they would all belong to herself, or maybe Sam, Jimmy or Vivienne.

She'd phoned Steven back the moment she'd spotted the cross and described it to him, so she wasn't surprised to see his office door standing open, waiting for her, as she came past.

She knocked briefly and stepped inside. He was already studying the paperwork in a folder. He looked up at her, his clear brown eyes also quickly reading her face. She knew she looked a little pale and a little tired. And probably a little tense too. 'It's nothing I can't handle,' she said flatly, reading his mind.

He nodded, respecting her professionalism in a way that both reassured her and, if she was to be honest, miffed her, just a bit. It would have been nice to be cosseted just a little – if only so she could tell him to leave it off.

'I had Handley run the initials straight away,' he said, by way of greeting.

She didn't really need to know if he'd had a hit, because he was already handing the file over to her. She took it and sat down, and he gave her a brief summary of what they'd found.

'Her name is Margaret Jane Vickary, known to her family and friends as Meg. She's been missing for four years,' Steven recited from memory. 'Divorced, no kids, she was a legal secretary with an Oxford firm. She had a flat share in Summertown with another professional woman, a dental hygienist. She had no family to speak of, both her parents being dead. It was her flatmate who reported her missing. She was believed to be having an affair with her married boss – this, again, from the flatmate. According to her, Meg was getting fed up with all his promises to leave his wife and kids and never delivering. The MisPer team thought it likely she'd simply given up waiting around and decided to leave for pastures new.'

'It's possible that she did,' Hillary pointed out. 'If she broke it off with the boss, he'd hardly be likely to give her much of a reference. I take it she never gave notice, just like Judith?'

'No,' Steven confirmed heavily. 'Nor did she collect the salary due to her. I've got Handley trying to find any trace of her, and I've asked him to try and cover the areas you couldn't manage on your own on the Judith Yelland case. He's promised a report as soon as he can. In the meantime—'

'We wait,' Hillary said heavily. 'If Meg Vickary has started again somewhere else, we'll find out about it.'

'I'm going to have to get a case file and preliminary review together and take it to Donleavy some time today. Tomorrow at the latest,' Steven pointed out.

'I know. If I ask him to let us have a shot at it – after all, the MisPers are cold cases – will you back me up?' she asked him quietly.

Steven looked at her in silence for a moment, at war with himself. On the one hand, it was shaping up to be a juicy case. Two missing women, maybe murder victims, and who knew how many more might be in the offing? Solving a serial killing that nobody even knew existed, and a cold-case one at that, was the sort of result that got officers noticed. And promoted.

On the other hand, the thought of Hillary actively turning the tables on her stalker by pursuing him as an on-going case, and putting herself in the firing line in the process, made him break out in a cold sweat.

'I don't want anything to happen to you,' he said.

Hillary smiled. 'That's not an answer.'

Steven smiled back. 'No, it's not, is it?' He tapped his fingers on the table top and thought for a while. Then he nodded. 'I'll back you up, as long as it's clear I'm SIO and we get more bodies on the ground to cover your arse.' He gave her a suddenly wicked smile. 'It's such a delightfully shaped arse, I don't suppose we'll go short of volunteers. Mind you, Donleavy almost certainly won't go for it, so don't get your hopes up.'

Hillary nodded. The commander certainly wouldn't like it, she knew. 'You leave Donleavy to me,' she said flatly.

'What are you going to do?' Steven asked, intrigued. He'd never quite understood the nature of the relationship that obviously existed between Donleavy and Hillary.

Hillary glanced at her watch.

'Well, right now, I'm going to review the Thompson file and go and interview more witnesses.'

Steven took the hint and gave a wry smile. 'OK. Keep me posted – on everything.'

'I will,' she promised.

She made herself a mug of coffee from his private stash, and kissed him hard and quick on the lips before she left. He looked satisfactorily both stunned and gratified by the unexpected assault.

Back in her office, she dragged her mind away from wooden crosses and forced herself to concentrate on the dead student.

On re-reading the murder book, she decided the Dwayne Cox situation could do with a second airing. She'd sensed at the time that something had been a little off about the good doctor. And since she had nothing better to do, she might as well rattle his cage and see what happened.

In the office, Jimmy looked at her a shade guiltily. He knew by now that she'd been told about his behind-her-back surveillance operation, and she smiled a 'hello' at him to show that there were no hard feelings.

With resignation her eyes alighted on Vivienne, who was sitting at her desk, of all things, actually buffing her nails. In all her years on the job, Hillary had never actually caught any female officer doing that particular chore.

'Vivienne, if I can tear you away from your work, would you like to pull the names of some of Dwayne Cox's ex-girlfriends, and we'll go and have a chat with them?'

Vivienne sighed and complied. Since hearing about the rumours about Hillary Greene and Steven Crayle, Hillary was definitely not her favourite person. She simply couldn't understand what the sexy super saw in Hillary. I mean, she had to be years older than him. Ugh!

Still, Hillary was her boss. So, with a few taps of her immaculately manicured nails on the keyboard, she managed to find two women who were still currently resident in Oxford.

'They'll do,' Hillary said, smiling as Vivienne shot her a dirty look.

CHAPTER ELEVEN

Angela Pryce worked in a branch of a nationwide branded coffee shop in Summertown. She was a tall, stick-thin brunette, dressed in dark-brown slacks, and wore a T-shirt bearing the coffee shop's logo. According to what little they knew of her, she'd never married, never run foul of the law, and was co-habitant with a man called Nathan Farrow, who worked in a car plant in Cowley.

Hillary and Vivienne took a corner table out of the way, with a pair of high stools settled around it, and after a quick perusal of the long list of drink options on the menu, decided on simple lattes.

Of the three waitresses and one waiter, the ex-girlfriend of Dwayne Cox was easy to spot. She had dyed red streaks into her long hair, and wore a multitude of gold chains around her somewhat scrawny neck. Although she could only be in her early thirties, Hillary, if she'd had to guess, would have put her closer to her forties. She had that tired, washed out, world-weary look of the middle-aged, but then Hillary wasn't altogether surprised. She doubted that the woman was working what amounted to a dead-end and busy job in the café for fun.

Just as she was thinking this, the pseudo-redhead spotted them and walked over.

'Miss Pryce?' Hillary asked. The waitress looked surprised, as well she might, since she wasn't wearing a name-tag on her T-shirt, and she obviously didn't know Hillary from Adam. Or Eve.

'Angie. What can I get you?' She probably asked the question automatically, and Hillary wondered if she did it in her sleep.

Hillary gave their orders, then showed her ID. Angela Pryce looked at first surprised and then wary.

'What's the CRT, then?' she asked, casting a quick look back towards the counter, obviously hoping that her boss hadn't seen the flash of the official ID.

'We work cold cases. We're currently taking another look at the Rowan Thompson murder. You were seeing a housemate of his around that time – Dwayne Cox?'

Angie's slightly worried look instantly cleared. 'Oh, yeah. Dwayne. Right. Gorky name, I always thought. Now there's a blast from the past, all right. But, come on, you don't think Dwayne did it, do you?' she half-laughed, half-frowned. ''Cause that's giving me the creeps, I can tell you.'

'It's just routine, Miss Pryce,' Hillary assured her, somewhat less than truthfully.

'Call me Angie. Hang on, let me get your orders, or I'll get it in the neck from Phil. I'll be back in a sec.'

Before Hillary could warn her that she'd need a few minutes of her time, she was gone. Beside her, Vivienne glanced around and cast the waiter a quick look. The lad looked to be in his late teens, early twenties, Hillary noted, and was a typical student trying to stretch the student loan by doing some part-time work. And although he was fairly good-looking, and caught Vivienne's scrutiny and returned it with an interested smile of his own, Hillary could see that the younger girl wasn't interested.

'Not your type, huh?' she asked, trying to be friendly, when Vivienne turned a cold shoulder his way.

'Not really. Besides, I've started seeing someone,' Vivienne acknowledged flatly.

Hillary smiled encouragingly. At least she'd stopped mooning over Steven, which would please him. 'Oh? Someone nice?' she fished.

'On the job,' Vivienne said, feeling pleased at being able to use some jargon at last. She'd heard someone say that on an American cop show recently, and was glad she'd remembered it. 'He's really buff, actually. Got muscles out to here,' she said, making a graphic gesture with her hands.

Hillary nodded, not really interested. Just then, Angie came back with their coffees.

'So, what can you tell me about Dwayne?' Hillary asked quickly, before she could just deposit them on the table and skedaddle.

'Oh, he was all right. Bit full of himself, but then, a lot of them are. They get into Oxford and think they're it.' Angie shrugged one thin shoulder, and glanced across towards the counter again. But her boss was busy taking money from a large family of Japanese tourists, and wasn't paying his staff much attention yet.

'I'm surprised you went out with him, then, if that's how you feel about it,' Hillary said drily.

Angie grinned. 'Yeah, well, I was younger and a lot more stupid then, wasn't I? Besides, Dwayne was good-looking. You seen him recently? What's he doing? Please tell me he's gone to seed and is working in Tesco's.'

Hillary grinned back. 'Sorry, he's working as a therapist in a posh clinic and is as handsome and smooth as ever.'

Angie grimaced and sighed. 'I thought as much. Wish I could have kept a hold of him, but it was never on the cards. We went about together for a month or so, then he went on to someone younger and prettier. But that was Dwayne,' she finished on a philosophical note.

'Did you ever meet Rowan, the boy who was murdered?' Hillary went on hopefully.

'Might have done. I remember reading about it – but Dwayne and I had finished by then, so probably not.'

'So you don't know how Dwayne took it?' Hillary asked regretfully.

'Nope. But knowing Dwayne, I don't suppose it did any lasting damage.' Then, catching her raised-eyebrow look, smiled grimly.

'I sound like a right sour bitch, don't I? And, to be fair, I think he was genuinely a mate of his. Dwayne always talked about him like they got on well, and all that. But, honestly, Dwayne was all about number one. He was determined to get a good degree, a good job, and a rich wife, in that order. He had, like, this life plan, and that was all that mattered to him.'

'He was ambitious?' Hillary clarified. Yes, that tallied with her memories of the slick operator she'd met at the clinic.

'Oh, yeah. Desperate for the good life, like the rest of us,' Angela confirmed with a snort. 'His mum and dad were only ordinary, like mine. But he was always determined to hang out with those who had money or class. And he liked to buy the best, no matter what it was. Food, clothes, the latest gadget. I suppose he felt he needed it, if he was going around with the sons of news-paper magnates and the other blue-nosed lot.'

Hillary nodded. 'And did he fit in with them? The elite, I mean?'

Angela smiled, somewhat whimsically. 'Oh, yeah. Funny thing, really, but he fitted in like he'd been born to it. That is, whenever we'd come across them, you know, the "in crowd",' here Angela made little comma movements with her hooked fingers, 'they'd always be pleased to see him. I could tell by their posh accents that they were well up there, and I half-expected them to look down their posh noses at us. But they never did. They always invited us to join them, and seemed to be glad Dwayne was there.'

Hillary nodded thoughtfully. Yes. And she had a good idea why. 'He took you to some nice places? He always had plenty of money, I suppose?' she asked craftily.

'Dwayne was always loaded. Not that he took me to Claridges or anything.' Angie laughed. 'In fact, we met some of the poshest people in the biggest dives. You know, how the well-off like to slum it?'

Hillary did.

'It always made me mad, that. Here I was, genuinely as poor as mouse droppings, and I wanted to go to the good places and live it up. And there they were, money to burn, and they wanted to hang out in dives. Stupid, if you ask me.'

Hillary smiled. 'Human nature, I'm afraid. The grass is always greener, and all that.'

'Yeah, I suppose. Look, I've gotta get back to work,' Angie said, noticing that the man who'd finished serving behind the counter was now staring at them.

'OK, Angie, thanks,' Hillary said, and took a sip of her coffee. The waitress nodded and resumed waiting on the other tables.

'So, what do you make of that?' Hillary asked Vivienne, who shrugged.

'It seemed like a waste of time to me,' Vivienne said grumpily. 'She never even met the murder victim.'

'But what she had to say about Dwayne was suggestive, wasn't it?' Hillary pressed, urging the girl to think.

'I dunno. She didn't like it that she was just a short-term fling. But then, if this Dwayne guy was good-looking and out to make a name for himself, she's hardly the sort of girl he'd hook himself permanently to, is she?' Vivienne said scornfully, giving Angie Pryce a dismissive glance.

Hillary sighed.

'She told us that Dwayne always seemed to have money,' she pointed out patiently. 'Now, think about it. If you're going to join the service, you have to cultivate a questioning mind. Never believe anything you're told unless you can confirm it to your own satisfaction. And always ask the who, how, when and why of it. Take this interview, for instance. How could a student, bogged down by loans, and coming from a strictly working-class background, always be loaded with money?'

Vivienne looked up over her coffee and thought about it reluctantly.

'Either he was having it off with ugly women for cash, or it was drugs, I suppose.'

Hillary nodded and smiled. 'OK. It's possible Dwayne was a

male pro – he had the looks for it – but given the fact that Angie told us that the posh people always seemed glad to see him, and accepted him willingly into their golden circle…. What does that say?'

'That he was more likely their drug supplier,' Vivienne said promptly. 'Big deal. I expect there's always plenty of them around Oxford.'

'Yes,' Hillary agreed, fighting back the urge to take the surly girl by the shoulders and shake some of the apathy out of her. 'But our murder victim Rowan had traces of an unspecified drug in his system when he died. And Dwayne Cox was one of his housemates.'

'But even if Dwayne did keep Rowan supplied with a high whenever he wanted one, he didn't die of a drugs overdose, did he?' Vivienne pointed out in triumph.

'No. But it might yet be relevant. Suppose they had a falling out and Rowan threatened to shop Dwayne to the cops?'

'That would be a motive, all right,' Vivienne conceded. She took a sip of her coffee as Hillary withdrew her mobile from her bag. 'Who're you calling?' she asked, showing some genuine interest at last.

'I have a pal in Narcotics. He asked me to keep him informed if I came across anything he could use,' Hillary explained.

'But that was all years ago,' Vivienne protested. 'I told you, when I first contacted the Drugs Squad, they told me it was nothing doing. It was all too long ago and vague for them to give a rat's arse.'

Hillary sighed again and began to press the digits. 'Think about it, Vivienne: where does Dwayne Cox work now?'

'Some fancy clinic. A relaxation place, or some such, for rich twits who want to chill out— Oh,' she added, in sudden realization.

'Exactly,' Hillary said succinctly. 'He's a doctor, with an eye to the main chance, who likes to make money, and one, moreover, who has regular access to a stream of rich people who want to "chill out".'

'You think he's a Dr Feelgood?' Vivienne said, nodding her head and stirring some more sugar into her coffee.

'Almost certainly. Once a drug pusher, always a drug pusher.' Hillary offered the maxim for what it was worth. Which, in Vivienne's case, probably wasn't much.

She keyed in the number of her mate and listened to the phone connect. When he answered, she gave him a brief, quiet update on what she had, careful not to be overheard in the busy shop. Vivienne half-listened and half-watched the waiter who was giving her some more interested smiles.

He was all right, Vivienne supposed, but he was hardly in Tom's class.

When she'd first met Tom she'd been impressed by his pecs, but little else. He wasn't as old as she liked her men, or as powerful. He was certainly no Steven Crayle, for instance. He lacked the super's stunning good looks and polish.

But since that initial meeting in the cafeteria he'd taken her out once or twice, and he'd sort-of grown on her. He wasn't so young that he was daft, like a lot of the uniforms his age. And his green eyes were really sexy as hell. Funnily enough, he hadn't seriously come on to her yet. Not that she'd mind getting more up close and personal, but it was up to him to make the first move.

And the fact that he hadn't done so yet was beginning to intrigue her. Was it possible, in this day and age, that he was a gentleman? That he was a genuine romantic, who wanted to do things the old-fashioned way? If so, he was the first one Vivienne had ever come across.

With some reluctance, Vivienne turned her attention back to what her boss was doing.

'So if you keep an eye on the clinic, and trace his source, you could get a nice little coup out of it,' Hillary was saying. 'And I wouldn't be at all surprised if a Dr Marcie Franks wasn't involved in it somewhere. I have an idea she was probably his fixer when he was up at Oxford. ... What? ... Yes, a biochemist. And I can't see any reason why they wouldn't have continued their trade once they'd both graduated. A quick background check on her finances will soon tell you whether or not she's living above her means.'

Hillary smiled at something the other guy said, and Vivienne drained her mug. She still couldn't for the life of her see what Steven Crayle saw in Hillary Greene. Not when he could have had her. She was years younger, and much hotter.

Still, he'd lost his chance. She wasn't the sort to hang around and pine forever. Somehow she'd have to invite Tom down to the office and show him off. Make Steven understand he was not the only fish in the sea. Who knew, if he got jealous enough, she might even give him a second chance.

After all, this fling he was having with wrinkly Hillary couldn't last for long, could it?

'And I'm sure your guv'nor would be well pleased shutting up operations on a swanky outfit like that place,' Hillary was still chatting into the phone. 'I don't know a copper alive who doesn't like to see the complacent middle classes come a cropper. You'll be on his Christmas card list for a couple of years at least.' Hillary laughed, listened some more, said, 'No trouble. Don't forget, you owe me,' and hung up.

Then the younger girl felt Hillary's sherry-coloured eyes on her and felt herself instinctively sit up a bit straighter and pay attention. 'You'll discover that it pays to give out and call in favours from as many friends and sources within the service as you can find,' she said. 'It's how the system works. And remember, you're here to take the villains down. Whether you do it yourself, or can help out a mate to do it, it makes no difference in the end.'

Vivienne tried to look impressed.

Hillary looked at her, knew without doubt that she was simply wasting her time and effort, sighed again and drained her coffee. 'Come on. We'll give the other girlfriend a miss. I think we got all we needed to know from Angie.'

'Right, guv,' Vivienne agreed, without much interest.

Hillary drove back to HQ in thoughtful silence. As they walked through the lobby and down into the basement, she told Vivienne to type up a report on the Angie Pryce interview and log it into the murder book. Then she followed the younger girl into the shared office and nodded at Jimmy Jessop.

'Jimmy, a quick word. Actually, it's nearly lunchtime, fancy a pint?'

'Always, guv,' the old-timer said with a smile.

'Don't let the brass hear you admit to that,' Hillary shot back with a grin of her own. 'Afterwards, we'll take a jaunt out to Kebler Road. I want to talk to Wanda Landau again.'

Vivienne watched them sourly as they headed out. All cosy and pals together! As if she cared. She sighed, turned to the computer and started to type up the report. Then she noticed she had email, saw that it was from Tom and smiled widely as she read it.

Hillary Greene was not the only one who lunched outside the office. Eagerly she grabbed her coat and bag and fled, the report on her morning's activities unfinished and already forgotten.

Hillary bought Jimmy his pint and a pie, and opted for the ploughman's and a cider shandy for herself. As she bought the loaded tray carefully back to their window-seat table, she heard her phone beep.

She was probably the only person she knew who didn't have a tuneful or comic ring tone on her phone. She put down the tray, took a sip from her glass and called up her messages.

Jimmy quickly tucked into his pie, just in case they had to shift. He'd lost count, over the years, of the number of times he'd had to eat on the run.

Hillary read the message briefly, frowned, then shrugged, and flipped the phone shut.

'Work?' Jimmy asked curiously, taking a hefty gulp of his beer.

Hillary nodded. She rarely got personal messages nowadays. 'But it can wait until we've eaten. It's not urgent,' she said, then smiled as the older man shot her an up-from-under look. 'Relax,

Jimmy. I'm not about to read you the riot act. Now, tell me about your mate and what happened last night.'

As Jimmy and Hillary quietly discussed her stalker, in a pub just a few hundred yards away, Vivienne accepted a glass of white wine and a plate of crab salad from Tom Warrington.

'This pub's nice. I've never been here before,' Vivienne said, glancing around. 'Is this the one with the reputation for being a gastropub?'

Tom smiled and shrugged. He'd taken off his tell-tale jacket, and in his plain white shirt and black trousers, nobody would immediately take him for a copper at first glance.

'I like to eat well.' He himself had selected a portion of steamed salmon on a bed of wild rice. 'So, how's your morning been?'

Vivienne rolled her eyes but told him. She kind-of liked it that he was so interested in her work in CRT and liked it even more that he was so obviously envious. 'I know you keep on telling me how you'd give your left arm to work down there, but seriously, it's right boring,' she finished. 'Take this morning, for instance. The girlfriend of one of the murdered man's housemates – what was the point of talking to her? We didn't learn anything new. Well, a bit, about the drugs maybe....' She paused to take a bit of dressed crab.

'Come on, that's got to be better than working in admin like poor old me,' Tom said with a smile. 'What's she going to do next, then?'

Vivienne shrugged. 'I dunno. Oh, yeah, she's going back to talk to the landlady. Who the bloody hell knows why, though – I mean, what can the old bat tell her anyway? If you ask me, Hillary Greene's no great shakes, no matter what her reputation is.'

Tom felt his smile tighten on his face, but he leaned back in his chair and let his foot nudge hers under the table. 'Taste the wine. It's Italian. Like it?'

Vivienne took a sip, and agreed that she did. She didn't normally like wine, preferring breezers and cocktails. Wine could be too sharp for her palate. But this one tasted sort-of creamy, and reminded her vaguely of vanilla.

Tom watched her eat and fought back his impatience. So Hillary was going back to Kebler Road. But right at the moment, she was out with old man Jessop, having lunch. Perfect. He knew just what to do next.

'I'm afraid we haven't got long. I don't get a full hour for my lunch break. What say we meet up again tonight sometime, and have dessert then?' he asked, forcing himself to smile like a lovesick calf.

Vivienne smiled over her wineglass. 'Got that line from a film, did you?' she teased.

Tom laughed and nodded. 'Damn, you noticed. I was hoping to sound smooth.'

'Play your cards right, and I might even give you coffee afterwards,' she said, this time doing the nudging with her foot under the table.

Tom tensed, and reminded himself it was all for Hillary. But this stupid, fatuous girl was seriously beginning to get on his nerves.

He wasn't sure how much longer he could put up with her. He wanted it to be Hillary sitting opposite him, laughing, talking, sharing wine, with that look of promise in her eyes.

She had to hurry up and solve her case soon or he would go mad. He could feel the frustration building up inside him. He just had to hold her in his arms soon. The moment, the very moment, her case was over, he'd make his move.

His heart pounded the more he thought of it. How would she react, their first time together? Would she be scared? Would she struggle? Or would she know, would she *understand*, and be sweet to him? He felt himself break out in a cold sweat.

'So how's the case going?' he asked, hoping that the desperation he felt wasn't too apparent in his voice. 'I bet she'll make an arrest any time soon, right?'

*

Their lunch finished, Hillary drove them back towards HQ. 'I'm going to have another word with Wanda Landau, see if she had any idea about Dwayne Cox being Rowan's go-to man for his highs.'

Jimmy nodded. 'If she was aware of there being drugs in the house, she might have had something to say about it. Specially with her fighting for custody of the kiddie, like.'

'That's what I was thinking,' Hillary agreed. She couldn't seriously see it, though. From what she remembered of the set-up, the landlady lived a fairly separate life from the students, being down in the basement and out of the way. Besides, surely Rowan and Dwayne would have been careful to be discreet. Still, at this point, she couldn't afford to overlook even the remotest leads.

'But first, something interesting might have come up. Want to take a brief trip to Traffic?' she asked.

Jimmy didn't, particularly, but knew she must have her reasons, so nodded contentedly. Besides, the pie and pint had gone down well.

Her reason for dropping in on the Traffic Division had just been seen to by a bored officer, and they were just in time to hear Darla de Lancie get a fine and several points added to her driving licence for driving without due care and attention.

Her telephone message had been from Sam, who'd picked up on the motoring offence thanks to a red-flag being sent down to CRT. She guessed that he'd fed the names of the main players in the Rowan Thompson case to Handley, and asked that a computer watch be put out, so that anything interesting on their suspect pool came to their notice straight away.

'Darla, hello again,' Hillary said, as Rowan Thompson's one-time girlfriend began to trudge down the steps towards them. She skidded to a somewhat comical stop, and a brief look of dismay crossed her face as she spotted the two of them.

Her eyes flickered from Hillary to Jimmy again, then restlessly, to the space behind them, and lingered longingly on the door and the freedom it promised.

Like a well-oiled machine, and in perfect silence, Hillary and Jimmy each took a tiny step towards each other, blocking the other woman's egress.

'I heard about the motoring thing,' Hillary said, making her voice sound both sympathetic and soothing. 'I hope it wasn't anything serious? No one was hurt?'

'What? Oh, no, nothing like that, thank… No. I just reversed into one of those bollard things. I wasn't drunk or anything. I blew into the bag and all that.' Darla tried for a nonchalant laugh, but didn't quite bring it off. 'I was just unlucky that a policeman was there and saw…. Oh, well, what's it matter? I'm normally a very careful driver. This is the first time I've ever had anything like this happen, so….'

She paused for breath, and Hillary smiled. Darla looked tired and pale and was acting very jittery. She might not have been drinking, but she could see why the traffic officer had been suspicious of her manner. She seemed to be all over the place. Not to mention, incapable of finishing a sentence properly.

'Do you want to go somewhere for a cup of tea? Sorry to mention it, but you seem a little stressed out,' Hillary said. 'I imagine things have been preying on your mind a bit just lately?'

'Yes. Well, obviously this thing with Rowan, to be honest. I still haven't told my husband about it, and I don't want to, but I keep thinking … oh well, it doesn't matter.'

Her inability to focus for more than a moment or two made Hillary wonder just how stressed she was. And why.

'Is there something you wanted to tell me, perhaps? About Rowan, or what happened back then?' she coaxed gently.

'What?' Darla went, if anything, even paler than before. 'No. No, of course not, there's nothing to tell. I mean, I told you everything before. It's just … the baby's teething, and now this stupid thing with the car, and I've got to get the tail light fixed and I'm just tired, that's all. It's not that I'm feeling guilty. About Rowan, I mean. I mean, I have nothing to feel guilty about.' Darla took a deep breath, and then made a determined move to walk around

Hillary and Jimmy on the steps in front of her. 'Anyway, I have to get back. I can still drive, can't I?'

'Of course, you can,' Hillary agreed. 'You weren't banned from driving or anything.'

'Right. I've got the car outside. I mean, it's not as if I've been banned or anything, is it. Sorry— that's what you just said, isn't it? Really, I don't know what made me say something so silly. Please, forget I said that, will you?' she asked, all in one breathless rush, then turned and all but ran for the door.

Hillary and Jimmy watched her go, both of them somewhat bemused.

'She's heading for a nervous breakdown at the rate she's going, guv.' Jimmy wasn't above stating the obvious.

'Yes,' Hillary agreed. But was it just down to sleepless nights, a teething baby, and the stress of keeping her past from catching up with her and her new husband? Or was something else troubling the woman?

'Could be a guilty conscience maybe?' Jimmy unerringly mirrored her thoughts. 'Not all killers are the cold-blooded type. If she did off her boyfriend, and now the chickens are coming home to roost, she might be up for a bit of confessing, if we press a bit?'

Hillary thought about it. 'Maybe. But we need something to press with, don't we? And so far, we've got nothing new. Best leave it for now.'

Tom Warrington was parked well back from Wanda Landau's house in Kebler Road, but he saw Hillary's old Volkswagen the moment it turned into the road. It was as if he was somehow attuned to her. He seemed to spend his every moment looking out for her, hoping for a glimpse. His heart beat faster and he leaned forward eagerly in the seat, anxious to see her.

He loved this part of the courtship. It was all so new and exciting. He felt like one of those lovers in the poems he'd started reading about recently. Hillary had been right to take a BA in English Literature. Keats had been a revelation to him.

It was yet another thing he had to thank her for.

Now he was looking forward to watching her find her next gift. He'd gone to some trouble to set the stage for it this time. Wouldn't she be surprised?

He watched her park and get out of the car, his heart falling to see the grey-haired figure of Jimmy Jessop emerge from the passenger seat. Damn. He'd rather she'd been on her own.

He watched them walk towards 8 Kebler Road, and wished he could have parked closer to get a better view. He'd have liked to have seen her face when she realized how clever he'd been. He briefly contemplated getting out of the car and walking casually down the road. He could easily cast a quick look into the garden as he went by the gate, and if she'd been alone, he might have done it.

But not now.

Still, he could imagine the scene, and he smiled, his green eyes flashing with glee. Then he quickly turned on the engine of his car and drove away. Once she'd found his present, she'd be clever enough and quick enough to scan the street for anyone watching, and a lone male in a parked car would be bound to draw her eye. She'd take down his licence plate and that would move things on to the next level much too quickly.

No, he would never underestimate her. It would be an insult to her.

Besides, they were having so much fun, weren't they? He didn't want it to end just yet, and he was sure she didn't, either. And the growing pressure he could feel to finally consummate their courtship was exquisite as well as painful. Already he was dreaming of the scenario every night. He'd even bought a black ski mask and gloves in preparation.

Tomorrow, he'd take a good look around Thrupp and scope out the best place to grab her.

As Tom Warrington drove away, banging his hands against the steering wheel in a frenzy of frustration and anticipation, Hillary pushed open the gate to number 8 and started to head towards the place where Rowan Thompson had lost his life.

Her eyes went from the path, to the steps leading down to the basement flat, and stopped there. She didn't even lower her eyes any further.

Because, there on the first step, was a wooden cross.

She stopped dead on the path, so abruptly, that Jimmy actually walked into the back of her.

'Oops, sorry, guv.'

Hillary said nothing.

Jimmy, wondering what the hold-up was, followed her line of sight, and saw the two pieces of carved wood. He swore softly.

Over their pie and pint, she'd bought him fully up to date on what had been happening, so he knew just what the strange offering meant.

Slowly, Hillary removed a plastic evidence bag from her pocket and walked forward. The cross was the same as the others, save for the initials.

This time, in black poker-work, she found herself looking at the initials GGT.

Another missing girl.

Maybe another dead girl.

Beside her, Jimmy watched her retrieve the cross, using the bag to pick it up and store it, and swore softly again. Although he hadn't blamed Simon for not nabbing the stalker when he had the chance, he wouldn't be human if he didn't find himself suddenly wishing that it was all over already.

This was the first time Jimmy had seen one of the crosses for himself, and it was giving him a very unpleasant feeling deep inside his gut.

This was nasty. And getting nastier.

'We'd better take this straight back to Steven,' Hillary said. 'We'll talk to Wanda another day.'

'Right, guv,' Jimmy said quietly. He looked at her anxiously, but she looked merely grim-faced and a little pale. It made him admire her quiet stoicism, but he was under no illusions as to how she must really be feeling about this latest episode. If it was making him feel churned up inside, it must be so much worse for her.

One thing was for sure: she was going to need someone to start watching her back on a round-the-clock basis from now on.

And he was sure that Steven Crayle was going to agree with him.

CHAPTER TWELVE

They were called to gather together in Steven's office the moment Sergeant Handley had done his computer magic. Luckily it didn't take long, now that he knew what he was looking for.

The moment Jimmy and Hillary walked through his door, they could tell by the look on the superintendent's face that GGT wasn't a bluff on the killer's part.

'Her name,' Steven began tersely, the moment they were seated, 'is Gillian Gale Tinkerton. She's been missing for nearly two years.' He tossed the computer printout to Hillary, who scanned it, even as Steven summed up the findings. 'He seems to be taking them roughly every two years or so.'

'At least there's no escalation yet, then,' Hillary said. Which was some comfort. Serial killers – if that's what they were dealing with – sometimes followed a pattern, whereby their killings started out few and far between, but then gained pace.

Steven nodded. 'There is that. As you can see, Gillian was twenty-nine when she went missing.'

Hillary glanced at the attached photograph and saw a slightly plump, pretty redhead with attractive freckles and big blue eyes.

'He doesn't seem to have a set physical type,' Hillary offered, for what that was worth. 'Age range is fairly consistent, though, until you get to me. Geographically they're all local to the area, but otherwise, don't seem to belong to the same demographic.'

'I agree. Gillian comes from a middle-class background, but

seems to have always considered herself to be a bit of a dropout,' Steven continued, mainly for Jimmy's benefit now, as Hillary quickly scanned the initial report. 'She was always trying out alternative lifestyles, according to those who knew her best, and even did a stint with some New Age travellers. She stuck with them for a while, apparently, but evidently couldn't hack it. She returned home to her parents a year or so later, who, by all accounts, were beginning to get thoroughly fed-up with her lifestyle choices by then.'

'So when she went missing, they thought she'd just got itchy feet again,' Hillary said, noticing that it had taken them six months before they'd reported her missing. It explained the delay.

'Right,' Steven agreed. 'They just assumed she'd turn up some-time with her tail between her legs and a story about running away to join a circus,' he confirmed.

'Except she never did turn up again,' Hillary said quietly, handing him back the file.

'No,' he agreed flatly. And met her eyes. One of them was going to have to say it, and it might as well be him. 'We now have three missing women, who for various reasons *might* have wanted to run away under their own steam, and *might* have succeeded in starting a new life for themselves somewhere. Or they might be dead.'

The last sentence lay flat and heavy in the room.

'And if they're dead, it's a pretty good bet that my stalker is the one responsible for it,' Hillary added calmly, determined to match his matter-of-fact professionalism. And there was no point in flinching away from it. She was potentially in big trouble, and they both knew it.

'And if he is, then he's playing games with you,' Steven carried on heavily. 'He wants you to know what's been happening and he's inviting you to take part. He's offering to play cat-and-mouse with you.'

'Either that, or he's just following his usual pattern,' Hillary pointed out. 'Perhaps all the other girls had gifts and texts to begin with. Then, when they didn't respond, the gifts turned to threats of one kind or another. In my case, the crosses. Who knows what the others received.'

'In that case, you're his next target,' Steven said grimly. 'I've set up an appointment with Commander Donleavy for four-thirty this afternoon. I've put together a file. For a start, we need to get you some round-the-clock protection, starting today.'

Hillary nodded. She didn't like it, but he was right. 'OK.'

Steven nodded, pleased but not particularly surprised that she was being so sensible and so calm about it, and then glanced across at Jimmy. 'So, how's the Thompson case coming on?' he asked. As a change of subject, it wasn't inspired, but he could sense that Hillary needed a little breathing space, and he knew that work was the best cure there was for her at the moment.

'We're plugging away, sir,' Jimmy said. 'Trouble is, we don't seem to be getting anywhere. As Inspector Gorman's investigation showed, there were plenty of people with a grievance against Rowan, with his girlfriend and Barry Hargreaves being the leading contenders, but so far we haven't come up with anything new.'

Steven nodded. 'Well, don't get too downhearted. It was only to be expected – this case was hindered by lack of evidence when it was fresh, so it's hardly surprising if we don't crack it this time round. Your success with your first case has probably given you a false sense of what can and can't be done. Believe me, I've never been holding my breath on this one. Sometimes you just have to admit defeat and move on. There are other cases to be looked at.'

'We're not finished here yet,' Hillary said stubbornly. 'The sticking point seems to be finding a motive that really makes sense. Nobody has an alibi, nobody seems to know anything, anybody *might* have done it. I felt it before, and I feel it even more strongly now: we've somehow missed something. Something weighty. Something with some proper meat on it.'

Hillary could hear the frustration in her voice as she spoke, but there was little she could do about it. The case *was* going nowhere fast. If only she could find just one person who had a real, solid reason for wanting the feckless, charming, predatory Rowan dead.

But she could find nobody around him who had anything to lose, important enough to be worth killing over. Would Barry Hargreaves really kill because his teenage daughters were starting to experiment sexually? Would Darla finally snap at all his infidelities, when she'd lived with them right from the start? Would Dwayne Cox really be scared into committing murder if Rowan had threatened to tell anyone about the drugs? After all, why would he? And it would have to be proved, and Cox would have been careful. And would Marcie get into a murderous rage just because Rowan kept trying to entice her lover away?

It all seemed too petty or nebulous. Not one of her suspects had any powerful, emotional, human, gut-wrenching reason to kill. That was the problem.

And then it hit her. Right there and then, as they sat in Steven's office, trying not to think about three missing and maybe murdered girls, and about the man who was stalking her so expertly.

Perhaps because she'd been thinking of something totally different, giving her subconscious a chance to work unhindered, she suddenly knew exactly who must have murdered Rowan, and why.

'I need my arse kicking,' Hillary said angrily.

Steven and Jimmy looked at her. 'Any particular reason?' Steven finally asked, amused.

'Because I should have known right from the start, and I mean the very start, who killed Rowan, and why,' she said flatly.

And told them.

When she'd finished, Steven rolled a pencil between his fingers restlessly. Jimmy was silent, cogitating. 'I'm not saying you're wrong,' Steven began cautiously. 'But it's going to be tricky. Very tricky. We haven't got a shred of proof, and aren't likely to get one at this late stage.'

'No,' Hillary agreed grimly. 'This is going to be a confession job, or the killer walks,' she stated boldly.

They were silent for a moment or two, thinking about this, and then Steven checked his watch. 'Do we move now or do we wait?'

'There's no point in waiting,' Hillary said, after a moment's thought.

'I agree. Do you have a strategy for interview?' he asked curiously. After all, she was right: if they didn't get a confession, the case would stay officially unsolved, even if all concerned were sure that they knew who the guilty party was. Which meant the up-coming interview was make or break for them. Not to mention the difference between justice, or not, for Rowan and his family.

Hillary shrugged helplessly. 'I play it by ear. What else can I do?' she asked. She was taking it for granted that she would take the lead on this, and with good reason. Steven didn't want the job – why would he, when she was known for her interview technique? Besides, it was her case, and woe betide anyone who tried to take it from her now!

Steven took a deep breath and nodded. 'OK. Let's do it,' he said.

In the mysterious way of things, it was quickly all over the station house that Hillary Greene had a hot lead on her case. Seemingly by osmosis, the desk sergeant caught scent of it on the wind and told someone from the Fraud Squad, who was having a belated meal with his mate in admin in the café and, before the hour was out, everyone knew she was on the point of yet another stunning success.

Tom Warrington was just going off shift when he overheard two old-timers from Juvie grumbling about how Hillary Greene had managed to close yet another murder case.

'I hear she's pulling in the prime suspect now. Whoever it is, the bastard doesn't stand a chance. I saw her interviewing a right scag once. She reduced him to pulp,' one of them said to the other.

But Tom didn't even pause to hear what the reply was. Suddenly, he was all but running for his car, barely able to keep the smile from his face. For so long now, he'd been denying himself the ultimate treat. But no more. Now, at last, it was here.

He knew just what he was going to do, and where he was going to do it.

His heart rate thumped. Before the day was out, he was going to hold Hillary Greene in his arms. And where it all went from there.... He felt his throat go deliciously dry. Well, that was up to Hillary.

Tom raced away to pick up his ski mask, gloves, and the large hunting knife he kept razor-sharp.

The first problem Hillary had to face was who to take into the interview room with her. Protocol said there had to be two, but it was tricky. Jimmy had gone to ask their suspect to come in for interview and, since he hadn't phoned back, there didn't seem to be any trouble about her being in any way uncooperative. Not that Hillary had expected that there would be.

Not yet, anyway.

But even if Jimmy brought her in without raising any undue alarm, she didn't think he was the best choice to sit in whilst she tried to get a confession. The suspect might see the presence of an older man as some sort of reprimand for her past behaviour.

Normally, of course, Vivienne would be an ideal choice, giving them an all-female gathering. And Vivienne wouldn't be seen as a particular threat or pose any sort of censure. The trouble was, Hillary didn't trust Vivienne as far as she could throw her. The other girl was bound to let her feelings show, and they wouldn't be kind ones either.

Sam Pickles was out of the question – not that Hillary didn't think it would do him good to get the experience, nor was she worried about him not keeping quiet, or letting his reactions adversely affect what was going to be a very tricky interview indeed. It was just that, as a good-looking young man, he had far too much in common with the murder victim to be viable.

Which left Steven.

And Steven, as, technically, the only serving and actively instated police officer on the team, also made sense. He alone had the power to arrest, anyway.

As they stood in the viewing room, waiting for their suspect to arrive, she glanced across at him. She still found him something of an enigma.

He was her brand-new lover. And her boss. She had no illusions about his ambition, and applauded it. She was no idiot, and knew that, at first, he'd only accepted her into his team because Commander Donleavy was a fan of hers and had probably twisted his arm. But she was fairly sure that he'd come to respect her strengths, and had confidence in her abilities still.

And he was obviously ready to start some sort of relationship with her. But what chance, realistically, did they have? Did he see this thing they had going as just a short-term affair? Or was he after something more? And if he was, how did she tackle that?

Sensing her scrutiny, he turned and looked at her, and again her heart picked up a pace. It made her exceedingly cross. OK, so he was physically gorgeous. And a fair few years younger than herself. Was that any reason to feel like a schoolgirl again?

Suddenly, she wondered if she was having a mid-life crisis. If she'd been a man, would she now have been thinking about buying a sports car and acquiring a twenty-something blonde bimbo with big boobs? Was Steven really her equivalent?

Or was she actually falling in love for only the second time in her life?

Given that the only other time she'd done so, she'd ended up married to Ronnie Greene, the thought did little to settle her already challenged nerves.

'A penny for them,' Steven said softly, his beautiful brown eyes watching her closely.

Not bloody likely, Hillary thought, and smiled one of her best smiles.

'Just to get things sorted out before we go in, sir,' she said, the last word firmly putting him in his place – which, right now, was her boss, 'I'm lead interview, yes?'

'Yes. You want me to sit in with you?' he guessed. Like her, he'd been reviewing the options, and had come to the same conclusions. She liked it that they thought the same, and seemed to fit together so well. On the other hand, it made her feel as nervous as hell. If it had taken him only a month or so to get to know her professionally so well, how long would it take him to start understanding how the rest of her ticked? The thought brought her out in a cold sweat.

'You think she'll feel more comfortable with me than any of the others?' he added, not understanding her prolonged silence.

Hillary quickly snapped out of it and got her mind back on the job. 'Yes, I think so. Of us all, you represent the least embarrassing option, as it were,' she agreed.

Steven nodded. 'You want me sit there, above all be quiet, and look as non-judgemental as possible, I suppose?'

'Right.' Again, he'd read her mind.

'OK. By the way, I've put back our meeting with Donleavy by an hour.'

'That's fine. I'm not thinking of prolonging this. If we don't get a confession within an hour anyway, we won't be getting one. And there's no way we can stretch it out, otherwise any solicitor will have a field day,' Hillary agreed.

Steven sighed. 'You're not looking forward to this,' he said, a statement more than a question.

'Not particularly,' Hillary said grimly. 'But it has to be done.'

Just then the door opened and Sam and Vivienne came in. Vivienne was looking excited, Hillary noticed. Sam looked far more subdued.

'They're here,' Vivienne said cheerfully.

'Right. You two, stay and watch,' she said flatly.

'Yes, pay attention and learn,' Steven added, making Sam almost come to attention. Vivienne shot him a hot look. No doubt she liked it when he was coming over all authoritarian. Beside her, Hillary could almost feel Steven give a mental roll of his eyes.

They left the two youngsters in the viewing room and walked into interview room three. They both sat down. A minute or two later, Jimmy Jessop opened the door and ushered in Wanda Landau.

Steven, seeing her for the first time, looked surprised. He knew the landlady was approaching seventy-four years old, but hardly looked it. She was dressed in a smart, mint-green linen suit, with narrow trousers and a jacket with a deep lapel, edged in emerald velvet. Underneath it, she wore a silky cream blouse, and a simple gold chain with a single pearl drop. Discreet pearl studs were in her ears, and her ash-blonde hair had been washed and immaculately set.

As she had when Hillary had first interviewed her, the woman barely looked sixty. Indeed, most would probably have guessed her age to be in the mid-fifties. Furthermore, Steven mused, as he pulled out a chair for the older woman to sit down, ten years ago she must have looked even better. She had the classic bone structure of a woman who'd always been beautiful.

Hillary set the tape recorder going, introduced herself and Steven and stated the time. Wanda, hearing the words 'Superintendent Steven Crayle' went slightly paler beneath the perfect make-up, but otherwise showed no other signs of alarm.

But she must be wondering why she'd been brought into HQ. And now was being interviewed by a very senior police officer.

She sat on her chair with her legs crossed, her handbag on the table in front of her and her hands clasped together neatly in her lap.

This, Hillary thought again, is not going to be easy. She had to try and think of Wanda as a delicate nut that needed cracking, which meant she needed to find just the right pressure points and give some very gentle taps. Setting about her with a crude hammer was definitely not what was called for here.

'Mrs Landau, thank you for coming in,' she began with a gentle smile. Wanda glanced at her, somewhat surprised to find that it was Hillary who spoke first. Of course, women of her generation would automatically think that the power lay with the man in the room.

A woman of her generation. Yes, Hillary thought. She had to appreciate just who she was dealing with here. A fairly well-heeled, former farmer's daughter. She'd had a good education, been a wife and a mother, and was a woman who was used to a steady order and a 'rightness' about how things were done.

'That's perfectly all right, Mrs Greene,' Wanda replied politely.

Hillary smiled. 'As you know, this is about Rowan's case.'

Wanda nodded. 'Of course.'

'Since I spoke to you last, we've been talking to everyone who knew Rowan: the other students in the house at the time, outside friends and, of course, his poor family.'

Hillary, who was watching her closely, saw the skin around her eyes contract just slightly at the mention of the word 'family'.

Of course. It would. Her own family had been the major source of disappointment, pain and joy in her life. It was the first little pressure point she needed.

She sighed. 'I'm afraid Mrs Thompson hasn't coped well,' she said regretfully. 'Her husband seemed much stronger, of course, but then men often are, aren't they?' she continued gently, almost chattily. 'They tend to keep a stiff upper lip, and hold it all in.'

'It's different for mothers,' Wanda said, then cleared her throat. Her voice had sounded tight and artificial to her ears, and she shot Hillary a quick, casual smile. But there was fear in her eyes, and Hillary felt her own nerves stretch tighter. As Steven had guessed, she wasn't looking forward to this.

'May I pour you a glass of water, Mrs Landau?' she said and, without waiting for an answer, poured a glass for the old lady and set it in front of her.

Wanda smiled her thanks but made no move to touch it.

Hillary suspected she wasn't confident that her hands wouldn't be shaking.

'Yes, I've noticed that it's always the mothers who suffer the most,' Hillary said. 'As you can imagine, after serving thirty years with the police, I've seen my share of horrors. And it's not only the mothers of the victims who have to pay, either. People tend not to think about it, but the mothers of the guilty parties go through hell as well.'

Wanda blinked. 'You're right. I hadn't thought of that.'

'But in Mrs Thompson's case – well, as you yourself know, there's nothing worse than losing a child. In fact,' Hillary carried on, still in that soft, gently chatting voice, 'you and Mrs Thompson have a lot in common. You both lost teenage children. Although in your case, I understand you simply don't know where your daughter is?'

'No. That's right,' Wanda said. 'Sometimes I think she's alive somewhere, maybe living a decent and good life with a man. That she managed to straighten herself out, maybe even married and started another family. Other times, I'm sure she's dead.'

She paused, and then shifted slightly in her seat.

'Of course, Mrs Thompson at least knows what happened to her son,' Hillary carried on softly. Then, just when Wanda was nodding, put in deftly, 'although that's small comfort to her when she has no idea why he was killed. And to her, the thought that her son's murderer escaped punishment has eaten away at her all these years.'

Hillary wanted to give time for that to sink in and do its work, so she reached for a glass and poured herself some water. Beside her, Steven sat quietly. His presence grounded her, made her feel less like someone hounding an old woman than someone with a nasty job to do which needed doing. His silent support felt good. Very good.

She'd been self-dependent and self-reliant for so long that the warm glow his support gave her worried her as much as it made her feel better.

She frowned, dragging her thoughts firmly away from Steven Crayle. But she had the feeling that that was going to get harder and harder the longer they were together.

'I'm sorry to say it, but both my sergeant and I came away with the feeling that Mrs Thompson was very fragile indeed,' she forced herself to continue carefully. 'She had the air of a secret drinker about her, do you know what I mean? Nothing of it showed, and yet her husband, for all his bluff and hearty manner, was obviously worried about her. I could sense the desperate effort it was costing her to keep up a good show in front of us. And that made me feel so much worse – by being there, and raking it all up for her again.'

Hillary sighed heavily. 'But that's what happens with cold cases, I'm afraid. People try and forget and put the past behind them, and then we come along and open up old wounds.'

'It does seem cruel,' Wanda said, with a distinct tremor in her voice now.

Hillary nodded. Time for the next gentle tap at the next sensitive pressure point. 'Yes. But so necessary, don't you think? People shouldn't get away with something as awful as murder, should they?' Hillary mused. 'Just think – poor Rowan would have been nearly thirty by now. He would have matured, and maybe lost a lot of that reckless cruelty the young can have. He might even have married, and be a young father himself. But all that's gone now. Mrs Thompson won't get to nurse any grandchildren.'

She paused, then sighed again. 'Speaking of grandchildren, how is your grandson? Ferris, right?'

'Yes, he's fine,' Wanda said shortly.

'Just taking his A-levels then?' Hillary went on gently.

'Yes.'

'So he's – what, eighteen?'

'Yes. Just.' Wanda shifted slightly in her seat again.

Hillary nodded. 'Not a young boy any more, then, but a grown man. That's the age they leave you to go off to university, or get a job, or find a girl of their own and move out and on, isn't it?'

Wanda said nothing.

'Rowan wasn't much older, in fact, when he died,' Hillary said. And wondered. Had she done enough groundwork? Was it time to move in? The thing was, Wanda was an intelligent woman. Pretty soon, she'd begin to realize what Hillary was doing and then the advantage would be lost.

No, it was now or never. She couldn't keep playing on her vulnerabilities for ever.

'The trouble with this particular case, Mrs Landau, is that I can't really find anybody who wanted Rowan dead. I mean,' she carried on, still in her most soothing, non-threatening voice, 'he led Darla a bit of a merry dance, but young women don't go about stabbing their unfaithful boyfriends very often, do they?'

'Darla was a sweet girl,' Wanda said stiffly.

'I thought so too,' Hillary said. 'Which is why I ruled her out straight away,' she lied. 'And although Marcie was a bit mad at him for trying to come between her and a close friend of hers, it was hardly a motive for her to stab him, was it? So it was hardly likely to be Marcie. And Dwayne was his friend. Now, Barry Hargreaves, of course, was a little different.'

Was it her imagination, or had the older woman tensed up just then? She liked to think so. It was an encouraging sign. If Wanda didn't want the innocent to suffer, it spoke of a tender conscience. And that's what Hillary was relying on.

'He had two twin girls. Fifteen years old at the time, you see. Did you ever meet them, by the way?' she asked casually.

Wanda managed a smile. 'Yes. Lovely girls. A bit of a handful for him, I thought. But he adored them.'

'Of course he did. So when we learned that Rowan, naughty lad that he was, had seduced them, well,' Hillary shrugged, 'you can see why we've been pressing him very hard.'

'I'm sure Barry wouldn't have done it,' Wanda said. 'He had a heart of gold.'

'Yes. Funny, but I had the same impression,' Hillary lied. 'And when I talked to his two girls, who admitted to dallying

with Rowan and with no hard feelings or any bad conse-
quences, I realized I was on the wrong track yet again.
Especially since they both swore that Barry never knew about
it. So, you see, I simply couldn't see who would want to kill
him. It was not as if anybody had anything really important to
lose,' Hillary said.

Then she let the silence extend, waiting patiently until Wanda
looked up from her studious perusal of her clasped hands, and
said softly, 'Except for you, Wanda.'

Wanda's breathing stalled a little, and she seemed to lose a little
more of her colour.

'Me? I don't know what you mean.' She tried to inject some
disbelief into her voice, but wasn't sure that she'd managed it.

'You were in the middle of your campaign to get custody of
Ferris, weren't you?' Hillary pointed out softly. 'And I can only
imagine how hard that must have been. You were not in your first
flush of youth, you were widowed, with no partner to help out.
The social services would have been very stringent in their investigation of you as a worthy guardian.'

Wanda said nothing.

'And I found myself wondering,' Hillary carried on gently,
'what would you have done if you'd thought Rowan could ruin
your chances of getting custody of Ferris.'

Silence.

'And then I thought,' Hillary carried on, 'why should that be?
Rowan Thompson, from all I'd been able to learn about him, was
a somewhat reckless young charmer, a bit of a sexual athlete and
predator but nobody had ever called him sadistic, or cruel.'

Silence.

'And then I realized what the problem must have been. So
many people had told me about Rowan's experimental nature.
Especially as far as his sexual exploits went. Barry's twin daughters were an example. As were one or two entanglements with
members of his own sex. And then I thought about you, Wanda.
You're still a very good-looking woman even now, if I may say so.

And ten years ago, you were what – merely sixty-four? Nothing, by today's standards.'

Silence.

'And if Rowan couldn't resist seducing Barry's twin girls, how could he have resisted luring an older, glamorous woman to his bed?' she asked softly. 'And who's to blame you? You no longer had a husband, and Rowan was a young man who would have been most persistent and charming and persuasive. Under normal circumstances, it wouldn't have mattered a fig.'

Hillary sighed. 'But yours weren't normal circumstances, were they?' she said softly. Sympathetically. 'You had social workers in and out, checking out every aspect of your life, poking and prodding and prying and looking for examples of bad behaviour or bad judgement on your part.'

Silence.

'What happened, Wanda?' she asked softly, leaning forward a little on her chair now, inviting confidences. 'I never knew him, but a lot of people have told me that sometimes Rowan didn't know when to stop. That he could be thoughtless and stupid. That morning, when you went to his room when all the others had left. Did he tease you? Did he say that he was – what, going to seduce the next social worker who came sniffing around – male or female? Or did he laugh, maybe, wonder out loud what they'd do if he told them that his landlady was another Mrs Robinson?'

Wanda Landau slowly raised her hands to her face, but she said nothing.

'Mrs Landau, nobody here thinks you are a cold-hearted killer. It's clear that whoever killed Rowan did so in a sudden fit of madness. The murder weapon being scissors that were on hand and a single stab wound, rather than a frenzied, repeated attack. All of that points to someone driven to a single moment of madness, when pressured beyond their endurance.'

Wanda sobbed once. But still said nothing.

Beside her, Steven sat quietly.

Hillary leaned once more across the table. 'Mrs Landau, I think there hasn't been a single moment since you killed Rowan when you didn't regret it. I don't think there's been a single night when you haven't been kept awake by remorse, or when you haven't woken out of nightmares. And I also think, all this time, that you've only been able to keep on going because of Ferris.'

Slowly, Wanda let her hands drop. Her make-up was ravaged by the tears that had been silently coursing down her face.

She nodded.

A breakthrough! But there was still a way to go yet.

'But, Wanda,' Hillary used her first name, carefully building up the rapport, 'Ferris is a man now. He doesn't need you any longer. You can't keep using him as an excuse. You have to face up to what you've done.'

Silence.

'To give Mrs Thompson some peace, at last.'

Silence.

'And to give yourself some peace too,' Hillary persisted. 'No matter what you think, whatever happens now, it can't be worse than all those years of silence and self-loathing. You know that nobody really gets away with murder, don't you, Wanda?' Hillary said gently.

And Wanda Landau nodded.

'Did it happen how I imagined?' she pressed softly. They needed her to speak for the tape.

Wanda managed a weak and shaken smile. 'Almost exactly. I … thought he wasn't serious at first. Flirting with me, letting me know what he wanted. Of course, I turned him down, but he was so persistent. And then … well. It had been so long, and I thought all of that was behind me. But it was wonderful. *He* was wonderful. It had been going on for a few weeks, and no one guessed. It was exciting – daring, even. But that morning, when everyone had gone, I went to his room to say goodbye before he left for the Christmas holidays and….' She took a deep breath. 'I don't know how it happened. How we got to talking about a social worker who was due for a follow-up interview the next day.'

213

Wanda shook her head. She looked dazed. 'I said something about worrying about them thinking I was too old to adopt Ferris. And then he started joking about it, saying if only they knew how … how sexy I was, and all of that, then they'd know how young at heart I was. I was appalled and begged him not to say anything. But instead of seeing how terrified I was, he seemed to find it funny. I tried to get him to see how serious it was, but Rowan never found anything in life serious or important. He said he'd reassure them how hot I was, and that I wasn't a dried-up prune, and he just when on and on like that, saying that he'd stick around and give me a character reference, and I was getting more and more desperate.'

Wanda's voice was coming in gasps now. 'But he just wouldn't listen. He wouldn't *understand.*'

Wanda's voice rose on the last word, then she slumped back in the chair. 'And I suddenly realized what an horrific mistake I'd made. Because I knew then, that he'd never understand. And that he'd ruin everything. I don't even remember picking up the scissors. They were just in my hand. All I do remember thinking is that I had to save Ferris, that I simply couldn't let him go into an orphanage or foster care. You hear such awful stories about them. About young children being abused. I knew I had to save him, you see?' Wanda looked at Hillary, desperate for understanding.

Hillary nodded. 'Yes. You couldn't save your daughter, but Ferris would give you a chance to redeem yourself.'

'Exactly.'

'But the only way you could save Ferris….' Hillary trailed off, feeding her the line.

'Was to make him be quiet,' Wanda said. 'So I stabbed him.'

She began to sob again.

Hillary let her.

After a while, she said softly, 'What did you do then?'.

Wanda looked surprised by the question. 'Nothing. Well, I think I washed the scissors in the sink, and my hands, and I …

yes, I think I just let the scissors fall beside him and then I went to my room, and had a bath, and put my clothes in a plastic bag.... They were ... stained, you see. And I walked to the park and put the bag in a bin, and just went home.'

Hillary nodded. She wasn't sure what the barristers – either for the defence or the prosecution – would make of all that, but that wasn't her domain. 'All right, Mrs Landau,' she said softly, 'I've got a pad and pen here.' She pushed the items across. 'I'm going to call my sergeant in now. He'll sit with you. I want you to write everything down. Everything you can remember. What you thought, what you felt, everything. And then sign it for me. Will you do that?'

'Of course, Mrs Greene,' Wanda said politely, reaching for the pen.

She looked relieved.

As she and Steven rose, the door opened and Jimmy walked in; as she'd known he would be, he'd been listening in with the youngsters.

Back in the observation room, Vivienne looked impressed.

Sam looked far more subdued.

'You all right, Sam?' Hillary asked, slowly feeling the tension draining out of her shoulders.

'Yes, guv,' he muttered.

'You don't look it,' Hillary said mildly.

'He feels sorry for her,' Vivienne said, a shade defiantly. 'So do I, sort of.'

Hillary nodded. 'It's all right to feel empathy for some of the people who do bad things, Sam,' Hillary said. 'We can all understand why some people end up doing something awful sometimes. But don't forget: Wanda Landau can speak for herself, and she can hire solicitors and barristers to speak for her. She can defend herself in a court of law. Rowan Thomspon can't. Rowan Thompson is dead.'

Sam blinked. 'Yes, guv.'

'Just remember whose side you're on, Sam,' Steven clarified

and endorsed simply. 'It'll mess with your head if you don't.'

'Yes, sir. It's just ... I don't know that I'd ever be able to do what you just did, guv, that's all,' he admitted miserably.

Hillary rolled her tight shoulders. 'I'm not proud of it, Sam,' she said flatly. 'But you'll learn, if you do this job long enough, that if something's got to be done, and it's down to you to do it, then you just have to bloody well do it. That's really all there is. Otherwise, you might just as well pick another career.'

Sam nodded thoughtfully. 'Yes, guv.'

It was earlier in the day than she'd normally even think of leaving work, but Hillary felt drained. Steven was processing Wanda Landau, and there was nothing she could usefully do at the office anyway.

She drove back home to Thrupp almost on automatic pilot. At this hour, the pub car park was deserted, and she parked in her usual place right in the corner, next to a stand of willow and hazel trees.

As she got out of the car and shut the driver's door, she was just reaching down with the keys in her hand to lock it, when an arm that felt made of steel slipped around her waist and pulled her backwards. Her startled gasp didn't have time to turn into a cry for help as she felt a sudden, clean sting on the side of her neck. This was immediately followed by a warm, trickling sensation, and a splash of red dripped down onto her blouse, quickly followed by another, and then another.

She was bleeding. The shock was sudden, cold, and almost overwhelming.

'Don't scream.' The voice that came from right behind her was half-whispered, half-growled. It was a good attempt to disguise a normal speaking voice, and Hillary felt the arms around her tighten in warning, threatening to cut off her breathing.

Her head started to pound.

Instantly, she understood two things. Firstly, her attacker was a man of vastly superior strength. Her hands had come up automatically to clutch his forearm which was lying across her collar-bone, and she could clearly feel the definition of rock-hard muscle under her fingertips. Which meant that he worked out.

Secondly, she knew instinctively that none of the moves she'd learnt in self-defence classes were going to be of any use to her in a situation like this. No matter how fast she might be, he would be quicker. He was younger, fitter and pumped up on adrenaline. So any backward kicks to his shin, or any attempt to use his own weight against him by trying to throw him over her shoulder would be futile and would probably only serve to enrage him.

Besides, he had what must be a razor-sharp blade to her throat. She'd barely felt it slice into her skin, but already she could feel a steady trickle of blood flowing from her neck. At least it wasn't gushing. He hadn't severed an artery. Still, the sensation of feeling her own warm blood trickling over her hand and onto her clothes was eerie and terrifying.

Even as she thought all this, she felt herself being half-lifted and half-dragged back into the stand of trees and behind a thick, yellow-spotted laurel bush. They were now effectively out of sight of any passing boat on the canal.

'I've waited so long for this moment.' The voice again, so close to her ear, she could feel his breath rustle against her hair, moving it a little with the strength of his excited, ragged breathing. She gave an atavistic shiver that snaked the length of her spine, and drew in a long, shaky breath of her own.

Shock was her biggest worry now. She had to keep her head and think clearly. If she could not fight her way out of trouble – and she couldn't – she had to think and talk her way out of it. She simply couldn't afford to let fear rule her. She had to think, damn it. Think! What did she know?

OK. He was her stalker. He was obsessed with her. Which meant that he craved attention from her. She had to engage with him, and fast. The knife at her throat could end her with just one twitch of his wrist.

She licked her painfully dry lips, and tried to ignore the loud thundering of her heartbeat roaring in her ears.

'So have I,' she heard herself say. Her voice was just a little croaky, but not too bad. She felt him stiffen slightly, as if taken by surprise by her response. That was good, right? Keep him off guard and guessing.

Then she felt her ear being kissed. She blinked, forcing herself not to recoil. Talk to him. Give him what he wanted. Make him want to keep her alive.

But what should she say? She didn't want to inflame him – she could end up being raped. And she didn't want to anger him either. But what would make him angry?

'I was beginning to think you'd forgotten me,' she said gently. That, surely, was a safe enough opening gambit.

'As if I could,' Tom whispered, closing his eyes briefly in sheer bliss. Her hair smelt so good. And it felt wonderful to feel her softer, feminine length pressed up against him. And now they were talking. Finally, she was concentrating her mind, her whole being, on him. It was nirvana. 'I would forget to breathe before I could forget you.'

Hillary dragged in another shaky breath, trying to think. Her phone was in her bag and her bag was still hanging by her side. Was the zip open? Could she reach down and reach her phone? Not without him feeling the movement of it, she was sure. And that would make him angry.

No. Concentrate. She had to concentrate on keeping him talking. He was waiting for her to reply. He'd said something dramatic, and she needed to respond in kind. He obviously saw himself as some great, heroic lover.

But her legs felt as if they were made out of water, and she could hear a primal scream echoing around somewhere in the back of her head. All she wanted to do was kick and struggle and scream, but she knew she mustn't. Panic, and fear itself, were her worst enemies now.

But her legs felt so weak they wanted to buckle.

Damn it, she had to grow a bloody backbone!

And had she forgotten she had a job to do?

'You've made it impossible for me to ignore you too,' she heard herself say. 'And the crosses were a good touch. They really got my attention. Raised it to a whole different level. Tell me about the missing girls.' If she could get some details from him, they might be able to locate their bodies.

'Let's not talk about them,' Tom growled in protest, shifting a little restlessly. 'They were mistakes. They were nothing. It should always have been you.'

Hillary felt her panic levels rise as she realized she was making him antsy. 'No, you're right. We're special.' She forced the words out and realized she was still holding on to his forearm. She let her index finger slide just a little up and down along his skin. She could feel the tiny hairs under her sensitive fingertips and felt a sudden rush of nausea make her feel dizzy.

She forced herself to swallow it down. 'I can tell you're very strong.' Flattery was good, right? It had to be. She wasn't much of a psychologist, but it was a fair bet that psychos had big egos, surely? 'But I don't even know your name. What should I call you?'

Tom Warrington chuckled in delight. 'Oh, my darling, you're wonderful. I knew you would be.' As if he was going to tell her his name! But here she was, trying to play him. It was fantastic. All of the others had just whimpered and cried, and got on his nerves with their stupid begging. But not his Hillary.

She was magnificent. He had a knife to her throat and she was still playing the game. It was almost too good to be true. Unbelievable. But it was happening. He'd never felt so alive. He felt like laughing out loud and shouting his triumph at the universe.

'You know my name,' he said, confusing her for a moment. 'You can call me anything you like. Lover. Soulmate. Love of my life. Yeah, how about LOL for short, for Love of my Life.'

His whispering growl sounded playful now, elated, and

Hillary's heart sank. He was getting too hyper. She could feel him getting jittery. She had to cool it down somehow. Slow it down.

Nobody was going to come looking for her, because nobody knew she was in trouble. She felt a wave of despair threaten to consume her as the thought came that she could die, right here, right now. And that would be the end.

She'd always known it was a possibility, of course, all the years she'd served on the force. She'd seen it happen to Mel, her old boss and long-time friend. And to others. Everyone thought it would never happen to them. But for every 'Why me?' there was always a harsher alternative. 'Why not you?'

'Hillary?'

Her name, whispered in her ear, dragged her back from the precipice.

'I was just running it over in my mind,' she lied, her voice back to being a little high, a little scratchy now. She forced herself to lower her tone an octave. 'Lol. I like the sound of that. It's manly but tender too.'

She felt his knuckles tighten in anger, making the blade slide dangerously across her skin in a second, shallow cut. 'Don't try and play me too much, Hillary,' he warned harshly. 'I don't mind you being naughty, but don't take me for a fool.'

Hillary froze, then forced a playful sigh. She made herself chuckle too. 'Just testing, lover,' she said softly.

Tom dragged in a quick, harsh breath. 'You're magnificent. You truly are. I want you so much it hurts.'

And with that, Hillary felt the first flash of anger lance through her. It felt more than welcome. It beat fear and despair hands down. Something finally hardened inside her.

If the bastard wanted to play, then play they would.

'But not just yet,' she said, her voice much sharper now, and stronger. She felt his surprise at the sudden shift in power, and knew she had to act fast to make him feel happy about it. 'It'll spoil it, otherwise, won't it?' She let her voice become cajoling now, and yet still a little teasing. 'We've got more self-control and respect for one another than to rush things, right? Nobody else would understand. They'd never have anything special like we have, and even if they did, they'd ruin it by being greedy and stupid. But not us. We're special. Right?'

She could feel her life hanging in the balance, as she waited to know whether or not he'd bought it. And she felt a moment of utter calm.

Tom Warrington sighed noisily. Finally! After all these years of trying and failing, he'd finally done it. He'd found the one. The one who'd been made just for him.

'I knew it. I knew you were the one. And you're right. You're always so right, my fabulous Hillary. It is way too early. We've got so much fun to have yet. Foreplay is almost the best part, isn't it?'

Suddenly the knife and the hand were gone.

'Don't turn around. Don't try and get a look. Don't spoil it,' he ordered. Then his lips were back at her ear, and Hillary tensed.

'I'll be around. And I'll see you later.'

Hillary heard the rustling of undergrowth behind her and let out a ragged sob, which she quickly stifled with the back of her hand. She mustn't reveal her weakness now.

She staggered forward quickly, thrusting her way past the concealing laurel and out into the car park. There she finally let her legs have their way and sank down onto her knees. For a few seconds, she stared at the backs of her hands, her mind hardly daring to believe that it was over. That she was still alive. Still breathing.

And then she watched the steady drip, drip, drip of scarlet onto the black tarmac. She was still bleeding. And he was getting away. What the hell was the matter with her? But even as she reached for her phone and speed-dialled Steven's number, she heard a car start up somewhere on the lane, and knew that he would be long-gone before anyone else arrived.

She heard Steven's voice, far, far away, and forced her hand to move, to bring the mobile to her mouth.

But what was it she needed to say?

'Evidence, I've got evidence.'

'Hillary?' Steven recognized her voice at once. 'Sorry, what was that you said?'

Hillary shook her head. She couldn't seem to get her thoughts to line up in a straight line. They kept skittering around. 'I'm bleeding. He had a knife to my throat. DNA evidence. Fingerprints maybe. You need to send someone.'

There. That made sense, surely?

She could hear, somewhere, a long way off, Steven's voice, getting more and more frantic, saying something. But she couldn't make out what it was. Besides, she was tired. Really tired. And she was suddenly feeling sort-of cold.

She let herself move forward, lying down on the sun-warmed black tarmac, letting her head rest on her forearm. She was going into shock, she knew. But that was all – she hadn't lost nearly enough blood for it to be life-threatening. Not yet.

So she should be heading for her car, driving herself to the A&E. But here she was, curling up into a ball like a big fat baby. She had to smile. So much for growing a backbone.

Somewhere, far away, she could hear sirens coming, but she ignored it.

Because, simmering away deep down inside her, beyond the tiredness and the numbness, she could feel her anger growing, and she needed to concentrate on that now. Because that was good. She was going to need it.

Because soon, she and Lol would meet again.

And the next time they did, Hillary Greene promised herself, things would be different.

Oh yes.

They would be very different.